D1636794

I KNOW
WHAT
YOU DID

I KNOW
WHAT
YOU DID

A NOVEL

CAYCE OSBORNE

**CROOKED
LANE**

NEW YORK

Copyright © 2023 by Cayce Osborne

Published in the United States by Crooked Lane Books, an imprint of The Quick Brown Fox & Company LLC.

Crooked Lane Books and its logo are trademarks of The Quick Brown Fox & Company LLC.

Library of Congress Catalog-in-Publication data available upon request.

ISBN (hardcover): 978-1-63910-329-4
ISBN (ebook): 978-1-63910-330-0

Cover design by Heather VenHuizen

Printed in the United States.

www.crookedlanebooks.com

Crooked Lane Books
34 West 27th St., 10th Floor
New York, NY 10001

First Edition: July 2023

10 9 8 7 6 5 4 3 2 1

For my friends and family:
Don't worry, I'm not naming names.

But you know what you did:
You cheered me on and didn't roll your eyes
when I talked about my writing.

Without you, this book wouldn't exist.

CHAPTER

1

SUBSTITUTE GYNECOLOGISTS ARE the worst.

A few weeks ago, I went in for my yearly checkup and got passed off to a sub. My regular doc was vacationing in Tahiti—paddleboarding on a dolphin, maybe, or skydiving with a parachute made from human hair. However rich people spend their leisure time these days. I grew up around wealth, so when I say shit gets weird when money is no object, I know of what I speak.

"You should read it," Sub Gyno said, voice full of himself.

He'd been talking, for a full minute at that point, about some book. I ignored him, putting my feet into the stirrups and scooting my butt down the exam table so my thigh muscles wouldn't cramp. I dialed my mental radio to my favorite Halestorm album and closed my eyes.

He blabbed about that damned novel all the way through my exam. His words were muffled by my thighs, and that suited me fine. I should've made more of an effort to listen, though. Not because he was worth listening to, but because he was relaying information that would turn out to be valuable. Listening might have saved me some grief—always high on my priority list.

I didn't know it at the time, but the book in question wasn't your average airport bestseller. A celebrity publishing goddess hadn't picked it from obscurity to release its brilliance onto the world. It wasn't special (blech) or precious (gag) or anything like that—I'm not one of those book-spine-sniffing, library-lurking reading obsessives, in case you hadn't figured that out already. The book was fiction, but it wasn't. It told the truth but wrapped it in lies. I might've called it ominous if I were into the whole foreshadowing thing.

But as I said: I didn't know that then. I continued to ignore Sub Gyno. This had zero impact on his one-sided conversation. And when I didn't respond, he only talked at me louder.

"I finished reading it today on my break, right before you got here." He raised his head to meet my eyes over the pink floral sheet draped across my midsection.

So that's why you were twenty minutes late.

I hadn't enjoyed substitutes when I was in school, and I liked them even less in my vagina. But my aunt Shelly, who'd taken me in after my parents died, had battled a very aggressive cervical cancer. Battled, and lost. I was now nearly the age she was when she died and never missed my annual Pap—certainly wasn't going to reschedule because of some jackhole sub. I was lazy about many things (laundry, nutrition, taxes, relationships) but not cancer. Aunt Shelly had busted her ass to keep my head above water during my four hellish years of high school. I repaid her efforts by making sure all her hard work didn't go to waste.

"Believe me, I don't normally read books about teenage girls."

Sure you don't, perv.

Anyone who says *trust me* or *believe me* cannot be trusted or believed. And you can trust me on that. But

I didn't give a rat's ass about the books he read or what he talked about during my appointment. I wanted it over with so I could get back to my crap day as soon as possible.

"One of my nurses left it in the break room, and I picked it up while I was eating lunch the other day. Could not put it down. Maybe because I have a fourteen-year-old daughter of my own."

May the patron saint of teenage girls protect her, because her father is a jagoff who steals books from his coworkers and will not shut up even though I clearly do not care.

"And that ending! It's going to make a killer movie. No pun intended."

He swirled a long cotton swab inside me like a cocktail swizzle stick.

"Movie?"

He'd tricked me into responding.

In my defense, he'd hit a weak spot—I loved movies. I loved stories, period, as long as I didn't have to read them. I was as obsessed with the movies I watched on Netflix as the tall tales I told myself to get through the day. Stories were the grease in my wheels. They allowed my brain to operate smoothly. They kept me from grinding to a halt, curling into the fetal position on my couch, and slowly starving to death because basic human needs like food and water were too much trouble.

Action movies were my favorite—snarky, badass main characters with good one-liners, backed by a loud soundtrack, featuring multiple car chases and at least one explosion. But books? No way. Reading left too much headspace for wicked thoughts to sneak in. Like a stray bullet, they'd rattle around in there and do serious damage. Books just weren't loud enough.

"David Fincher is attached to direct. So you know it'll be good."

"I'll wait for the movie version, then."

He sat back on his crotch-height stool, pulled off his latex gloves, and patted my knee like I'd been a good girl. In my experience, male gynos had no idea what it was like to get a speculum shoved inside them—and it showed in their bedside manner—yet they were still damned certain they knew everything. I imagined shoving the shiny metal instrument somewhere he would find very uncomfortable and smiled.

He took this as encouragement.

Damn.

"Oh, no, you should definitely read it. You, of all people!"

I looked up and he was staring at me, a half grin on his too-tan face. Apparently I'd missed something, and this exclamation required a response.

I sat up, shifting my butt backward on the table so I could take my feet down. The flesh-colored exam gown slipped off my shoulders, exposing the black-and-gray tattoos that covered my upper arms, elbows to collar bones.

"Uh, what do you mean me, of all people?" I asked when I saw him eyeing the black script winding along the inside of my right bicep.

I yanked the gown back up. When people saw the tattoos, they tended to want the stories behind them. That's why I kept them covered. Mine didn't mean anything other than I'd had some blank skin and one day decided to fill it. Nothing about me made a very nice story, and that went for my ink as well.

Sub Gyno looked at me like I'd asked a stupid question. But I knew something he didn't: there are no stupid questions, only stupid men who waste my time.

"Well, like I told you, because of your name. It's not like it's . . . common."

I fixed him with my best blank stare. And I wasn't faking. I had no idea what he was talking about. Maybe he didn't either. For the first time that day, he seemed unsure of himself. The thrill of his discomfort zinged through me like the sting of a tattoo needle.

"I mean, it's not like your name is Jane Smith or something."

"Why would my name be Jane Smith? My name is Petta."

My name was Petal, actually, and I hated it. I'd lopped off the *l* years ago and made people call me Petta. Because I was no flower, and *Petal* had brought me nothing but trouble.

He wouldn't let it go—this thing about my name and the book and whatever they had to do with each other. His next victim was probably drumming her fingers in the exam room next door while he ate up my day like it was a bottomless basket of chips and salsa.

I don't like to dwell on what-ifs. It's my personal policy not to, in fact. But now I wonder how much longer I might have continued living in blissful ignorance if I hadn't antagonized him into explaining the name thing.

"You . . . no. What I mean is, have you ever met another Petal Woznewski?"

"I go by Petta."

"Sure, sure," the doc said, waving his hand between us as if the way I wanted to be addressed didn't matter.

I shrugged. It was my go-to gesture, more polite and less effort than swearing under my breath.

He stood and bumped his stool backward with the heel of his hideous square-toed oxblood oxford. It rolled across the linoleum floor and crashed against the wall.

"Okay," he said, with the finality of a door slam.

I'd succeeded in annoying him into giving up.

Excellent.

"Nurse will call if the Pap shows anything."

He was halfway out the exam room door—I was already hopping down off the table, gripping the loose neck of my gown, eager to put my street armor back on—when he paused.

"*No One Suspected*. That's the name of the book. I forget the author. But read it." He pointed a finger gun at me and I knew what was coming, my face already collapsing into a proactive grimace.

"Doctor's orders."

He pulled the trigger and the exam room door snicked closed behind him.

* * *

My Pap was clear. I got the results by email a couple days later. Still, the appointment left a hangover no amount of greasy food or napping could fix. All because of that damn book. I'd left the doctor's office with no intention of ever thinking about it again—certainly not reading it. But that was before the book began to stalk me.

I know that sounds crazy paranoid, but it's true. It showed up in the store windows I passed on the street and popped into my Amazon daily deals emails. Ads for *No One Suspected* blared over my head from the mammoth screens in Times Square.

The Square was on my weekday walking route from my studio apartment in the Garment District to the nondescript high-rise where I performed soothingly mechanical data entry forty hours a week. But after the book stalking started, I took the long way—using Thirty-Eighth Street over to Fifth Avenue, up around Bryant Park—not wanting to see that black-and-green dust jacket flashing down at me like a lightning bolt from above, ready to fry my ass with one zap.

I had the option of working from home and had done so for many months the year before (along with the rest of humanity), but being cooped up inside my tiny apartment was like being trapped inside my own head. In other words: torture. Every time I left the apartment was an exercise in proving to myself that I could exist in the world, that I had the basic social skills needed to interact with different people in changing environments. I was a championship-level introvert, but knowing I could function outside myself made me more human, and sometimes I needed to feel that.

Then there was the walking. Another thing that made me less of a pod person. There's nowhere in the world like NYC for walking. I'd get a good, loud album pumping through my earbuds, something to match my mood and the energy of the city, and I'd walk. I would stare straight ahead, waiting for the next block to appear on the concrete horizon, focusing above the crowd to avoid accidental eye contact. I kept my head up and ready. Even on the days I'd rather slouch and study the toes of my boots as they pounded mile after mile of sidewalk, I kept my chin lifted. It was dangerous to hide too far inside myself. Especially in the big bad city. I needed to see what was coming at me before it was too late.

Avoiding my usual walking routes and ignoring the existence of the book worked, at first. I went a whole day without seeing or thinking about it. Every time a bookish thought would bob up, I'd push it back down, under the surface of my consciousness, begging it to drown already. Then the Monday after my doctor's appointment, on my way home from work, I passed yet another copy of the book in a drugstore display window. But this time, I didn't look away.

The words #1 NEW YORK TIMES BESTSELLER were printed in a blocky font above *No One Suspected*.

"Damn. That explains why it's everywhere."

A passing dog walker, tangle of leashes clutched in his fist, gave me and my mutterings a wide berth. I waited until he passed.

"Okay, fine. You win."

I walked into the Duane Reade, bracing myself to play out a one-woman game of hide-and-seek. Yeah, I was seeking my connection to the book. And at the same time, I was hiding. A long time ago I'd carved out a place, deep inside, and secreted away my past. But before I even picked up *No One Suspected*, my gut was giving me spoilers. It knew the book was connected to my childhood. It knew that butt-ugly skeletons had been ripped out of my closet, put on the page, and made into literary entertainment for the masses. And I needed to figure out not only how, but why.

It was summer rush hour, and the store was packed with sweaty patrons who, if the smell was any indication, were shopping for deodorant. A narrow shelving unit, where the store stocked magazines and a few recent book titles, held half a dozen copies of the book. I slid one from the back of the display. Its black cover showed the silhouette of a cabin with a cluster of trees in the background. The moon was high and bright, casting long shadows. The author's name was printed small at the bottom: *ME Littleton*.

The title was embossed in alien green across the midnight sky: *No One Suspected*.

A woman rushing toward the tampon display body-checked me from behind. The book fell from my hands and skidded across the floor. I retrieved it, dusting it off. The bottom of the spine had crumpled when it hit the floor.

Take that, asshole.

I considered "accidentally" dropping it again to see what other damage I could do. Instead, I opened the front cover. The title page repeated the name of the book and the author. I'd never heard of ME Littleton. And I was no closer to figuring out why Sub Gyno had insisted I read this book. But then I turned to the dedication page.

Normally, grateful authors use that space to thank their children, or their spouse, or their saintly high school English teacher for inspiring them. But ME Littleton had no such dedication. They'd used the page for a different purpose. It read:

I know what you did, Petal Woznewski.
Now everyone else will too.

The store disappeared. I floated away from my body, and a white, roaring void of panic enclosed me like an iron lung.

I dropped the book like it'd sprouted fangs and stumbled out of the Duane Reade. Maybe fresh air would help bring me back to myself. It didn't—or maybe it did, and that was the problem. I was too much myself, all raw nerves and exposed wiring. I craved the contained safety of home but wasn't ready to be alone with my thoughts. Or the threat spelled out in the book. Or my thoughts about the threat in the book.

I put in my earbuds, cranked a Garbage album until my eardrums ached, and started walking. It took hours, zigzagging across the city, but by the time dusk fell, my head had cleared. I checked the time. It was after eight. Gus had been off work for over an hour. I weaved out of the foot traffic on the sidewalk and leaned against the front window of a Jollibee. The smell of fried chicken seeped into my T-shirt as I pulled my phone out of my back pocket.

Tonight?

Gus answered my text in seconds. Like maybe he'd been expecting it, which made me both smile and feel sorry for him.

Affirmative. Ordering our usual now.

Gus and I were friends, and sometimes more. Other times less. I had a periodic need to cling to a warm body, which lasted until I got too dependent on that warm body—or until it started to cling back. When that happened, I'd stop returning his texts and he'd get the hint. But we'd always start up again when I got lonely. I'm prone to loneliness, a weakness I'd worked hard to hide (and when that didn't work, ignore). But I always caved and went back to Gus. Our on periods lasted much longer than our off.

After a few of these on-off-on cycles, some hurt feelings (him), and loads of conflict avoidance (me), we'd arrived more or less on the same page. Friends with benefits. The benefits coming first and the friends more from his persistence than anything else. I wasn't a very nice person and could be downright ornery at times, but for some reason Gus liked me. I can't say that was a point in his favor. My guess? He thought he could save me, shake me out of my perpetual funk. And I let him believe that was possible.

His apartment was a few blocks from mine in the Garment District, and we worked in the same building. He was one of the day-shift lobby security guards. Even before we were involved, I saw him every morning as I went into work. And again every evening as I left. We'd run into each other in the neighborhood too, at the deli or the Duane Reade or on the sidewalk. New Yorkers live at their own rate and rhythm, harmonizing with the city in a unique way. Some are social night owls, others are introverted early risers—and vice versa, mix-match, and everything in between. Occasionally, I'd find myself in the same groove as someone else. I'd see them at the Laundro-mat, or pulling their garbage out to the curb, or leaving their apartment for work at the same time as me. Gus was one of those someones. We were opposites in almost every way but similar in our rhythm. We'd see each other all the time, by accident. Eventually, we started running into each other on purpose.

Back then, Gus was going through a rough time. His mom was dying, and because he was the only one of his siblings who wasn't married with kids, he became her primary caregiver. Between her and work, he had only about 10 percent of his time and energy to devote to me. That suited me perfectly. We could wrap up in each other in our dark, needy moments—the ones that fell through the cracks between our depressing days—and became each other's bright spots.

It took a while, but eventually Gus wanted more from me. More than I knew how to give.

After his mom passed away, his life normalized. Mine was still shit. The more time we spent together, the more I felt like an obligation—one more woman he had to take care of. As the older brother in a fatherless household, he'd helped raise his sisters. Then he'd watched his mom die. Now he was trying to help me to . . . I don't know. Join the living, I guess?

It wasn't in me to let him, and that led to our first off period. My soft, squishy center—ask me and I'll deny its existence—was buried under hard layers of shame, fear, and regret, all held together by sheer stubbornness. I told myself it would take more than a big, slobbery puppy like Gus Johnson to crack me open. But that didn't stop him from trying.

I beat the Postmates to his door by fifteen minutes. We sat together on the floor, resting our backs against his fuzzy brown couch. He shared his moo shu and I shared my extra-spicy kung pao, and he told me about his day.

The deli had put mayo on his sandwich instead of mustard.

The 911 operator had put him on hold.

Blah, blah, blah.

I let him talk, nodding along as I chewed—the whole time waiting for the moment he'd run out of chatter and the food would be gone and we could get to the sex part. Then maybe I'd be able to erase the image of my name in black print on a dead white page.

The sex was good—it was always good. Gus knew how to be rough and gentle in all the right places, at all the right times. Another way we were in rhythm. His hands and his lips and the friction of his skin on mine made it easy to concentrate on the heat between us and only that.

I liked to stay over at his place after. He could always scour my brain clean enough to sleep. If I got up and walked home, the spell would be broken. And if I was being honest with myself, I liked the comfortable weight of his arm across my hip as we lay in bed. His hand cupping the squish of my belly. Gus was a gift; one I didn't deserve.

That night, after we finished, neither one of us was tired. I was hoping for round two. I waited for him to be ready and considered rolling on top of him and wiggling around to move the process along. But then he started talking, picking up where he'd left off: the litany of small disasters that had made up his day.

Join the club, I wanted to say. But that would only invite questions, and in general Gus and I avoided those. On any other night, I would've given up on round two and sunk into the deep buzz of his words, letting them lull me to sleep. But it wasn't any other night—it was one of those days.

"It was one of those days, you know?" Gus said, and I huffed out a knowing chuckle. "Everything that could go wrong, did go wrong."

"I'm familiar."

"The bomb threat was only the beginning."

I sat up. The bed sheet slipped down, bunching around my waist. I was naked, but never self-conscious around Gus. He enjoyed every fat roll, scar, and tattoo—he proved this, enthusiastically, each night we spent together.

"You didn't tell me there was a bomb threat. They didn't evacuate us."

I worked on the twenty-seventh floor and hadn't heard a thing.

"Yeah, that's why I called 911. I mean, I guess it wasn't an actual bomb threat. More like a suspicious package. Outside the east entrance. I had to call it in, just in case."

"Hmm." No bomb. I was losing interest again. I huddled back under the covers and tried to summon sleepiness. I imagined the bed was a warm tortilla and I was being wrapped in it, burrito-style.

"Turned out it was nothing. Somebody's gym bag they set down while they were texting and forgot—Oh, shit! Can't believe I forgot to tell you!"

As I waited for him to come out with it, he rolled across the bed, leaning over his side to dig underneath the discarded clothes littering the floor. The bed sheet and blanket, wrapped around his torso, went with him as he leaned. The air-conditioned room made a shiver break across my skin.

"What are you—"

He didn't answer, still searching the floor. I was getting irritated. I was chilly and wanted more sex or sleep, preferably both, in that order. I didn't care in the least what he'd forgotten to tell me. I considered putting my clothes back on and leaving.

"When the bomb squad emptied the bag, there was a book in there."

Oh hell no.

He was still pawing at the floor. I could barely hear what he was saying over the roar in my ears.

". . . bag contents were spread out all over the concrete bench—that long one outside the east entrance the skateboarders like. I was bored, waiting around for the all clear from the officer in charge. And the book was just sitting there, so I picked it up and read the blurb on the back."

Gus sat up, having found what he was looking for—what I dreaded. A copy of *No One Suspected*, which he held out to me like a dime-store Santa with a gift for a needy child.

"They wouldn't let me keep the one from the bag. I stopped at Duane Reade on my way home to buy my own copy—I had to show you. Because guess what? There's a character in here with your exact same—"

I shut out his voice, tried to ignore what I was seeing: *Gus's copy of the book had a crumpled spine.* It was the same one I'd dropped on the floor earlier that day, in our neighborhood Duane Reade. Somehow, that spooked me more than anything else. Like I was destined to have this copy of this book in these hands—my hands.

I knew then. It would no longer be enough to change my route to work or avoid looking in store windows or curate distractions. This book was not going to leave me alone. I would have to face it sooner or later.

But not now. Not with Gus here to witness it.

I was out of bed and dressing in seconds.

"Hey! Where you going? I thought maybe . . . round two?" Gus's expression was equal parts surprise and disappointment.

I hooked my fingers through the loops on the back of my navy Doc Martens boots and pulled them on before I realized I hadn't put my pants on.

I kicked the boots off, found my jeans, and yanked them on. My favorite gray T-shirt—a photo of young Samuel L. Jackson with a cigarette hanging from his lips and the words *Hold on to your butts* across the front—was hiding under Gus's uniform. It was inside out, but I didn't care. I ducked my head inside it, eye to eye with Sam for the time it took my head to emerge. My bra was somewhere in the room, but I wasn't going to take the time to look.

"Text you tomorrow," I tossed over my shoulder as I grabbed my backpack and scurried toward the door, Docs in my arms. But I knew I wouldn't. The book had come between us. I let myself feel guilty about that in the span of time it took me to put my Docs on in the elevator. Then I let it go. I preferred to swallow my self-hatred in small bites. That way it couldn't choke me.

Outside, it was dark. I checked my phone: eleven o'clock on a Monday. The street traffic was light. The air was humid and smelled like hot garbage. Gus's words dogged me the three sweaty, panicked blocks to my apartment. It wasn't until I was inside, and I'd flipped the dead bolt and leaned my clammy forehead against the cool steel door, that I processed why I was so freaked out.

There's a character in here, Gus had said. *I picked it up and read the blurb.*

When I'd examined the book at Duane Reade, I'd seen my name in the dedication. Bad enough, right? But it got so much worse. He'd read my name in the blurb, not the dedication. That meant my name was in both places—as a warning on the dedication page, and as a character in the story.

"What the actual hell?" I asked my empty apartment.

It didn't answer, which made the lonely silence fall heavier. I rolled a joint and smoked until my head—the blaring alarm bells, the questions, the scream of my own name—went quiet. I pulled my laptop into bed with me and opened Netflix, clicking on an old Christian Slater action movie from my Watch It Again list. I wouldn't be able to sleep, but the movie would help quiet my demons.

I've always loved Christian Slater. His smile lets you know he's in on the joke. Even when, like in *Broken Arrow*, John Travolta gets all the good one-liners.

2

B Y THE TIME I dragged myself out of bed, the morning was an unraveling rope threatening to snap. Tuesday was one of my days off, a small mercy. But I had nowhere to go. I manufactured a few errands, hurrying out the door in yesterday's T-shirt (Sam Jackson, still inside out) and jeans to replenish household supplies I didn't need. I walked the fourteen blocks to my favorite headega: part head shop, part bodega. I'd picked up a moderate pot habit in high school, and my smoking preferences had been formed back in the days of pipes, joints, and for those who were into larger contraptions, bongs. No gummies, none of that vaping nonsense for me. I was all about that sweet smoke, herby and skunky, and the satisfaction of a well-rolled joint or tightly packed pipe.

At the headega, I grabbed a basket and walked up and down each aisle. I took my time, searching for treasures. By the time I reached the front counter, I had rolling papers, sesame sticks, soy sauce, and rye chips in my basket. I impulse-bought a fancy soy sauce decanter at the register. It was shaped like a gold-and-orange koi fish. All the while, Pat Benatar raged through my earbuds. I nodded my thanks to the clerk, stuffed my booty into my backpack, and walked on, detouring toward the Upper West Side in search of my favorite hot dogs.

Lunch was a juice and two mustard-onion-relish franks at Gray's Papaya. They were nutritionally deficient but tasted good, which was all I was after. It fueled me across Central Park and up Fifth Avenue. I walked until I hit Marcus Garvey Park in Harlem. The grassy areas were full of families and couples. I avoided them, sitting down on the bottom step of a wide stone staircase that led up to the park's Acropolis. The bottoms of my feet throbbed. I extended my legs, feeling the muscles stretch and lengthen. The walking had lulled my body into a trance, and the humming dread had subsided.

Too tired to walk all the way back down Fifth, I hitched a subway ride home. When I first moved to New York, I could've walked the whole of Manhattan with energy to spare. Not anymore. My age had started showing up in physical ways: a twinge in my knee, the need for a good mattress, and the inability to stay up all night getting into trouble.

But I was heading for a different kind of trouble as I stopped into my neighborhood Duane Reade on the way home, bracing myself like an outclassed boxer waiting for the next roundhouse.

The copies of *No One Suspected* had multiplied overnight, like gremlins.

"Did someone feed you after midnight?" I asked them. Their covers stared back at me, unimpressed.

I plucked one off the shelf and tucked it under my arm. I knew if I hesitated, or opened it there in the store, I'd change my mind. I wandered the snack aisle for dinner provisions and waited in the checkout line like it was my own funeral procession. After paying, I pushed the book to the bottom of my backpack, burying it under my other purchases.

I didn't let it out again until I was home, safely sprawled on my broken-down sofa. It was dark outside my window, and I was one joint and a half gallon of cucumber-lime Gatorade into the evening.

The book looked the same as yesterday: green writing, creepy cabin, dark shadows. I was too chickenshit to read the jacket blurb right away, so I turned to the inside back flap, expecting to find a photo and biography of the author. ME Littleton—a pen name if I'd ever heard one. But there was no picture, and only one line of text.

ME Littleton lives and writes in Madison, Wisconsin.

I'm not prone to emotional vomiting, but the Gatorade came out in a gush, drenching the cushions of my paisley couch. My childhood in Madison was something I never thought about—I spent a good portion of my days actively suppressing that time of my life. I'd gotten quite good at compartmentalizing and didn't see it as a bad thing. Those years had been too difficult, too heavy, to drag into adulthood. I'd let the weight of my adolescence sink into the churning ocean of my past. But now it was rising—the long, bad years and good, fleeting moments of my Madison memories returning.

For some reason, the smells came back to me first. The dank fishiness of a cool breeze off Lake Mendota. The yeasty steam of fresh-baked Bagels Forever. The powdery floral perfume of my best friend's hair spray and her too-sweet Dr Pepper Lip Smacker. The dewy-grass and fresh-pavement scents of sneaking out at night without permission.

To say my formative years were difficult would be an understatement.

Here are the highlights: my parents died young, I was passed on to a firm but kind aunt, and I barely survived four tumultuous high school years after the death of my best friend. On top of all that, life piled the usual teen-age friendship drama and raging emotions. Basically, teen angst turned up to eleven, with a handful of significant deaths like maggot sprinkles on a shit cupcake.

My hard edges weren't put on. I'd come by them honestly. New Yorkers were supposed to be brash and tough, but I'd been both while still a Madisonian. Every soft bit of me had been lopped off long before I left my hometown. I was a human sea urchin: tucked protectively into a ball, aiming my black spikes at the world. I might have a thing for spicy food, but I worked hard to keep the rest of my life as bland as American cheese on Wonder Bread.

I knew the book was about to change all that, even before I started reading.

Because there was only one reason someone would write about me.

I lit a second joint before reading the blurb on the back. The story it described was familiar and foreign, all at once.

> On a moonlit night in 1991, three girls went into the woods. Only two returned . . .
>
> Miriam Rowley was a beautiful and charismatic fourteen-year-old, beloved and envied by her class-mates. Until the day she turned up dead, alone in a Wisconsin forest, with no signs of foul play. For decades, her death was labeled a tragic accident. But there were rumors, and many whispered suicide.
>
> Izzy Jacobs, Miriam's best friend, knows gut-wrench-ing details about what happened to Miriam that night. After thirty years, she's ready to face the truth and set herself free.

What happened when Miriam, Izzy, and their new friend Petal Woznewski snuck out of their homes in the dead of night? Petal knows, but she guards her secrets well. Izzy won't be able to bring the truth to light alone.

Samson Bull, the detective on the case at the time, has never forgotten Miriam. Instinct told him there was more to her death than the evidence showed, but under pressure from the girl's wealthy family, he ruled it accidental. When Izzy tracks him down in 2021, Bull is long retired. But he cannot refuse her invitation to delve back into the one case that has always haunted him.

Together, Izzy and Bull set their sights on a heartless killer.

"Such a load of crap!" I screamed.

I kept screaming—until my throat was raw and my upstairs neighbor used his feet to beat a drum solo on the floor, our agreed-upon *shut up* signal. A second bottle of Gatorade helped my throat, but it didn't wash away the pit in my stomach. The book contained too much truth, and too many lies. A tangle I might never escape.

Miriam Rowley and Izzy Jacobs were names I'd never heard—fictional versions of the real girls I'd known. And there was no Detective Bull. Not then, and (I confirmed after Googling) not now. There had been a secret night, though. One I'd never spoken of to another living human. Not to my aunt Shelly, not to Gus. Not to a priest or a psychiatrist or a stranger. A night when I sneaked out of my house to meet my two friends, during the spring of my freshman year of high school. Ours was a third-wheel, ever-shifting friendship. Iridescent—flashing bright pink one moment, a dull lavender the next. I'd never been certain who was in favor and who was out, whether we were bound more by love or by hate. The friendship ended forever that night, when only two of us lived to see the next morning.

The truth of that night was my deepest darkest—one of the top two crappiest things in a crap childhood. And now, my secret was number one with a bullet in the *New York Times*.

Figuring my night couldn't get any worse, I cleaned the vomit off my couch, opened a fresh bag of Twizzlers, and started to read.

Excerpt from
No One Suspected

1990

MY NAME IS Izzy Jacobs, and I was Miriam Rowley's best friend. I can't tell the rest without getting that out first, even though it says more about me than it does about her. We were each other's number-one person, even if she didn't act like it all the time. She had her moods; anyone who knew her would tell you the same. But Miri was mine, and I was hers. We were the perfect pair. Friends since we were little.

Until freshman year of high school when Petal Woznewski transferred to our school.

Everyone felt sorry for her. And it wasn't only because she was saddled with that god-awful name: Petal. She was no wilting flower, that's for sure. Before Miri and I knew her, she'd lived with her parents in a fancy, east-side area of Madison called Maple Bluff, on the same street as the governor's mansion. Her mom and dad had died in an accident the spring before we started high school. When people whispered about the Woznewskis—which they did often that summer and fall—it was with raised eyebrows and air quotes around the word "accident."

Afterward, Petal had to move in with her aunt on our side of town—the west side—and she joined our incoming

freshman class at West High. Entering high school was like
jumping into a spot in the ocean where several currents met:
kids from different middle schools pouring together into the
same churning hallways that smelled of sweat and bleach and
wet paper towels. Miri was my life raft in that ocean. We'd
been in the same schools all the way back to first grade. We'd
bonded early, like soul mates, the way young girls sometimes
do. I thought we'd be friends forever, even though Miri was
my opposite in almost every way: fun and beautiful, rich
and privileged. I drank her in like nectar, adoring a girl who
thrived on adoration. Perhaps that's why we worked. There
was a natural, often unhealthy, codependence to our friendship that I didn't recognize until we'd dipped our toes into
the high school waters.

Miri and her family lived in a big Tudor house in Shorewood Hills, a neighborhood nestled along the southwest end
of Lake Mendota, populated by rich and noteworthy west-
siders. I lived with my parents in a tiny one-bedroom duplex
in a nameless part of town. Less than two miles separated our
houses, but we came from different worlds. Miri's bedroom
was bigger than our living room, in the corner of which I
slept on a pullout. Sometimes, when my aunt and uncle were
fighting, my cousins would sleep over and we'd all cram onto
the queen-sized pullout together like poorly packed sardines.
Our house was comfortable and clean, but the kind of worn
and dingy that hours of scrubbing couldn't improve. I never
invited anyone over. Especially not Miri.

In high school, living in a named neighborhood like
Shorewood Hills or Maple Bluff (technically, both were vil-
lages within the city of Madison) began to matter in a way it
hadn't in middle or elementary school. People looked at Miri
and me and wondered how we could possibly be friends. We
were so different. And when the infamous Petal Woznewski
showed up, freshly orphaned and formerly rich, Miri rushed

to make friends with her. From the outside, their friendship made much more sense than the one I'd built with Miri.

That was the first time I understood that status and notoriety mattered to Miri—they weren't just part of her life, but a priority—and that my lack of both might become a problem. This discrepancy had always lurked underneath our friendship, like an alligator trolling a swamp. But it took Petal's arrival for the gator to surface.

Miri might have been dazzled, but I saw through Petal's tragic new-girl shine. I seemed to be the only person in the whole school who didn't fall all over themselves to make her feel welcome or tell her how sorry they were for her loss. Maybe it makes me a bad person, but I didn't pity her. She was beautiful, for one thing, dark haired and amber eyed, whereas Miri was a strawberry golden ray of light with eyes like a clear blue sky. They made a striking pair. But worse than that, Petal was boastful, broody, and basked in Miri's attention. She didn't care that her parents had died, either. She only cared that she had been inconvenienced—forced to leave her mansion and passed on to a boring, middle-class spinster relative.

I knew this because Petal talked constantly about the giant lakeside home she'd lost. It had a pool, a four-car garage, and a boathouse with room for a pontoon and a ski boat. She told us about the game room with a pool table and foosball and Ping-Pong and an actual Las Vegas slot machine that spit out real quarters. Miri asked a million questions, egging her on, feeding off every detail. They had so much in common, at times it was like they spoke their own, moneyed language. Words like *Pfister*, *Osthoff*, and *Miscauno* came up as they discussed their Wisconsin summer getaways. I'd finally catch on, and then they'd switch it up, tossing off foreign-sounding phrases like *Tensing Pen* and *San Souci*. Places their families vacationed in the winter, on some Caribbean island. Perhaps the Caymans, or Jamaica.

Their fancy Madison homes had stood on opposite shores of Lake Mendota (we were reading *Gatsby* in lit class that year, and I started to draw alarming parallels). The lake waters had baptized them both with the same privilege, one I could never understand.

When they talked about boat rides and country clubs and horseback riding lessons, I stayed silent. Miri would accuse me of sulking, but I wasn't. At least, that wasn't the only thing I was doing. I was using that time to strategize. Because the dynamics of my friendship with Miri had begun to shift. Something vital was slipping away, dissolving, and I wasn't going to let it—or let Miri—go without a fight.

3

THE BOOK'S OPENING pages brought back the storm that had raged inside me after my parents died. Had I really been the braggy teenager described in *No One Suspected*? Maybe from the outside. Yeah, I'd played off my tragedy like I didn't care. But that was survival, not reality. And I knew I'd talked about my old house too much. Though not for the reasons the book implied.

I didn't miss the grand staircase in the foyer or the backyard pool of our Maple Bluff house. If I never played another game of foosball, I wouldn't have cared. It was the people I wanted back. I craved the mom and dad who had walked those stairs, swum in that pool, and played at the foosball table—the parents I no longer let myself think about or mention because what had happened to them was too crushing. I'd had it good, for a while. Until the morning I don't like to remember.

All I know for sure is their Lincoln was left running in the garage, and the next morning I found them. Side by side on the bed in the above-garage guest room. They were cold and dead and stiff and looked so much like oddly posed museum figurines that I told myself someone had recreated my parents in wax. That's how I was able to shit-kick the panic and make it out of that room and back to the land of the living.

With my new friends at West High, I could only express the pain in terms of the life I'd had to leave behind. I couldn't talk to them, or to anyone, about the people who'd chosen to die, leaving me behind. So I buried my parents, moved in with my aunt, made new friends, and tried to be a normal teenager.

I kept this act up for about seven months. Then I started to crumble, just in time for Petal's Teenage Trag-edy, Act Two. That terrible night and its deadly severing of friendships covered the memory of my parents in a new layer of trauma. I wasn't even a fully baked person yet, and the main life lesson I'd learned was that everything was crap and the only way to survive was to bury and ignore. Ignore feelings and friends, bury the past deep. Harden my shell and grow spikes and self-medicate so nothing could surface and no one would get close.

But now my entire backstory was sitting in my lap. Exposed to the light of day, for the entire world to read. ME Littleton, whoever that was, claimed the book was a work of fiction. But the author was borrowing more from my flesh-and-blood past than anyone had a right to. That was infuriating as hell, but stronger than the rage was one huge, pressing question.

Why?

Once I opened that mental box of whys, questions flew like angry wasps from their nest:

Why target me?

Why now?

Why in a book and not to my face?

I set the book on my coffee table and wiped my hands on my jeans, as if I could rub away the stain it had left on me. The title glared from the front cover. *No One Suspected.* With a generic mystery title like that, the story could've been about anything. But it wasn't about anything. It was about me. About my friends. And what we'd done.

I kicked out with my right foot and sent the book rocketing off the table. It hit the laminate wood floor with a *thunk* and slid across the room like a puck on a hockey rink. It came to a stop underneath my shelving unit, below my favorite DVDs (*Speed, Run Lola Run, The Matrix*) and my smoking paraphernalia. The title smirked and smoldered, despite the colony of dust bunnies nesting under the shelves, in the same green as the digital rain from *The Matrix.*

I hauled myself off the couch and stuffed the book in the freezer. I hid it behind a carton of pistachio nut gelato and dug my laptop from under the pile of clean clothes I hadn't had time to fold. No, that's a lie—as always, they'd remain slumped at the end of my bed until I plucked jeans, T-shirts, and underwear out one by one as needed. In bed, under the covers, Netflix delivered an action movie straight into my veins—*John Wick* turned up to full volume, earbuds in so I wouldn't piss off the neighbor more than I already had. I stared at the screen until my eyes burned and the images blurred. I told myself the tears were for Keanu and his dog. No one else. Certainly not for myself.

* * *

It was the sun that woke me, streaming in through my window and hitting me like a punch. I winced and shifted until my face was in shadow. I rubbed my eyes until the world came back into focus. My laptop, tipped backward on the bed next to me, wanted to know, *Are you still watching?* I slapped it closed, noting the time. I was due at work in thirty minutes.

I texted my supervisor.

Ate some bad clams last night. I'm a mess, can't come in today. Will try to get some work done from here.

We both knew I wouldn't. I was a silent, efficient-bordering-on-obsessive employee 99 percent of the time. When my attitude and motivation tanked during the other 1 percent, my boss let it slide. I'd take a sick day or two and be back in the office like new. I probably could have told her the truth in my text—that my eyes felt like two piss holes in the snow, that my brain was jelly, that my entire system of self-protection was crumbling around me—but then she'd be obligated to recommend mental help and a longer leave of absence, and I didn't want to put that on her. We had our own way of communicating, and it worked. *Bad clams* was code. Our relationship, despite a generous dose of lies and avoidance, was one of the healthiest I'd ever had.

Feel better, she texted back. And I did, a little.

Breakfast was a joint followed by a can of cold brew and a large bowl of my BOC Blend. Breakfast of Champions, copyright me, perfected over many mornings of rigorous experimentation. One third Cap'n Crunch for a vanilla-caramel note, one third Cocoa Pebbles for chocolate and depth, and one third Wheat Chex because I'm a grown-ass woman and can't eat sugary garbage all the time. At least that's what Gus says. I added in the Chex after he kept harping on about me having the eating habits of a ten-year-old whose parents had given up. He'd meant for me to switch to eating just the Chex, but I misunderstood on purpose. It's a thing I do. He knows but doesn't call me on it. He's smart enough to take the small win. I like that about him.

Also, he happened to be right about the Chex. Having them in the BOC makes the garbage taste even better.

The book was still chilling in the freezer, but I could feel its presence in the house the same way the air is heavy and electric before a storm. My upstairs neighbor was always burning sage for one bad vibe or another— it drifted down through the ventilation system every few days—and I considered asking him to come down and burn some in my apartment. But the only burning herb I had any real faith in was marijuana, so I rolled a fresh joint. After three puffs, I'd gathered the courage to open the freezer door.

I'd thought about leaving the book in there for eternity, letting it warp in the damp chill and become part of the lumps of frost that were taking over my small freezer compartment like tumors inside a body. Maybe I could hold out until a new bestseller knocked it off the shelves and it disappeared. My life would go back to being the same.

Could I deal with more of the same?

More barely surviving, more clawing through each day. I was running on fumes, and hadn't realized it until the book crept into my life on little rat feet. My past had been feeding on me for years, leeching the nutrients from my blood until nothing but salty water ran through my veins. It was time to tie off my past once and for all, wrap a tourniquet around the place where the dead part of me met the living. Hopefully, whatever was left after the amputation could survive.

I retrieved the book and dusted away the layer of frost ghosting the cover. It opened with the crack of a person falling through thin ice. I settled into the couch and picked up where I'd left off the night before, skimming through the rest of the book's opening chapter. It told the story of a jealous girl named Izzy (not her real name—I knew her as Jenny) becoming distrustful of Miriam's (Megan's) budding friendship with the new girl in school. The me-girl, Petal Woznewski.

I tried to stay detached from the story, to zoom out and read as if it'd happened to someone else. It worked, for a while. The book was written from Izzy's/Jenny's point of view, which helped me keep that distance. But every page brought back a new memory or a forgotten detail, each more painful than the last, until I was right back there—until adult Petta was eaten alive by teenage Petal. But I didn't let myself stop, and soon the story consumed my focus.

Midmorning, I got a text from Gus. He wanted to know why I wasn't at work and if I was sick or if it had anything to do with how I'd left his apartment the other night and could he bring me some dinner, maybe chicken soup or saltines or something.

I could've asked him to send over a personal chef trained in ancient Persian cooking techniques, and he would've figured out a way to do it for me. The thing about Gus was, he didn't know how not to be a good guy. Even when that wasn't what I wanted. No matter how many times I batted away his kindnesses and refused his offers of help, he never gave up on me. If he had a last straw, I hadn't found it yet. And not for lack of trying.

I ignored his texts and went back to the book. ME Littleton knew—and wrote about—intimate details of my real-life teenage relationships. Details I hadn't thought anyone else noticed or remembered. I hadn't recalled them myself before reexperiencing them in the pages of *No One Suspected*.

How was that possible?

I didn't have a good answer for that.

But there was plenty in the book that had been common knowledge too. Even if I'd wished it'd been kept private.

The shocking death of my parents had been splashed across the local news. It was impossible to get the stain off me, even at a new school where I knew no one. Other students would whisper and point in the halls, thinking themselves clever and stealthy when really they were clumsy and obvious. I hated them for it. In class, the teachers would ask me to stay after so they could shower me with performative support or pity or pamphlets about processing grief. None of it helped me keep the low profile I was trying so hard to cultivate.

Then I met Megan. She saved me, at least for a while. She didn't point or whisper. Instead, she walked up to me after fifth-period gym, in the locker room on the Thursday of the first week of school. She was a stranger then, and I didn't know what to expect from her. Confrontation? Condescension? She wasn't one of those high-profile, ultrapopular girls, but she glowed all the same. I couldn't imagine what she wanted with me.

I'd noticed the two of them, Megan and her best friend Jenny, even among the four hundred something other students in our freshman class. They were inseparable. But on that first meeting, Jenny hung back, half hidden behind her locker, watching Megan approach. I didn't think anything of it at the time, but after, it made sense. Jenny preferred waiting in the wings until she got a read on the situation, and then she'd follow Megan's lead.

Megan was beautiful, her thick hair gleaming like the copper on a new penny. I stood my ground as she walked across the locker room, wiping my face of all expression.

"Hi. Petal?" She said my name like she wasn't sure if she was pronouncing it right. She hadn't been the first (and wouldn't be the last) to turn my name into a question. "I'm Megan. Anyway, I know you're new, and um, everything . . ."

No one ever said what had happened to my parents out loud, as if by saying the words, they'd make death more real. They referred and alluded, mouths collapsing into sympathetic crumples or stretching into small, toothless smiles.

"So, yeah, me and Jenny," she continued, pointing over her shoulder at her small, blond friend, "we're going to have a manicure party at my house after school. I live in Shorewood." She said this like it should mean something to me. It didn't. Not yet. "You wanna come?"

I hated nail polish, the sharp, chemical smell of it and the tiny brush that was clumsy in my hands and the way the thick liquid felt goopy as it dried, hardening the skin around my nails where I'd colored outside the lines. But it wasn't the manicure that mattered. It was the invitation. Painting nails was something normal teenage girls did.

"Yeah, okay," I said, turning my face into my still-open gym locker so Megan wouldn't see the unshed tears pooling in my eyes. I was grateful that someone, anyone, wanted to hang out with me—to treat me like a person and not a curiosity or a cause or a victim. I would've jumped headfirst into a vat of nail polish to get one shred of normalcy back.

"Great. Meet us at the Regent Street bike rack after school. You can ride with us."

Then she twirled away, leaving behind the scent of hair spray and gummy bears.

After the last bell of the day rang, I ran to the pay phone in the cafeteria and left a message on my aunt Shelly's office answering machine. She probably wouldn't have noticed if I didn't come right home after school; her work hours at the university were long and unpredictable. But the call was more of a performance than a check-in. I called so she'd know I wasn't sulking in my room until dinner, the way I had every other day since school started. I called to show off my brand-new friendship, and prove

I was trying. She wanted more for me than I wanted for myself, and it had become a roadblock between us.

When I made it to the bike racks, rushing and out of breath because I was afraid the other girls would leave me if I was late, only Megan was waiting. No sign of Jenny. Megan was scanning the sidewalk and waved me over when she saw me. As I approached, Megan leaned through the passenger-side window of a wood-paneled Wagoneer to say something to the driver. Megan's family had a live-in nanny for the younger children—an au pair, they called her, a twenty-four-year-old woman from Portugal they'd hired through a service. Each afternoon, the au pair would load Megan's twin younger siblings into the Wagoneer to pick Megan up from school. Riding the bus wasn't an option in Megan's world, and until she had a car of her own, she hitched a ride with the help.

Megan waved good-bye to the kids in the back seat, and the Wagoneer pulled away.

"Jenny's late," Megan explained, her voice tight with irritation. "And the kids were going berserk in the car. I didn't want to make them wait any longer."

"Sure," I said, still out of breath from my rush to meet her. I wasn't sure what to do or say next. Did this mean our plans were off? Had Megan changed her mind?

"She'll be here eventually," Megan said. "Her cousin can give us a ride."

I watched the departing buses, stuffed full of my classmates.

We chatted to pass the time; I don't remember now what we talked about. All I recall about those long minutes waiting for Jenny was that Megan's mind was not on our conversation. The girls appeared to be great friends, but I learned that afternoon there was more to their relationship than being inseparable—and Jenny's lateness had brought it to the surface. An undercurrent, maybe. Or a guitar string of tension Jenny had plucked. The air in front of the school, smelling of bus exhaust and cigarette smoke and sneaker rubber, vibrated with it.

When Jenny sauntered up, she had her cousin in tow. Ericka was older, a junior I think, and conservatively dressed, with her nose buried in a small leather Bible.

"Sorry," Jenny said carelessly, eyes anywhere but on Megan. "I had to get some books out of the library for my history report."

She looked over at me.

"Right. Hi. I'm Jenny."

"Petal," I said. "Megan invited me."

"Oh, I know. She told me." She smiled, but it flickered and was gone.

Jenny held her backpack with a single finger hooked through the loop at the top. It sagged in on itself. I doubted there were any books in it at all. Megan didn't seem to buy her excuse either.

"I sent Beatriz home already," she said pointedly, the vocal equivalent of bared fangs.

"Oh, no worries." Jenny talked a good game, but there was a tremor in her voice.

Megan cleared her throat, a warning. Jenny blinked as if she'd been smacked.

"Sorry I was late, but there's no problem, really. Ericka can drive us. Should we stop at Bagels Forever on the way? I'm starving."

At the mention of her name, Ericka began to walk, past the bike rack and up Regent Street toward the long line of student cars parked along the curb. We all followed.

I have no idea what Jenny and Megan's friendship was like before I arrived at West High, but my entrance seemed to cause a dynamic shift. Jenny asserted her power and position as Number-One Friend. Megan became increasingly irritated at not being immediately obeyed. And I was caught in the middle.

It took a long time for things to feel comfortable that first day we hung out. Jenny bought us all apology bagels. They were only twenty-five cents each, but I got the sense she couldn't easily spare the dollar. Ericka said only one word the entire ride—"Sesame," the flavor of bagel she wanted—and then dropped us off at Megan's house with a grim expression.

Up in Megan's fit-for-a-princess bedroom, the three of us chewed on our snacks so we wouldn't have to talk— pumpernickel for me, blueberry for them. We marveled over Megan's full rainbow of Wet n Wild nail colors. Jenny chose neon orange, applying the polish expertly. Megan wavered for a long time, asking me what I thought, ignoring Jenny's opinion, and settling on a color she called Tiffany blue. It looked like plain old light blue to me. I painted my nails a red so dark it was almost black, like a thick layer of dried blood. By the time the nail polish was put away and the fumes had dissipated, our silences had become easy rather than tense.

Megan and I bonded quickly after that. I figured she was one of those people: the shiny girls everyone is drawn to for reasons no one can articulate except to call it some sort of charisma or beauty or magic. But now I don't think it was that at all. Or not only that, at least. For me, Megan was the right person at the right time: someone with the power to pull me into her world so I didn't have to live in my own. And Megan's world was familiar in ways that were comforting—the ease her wealth brought, the casual way it was displayed and discussed, the spacious luxury of her house. She made me feel at home, the only consolation I'd felt since my parents died.

All the details of that first meeting were in the book. Our introduction, exactly as I remembered. It might've been plucked right from my gray matter. Megan was called Miri and Jenny was Izzy, but the locker room, Jenny making us wait, Bagels Forever, and Wet n Wild—all of it was in those pages. Only three people could have written every moment of that day in such detail: me, Megan, and Jenny. The only three who'd been there. The process of elimination was easy.

I hadn't written the book. That was one thing I was sure of. Grouchy and self-hating and a messy bitch? Yes, me to a capital T. But psychotic and delusional? No.

Megan hadn't written the book. She'd been dead for decades. The blurb on the back of *No One Suspected* got it just right: her death had been labeled a tragic accident, but there were rumors, and many had whispered *suicide*.

That left Jenny. The story was in her voice. But why would she dredge the past up now, in a way destined to throw both of our lives into chaos? It made no sense: Jenny would *never* expose secrets she had more reason to keep than I did. And why not warn me if she was going to spill her guts? Was her desire to attack me?

Jenny and I had sworn never to speak of Megan's death. Those secrets would go with us to the grave. *We didn't see Megan that night; we weren't there*—that's what we'd said when the police asked. Megan had been alone, drowning her teen drama queen sorrows in vodka, and suffered a tragic accident.

Lies.

Megan hadn't been alone. Jenny and I were there. But telling that truth wouldn't bring Megan back—not then, not now. Not ever. Jenny and I had agreed on that, at least. That was our pact, sealing and ending our friendship in a single moment. A licked envelope, never to be opened.

I put down the book, hands shaking, and cracked a new bottle of Gatorade. I poured it down my throat until I was gasping for air. New questions cropped up like weeds in an untended graveyard. I drank like I could wash them away.

Why was I the only character in the book who hadn't been renamed?

It felt pointed, and personal.

Why disguise the truth as fiction?

If the author wanted to call me out, why not write a true crime book? Wasn't that sort of thing trendy?

No matter the answers, one thing was clear: *No One Suspected* was a gun with its laser sights set on me.

The secret of Megan's death had festered inside me for decades. I'd been certain it would have done the same to Jenny. Maybe it was as simple as that: she was tired of keeping silent and wanted to have it out, with me and with the past. The novel was a revenge tale—even a chapter into the book, I could see the Izzy version of Jenny had it out for Petal. Maybe that was the purpose of publishing it. Real Jenny's revenge on the real me.

It was a story arc any book or movie lover could get behind: rebalancing the scales of justice. According to the book blurb, Izzy was obsessed with making someone pay for the death of Miri. She wanted to become the hero of the story.

It might have made sense that Jenny would want me to pay too.

But there were two problems with that plotline.

One: My life wasn't a book or a movie. It didn't conform to story arcs or provide an audience with easy answers or satisfying endings. Nothing about me was easy or satisfying, and I considered that a point of pride.

Two (and this is the big one): I hadn't killed Megan. But I had watched her die.

CHAPTER

4

THE BOOK READ like a warning shot. One I couldn't ignore, even if I'd wanted to. And I surprised myself with how much I didn't want to ignore it. The mysteries surrounding *No One Suspected* had layers, and I wanted to peel them away like the hangnails that plagued my ragged thumbs. Even if the reveal left me raw and bleeding.

"Jenny."

I whispered her name into the purple, early-evening light of my apartment, testing. I hadn't spoken it in decades, yet it still sounded the same on my lips. I couldn't picture the adult face that would match. So much time had passed. What did middle-aged Jenny Isaacs look like? Was she still a small, hungry-eyed blond, or had the years changed her as much as they'd changed me?

My laptop's battery light blinked orange. I'd forgotten to plug it in. I dug out the charger and set myself up at the two-seater café table that occupied my studio's barely-there transition from kitchen to living room. The laptop had come back from the dead by the time everything I needed was arranged in front of me: a pack of Trident original flavor, a stubby bottle of Coors Banquet, a freshly rolled joint, and a bowl with a mixture of sesame sticks and rye chips.

The world revolved around social media—at least that was what I'd heard. I didn't touch the stuff. It was a travesty, if you asked me, experiencing life through a screen instead of having boots on the ground. And what good would Facebook or Twitter have done me? The last thing I wanted was to draw attention to myself, virtually or otherwise.

But I knew Facebook had its uses, both shameful and worthwhile: Stalking exes. Checking to see if your elementary school teachers were still alive. Admiring photos of your cousin's latest drag performance. And tracking down old classmates, of course.

It was that last one that got me. For the first time in my life, I intentionally opened Facebook. Or I tried to—I couldn't get far without an account. I hated the thought of an online Petal existing within the suffocating, white-and-blue confines of Facebook. There were too many versions of me out there already, thanks to *No One Suspected*. But my curiosity was more powerful than my loathing. I made a profile. The task became a lot less of a chore once I realized I could use my real name without having to be the real me. Then I leaned into it. Hard.

Facebook Petal added 1990s Janeane Garofalo as her profile picture—not too far off from my actual, current look. Same slightly Goth vibe, but with thicker eyebrows and less brown lipstick. Fake FB Petal worked as a full-time Walmart greeter near Baltimore. She was "In a Relationship with Myself" and had recently celebrated her cockatoo Murray's fourth birthday with a birdseed cake in the shape of Murray himself.

Google's image search truly is amazing. Imagine it, and you can find a picture of it. And then pretend it's your own and repost it on Facebook.

Jennifer Isaacs Madison Wisconsin, I typed into the search bar. A few faces popped up, none of them her. The ages were all wrong.

Puff, crunch, sip. My refreshments kept me going when I wanted to slam the laptop closed in frustration.

Next, I tried *Jennifer Isaacs 1990 Madison West High School*.

The school's official page popped up, but that was no help. It was all student access and parent portals and event calendars and daily schedules.

Still no Jenny.

The *Go Regents West High Class of 94!* reunion page begged for attention from the sidebar of suggested groups.

"Finally," I muttered. If anyone was willing to get fake-nostalgic over old classmates, it would be these people. But the group was private. I'd need to request membership. As myself, a real member of the class of 1994.

Ugh.

"Ugh. But when in Rome . . ."

I wasn't the only one wasting a Wednesday night online. My request to join the group was granted in five minutes. This allowed me access to hundreds of blurry pictures, taken the nineties way: on compact film cameras, developed at the local drugstore, scanned and uploaded years later onto the internet. Familiar teenage faces, some smiling and some snarling. And then there was—may a greater power smite me if I ever tie another flannel around my waist—the fashion. Hypercolor T-shirts, baggy Gir-baud jeans tight-rolled at the ankle, Benetton sweaters, and giant scrunchies. Converse sneakers too, but those never seem to go out of style.

I shoved a handful of sesame sticks into my mouth and scrolled the photos. I wasn't in any of them—no surprise. But Megan was there, even though she hadn't lived to see the end of our freshman year. It seemed that anyone who'd preserved her impish grin on film had uploaded a photo, trying to claim a sliver of the notoriety that went along with her untimely death. Occasionally, I'd see a blond smudge lurking behind Megan in a photo. Jenny. In one, I could see half of her face, staring down the photographer. But old photos of Jenny were no help to me. And she wasn't a member of the Facebook group—I checked.

I scrolled back through the years until my fingers ached. The Megan posts came in waves, a new one every other year or so, poking at her memory like a fading bruise. Testing to see if the old wound was still painful.

Hey, anyone remember that Megan girl who died freshman year? That was so sad! someone would post, as if they were the first to resurrect her.

Underneath, a predictable cascade of responses:

I had gym class with her. We were badminton partners. She was so sweet.

I probably shouldn't say, but I always sensed there was a darkness in her. I wasn't all that surprised when she died. Still sad, though.

RIP Megan. Gone but not forgotten.

No one on the reunion page had much to say about the real Megan. The girl I knew. There had hardly been a chance for most of them to get to know her, and too much high school still to survive after she left us. The shock of her death got buried: under the boys' basketball state championship, first loves, school dances, college admissions. It got buried because Jenny and I, the two people who should have kept her memory alive, lied about where we'd been that night, and never spoke of Megan, or to each other, again.

My beer was empty. I went to get another and downed half of it in a few long swallows.

After Megan, I'd stopped trying to make friends. I'd done a pretty shit job in my first attempt at West High, and I felt jinxed—first my parents had died, and then Megan—or like I was poison. That sounds dramatic. Okay, I wasn't poison. But I was bad news, and unlucky to boot. Not that people lined up to hang out with me. I was pleasant enough to my classmates but cultivated a low profile. Not too friendly, not too abrasive. I wanted to be unremarkable, to disappear. I concentrated on graduating so I could get the hell out of Madison and never look back.

Jenny hadn't fared any better. After Megan died, she spiraled into an angry depression, acted out, and by the end of freshman year could often be found getting high on the Regent Street heating grate where the stoners gathered. A few months into sophomore year, she was finally expelled for throwing her biology textbook at a teacher. Not her biology teacher, but some poor bastard on cafeteria duty who'd asked her to put her tray away.

Everyone knew she and Megan had been inseparable. No one was surprised when she fell apart.

The reunion page was bringing back memories, but that wasn't what I needed—or wanted. Which was to locate Jenny. So I added my own post to the mix.

Anyone remember Jenny Isaacs? She was only at West for Freshman year.

I waited, hoping for at least one response. After fifteen minutes I got one, but it didn't do me any good.

Uh, who? Nope.

I didn't recognize the poster's name and was rapidly losing faith in the whole Facebook sleuthing idea.

She was friends with Megan, the girl who died, I explained.

Uh, still nope.

If anyone knew where Jenny was now, they weren't on Facebook that night.

I'd witnessed the cafeteria hissy fit that got Jenny expelled but had never seen her again after that. Before long, it was like she and Megan had never walked the halls of West High at all. Had Jenny stayed in Madison, gone to college? The internet was giving me nothing. Her less-than-unique name made it harder to find answers. She was a Jenny and I was a Petal. That said everything about how much we had in common. Megan had been the only thing holding us together. Then she died, and the fire that fed our friendship went dark.

So did we.

Despite my Facebook fail, I wasn't ready to give up on the internet entirely. Mostly because it allowed me to continue searching without leaving the safety of my apartment. My sleuthing tangents were plentiful, and the internet rabbit holes were deep. I combed through white page listings and neighborhood directories. I paid for one of those people-finder sites, but none of the Jenny Isaacses it found matched the person I'd known. I scrolled through *Jennifer Isaacs* images on Google, in case a familiar feature caught my eye, but none did. Searching for one Jenny among millions was a dead end, and the six-pack of Coors proved no help.

Burp.

*   *   *

I'd passed out on the couch. The squeal of brakes from an early-morning delivery truck woke me. Every inch of my body screamed with an ache or a pain or a grumble. It was a bummer I couldn't crash anywhere I wanted anymore, at least not without consequences. Just thinking about a bad night's sleep could give me a neck ache. I wouldn't go so far as to call myself old, but I certainly wasn't a youngster anymore.

The first thing I saw when I pried my eyes open was the book. Waiting facedown on the coffee table, corner of the page turned down where I'd left off reading. My laptop, its belly full of charge, had gone to sleep on the kitchen table. I relit my half-cashed joint from the night before and poured myself a heaping bowl of BOC. Three spoonfuls in, I Googled the book.

No One Suspected, by ME Littleton, published by Roebler House Books.

Soon to be a major motion picture!

Roebler House was based in New York City, an imprint of a larger megapublisher. On the About Us page of their website, each editor was listed alongside their books. A smiling woman with a head of dark curls had acquired *No One Suspected*. If anyone would know who ME Littleton was, it was her. But of course it couldn't be as easy as a phone call—the website didn't offer up her contact information. There was an address, only a few blocks from my own place of work. I'd probably passed the building dozens of times on one of my lunchtime rambles—never suspecting that anything to do with me could be going on inside.

The thought of marching down to the publisher and confronting the editor in person made me want to crawl under my weighted blanket with Netflix and a year's supply of Takis. I was much better with a computer in front of me or, if pressed, on the phone. The lack of email addresses and phone numbers on the website was annoying. How did people get in touch with them?

But there was a better question: What was I going to say if I did talk to the editor?

I ran a version of that conversation through my head.

Hi. My name is Petal Woznewski. Yes, like in the book. Yes, really. No, I'm not crazy. I promise. But here's the thing: I didn't enjoy being threatened in the dedication, and what I enjoyed even less was reading about my dead friend Megan. Yes, I know there's no Megan in the book. The author used my real name but made up . . . You know what? It doesn't matter. [Long pause for listening and silent swearing.]

Yes, I know it's a novel. Yes, I know that a novel means it's fictional. Yes, I know fictional means it's made up. I'm not a complete moron.

Click. Even in my imaginary conversations, I got hung up on.

No wonder they didn't post their direct numbers online. Anyone might call and spew crazy at them. Or worse—try to pitch them book ideas.

But there was another way. What if I didn't lead with the crazy? What if I appealed to their deepest desire: to sell more copies of *No One Suspected*?

I hunted the Roebler House website for a number, any number. The only one I could find was a general line listed under the website's Media and Public Relations drop-down menu. Close enough. I took a few minutes to get my story straight. I checked the time: just after eight o'clock in the morning. I waited thirty minutes before calling, finishing the joint and settling into the perfectly saggy cushions of my couch, where I wouldn't be tempted to shove more cereal in my mouth.

Where was my phone? After ten minutes of searching, I found it still in the jeans that sat in a heap on—of all places—my one square foot of kitchen counter space. I returned to the couch and dialed.

"Roebler-House-how-may-I-direct-your-call?" The receptionist spoke so fast, her greeting came out as one long, run-on word.

"Wow." I hadn't expected to be confronted with an actual human so quickly. I'd thought I'd have to wade through a robo-directory first. "Okay. Sorry. I'm calling— I represent a group of Instagram influencers who would like to partner with Roebler House on a promo for one of your books."

"Hold, please."

There was no hold music, only a loop of recorded advertisements for their books. I was parked there for several minutes, listening to glowing reviews for (you guessed it) their latest smash, *No One Suspected*.

"Roebler PR, this is Gwen?" Her voice went up at the end of her greeting, as if she weren't entirely sure who she was. I knew exactly how to play her.

"Gwen, hi! I've heard such great things about you! My name is Polly Marsh." If you want people to cooperate, it's always good to show you're listening by working their name in right away. Compliments don't hurt, either. I'd done my time in telemarketing. Hated it, but learned a lot about people. "I've got a group of Insta influencers who are super, super excited about one of your new books. They'd love to do a collab. Your sales will totally blow up."

Occasionally, when I needed a breather between movies, I looked up online gossip on my favorite action stars. Not proud, not sorry. Lingo like *Insta* and *collab* had burrowed into my brain uninvited. Never imagined it would come in handy, but here we were.

"That sounds amazing. Which title?"

"*No One Suspected.*"

"Oooh, that one is so totally hot right now. But we could always use more promo. Who do you represent, and what kind of collab did you have in mind?"

"Well, my bookstagrammers would love to do an Insta Live with the author."

"Oh. Yeah, no. Littleton's not doing interviews. But if you'd like to submit your questions in writing, I'll see what I can do. I'll need to see your clients' follower count and engagement numbers first, of course."

"Oh, bummer. Not even a phone interview?"

"Yeah, no. It's in the author's contract. No publicity."

"It makes sense why there isn't much information out there about her. Him? Is Littleton a pen name? Maybe you guys have a more extensive bio that we could make work for our purposes."

"Sorry, I can't tell you any more than what's printed on the book jacket."

"Aw, come on, Gwen. Just one tidbit? I'd love to work with Roebler House, and the angle we're going for is to get a scoop on the author. Our follower counts are six-figure."

"Ugh. I really wish I could. The author values their privacy; that's all I'm allowed to say. Sorry. I'd, like, totally get fired if I spilled."

"Right. Okay. I'll get back to you if we can work something out."

"If you have a strategy one-sheet you could email—"

I hung up on Gwen.

After repressing the urge to chuck my phone at the wall, I texted my boss for another sick day and took a few minutes to dissect this new piece of the puzzle. I turned things over in my head. Jenny was impossible to find, and ME Littleton didn't want to be found. Coincidence? I believed in the kismet of coincidence as much as I believed in happy endings, or talk therapy, or myself.

The author had built a buffer of anonymity around themselves, despite the public nature of *No One Suspected*'s success. Or because of that success, maybe.

Had anyone on the internet figured out who Littleton was? Surely the entirety of the World Wide Web was a better detective than one grouchy, no-longer-young woman with no social media skills.

Who is ME Littleton? I asked the Google gods.

People magazine, *Entertainment Weekly*, and dozens of blogs had featured the book, but they had no more information on the author than I did. Over and over, the single bio line from the book jacket was parroted. There was a Reddit thread—I had to pause for ten minutes and four more bites of cereal to figure out what the hell a Reddit thread was—speculating about why the author was so secretive.

The general consensus: yes, ME Littleton was a pen name. Probably for an already-famous author who wanted to try writing something new, they speculated. But I doubted that was the case.

And no: no one knew who was behind the mask, though many obsessive readers were curious. Turned out they'd done some Googling of their own. And they'd found no record of any "ME Littleton" ever having lived in Madison, Wisconsin.

I tossed the phone on the couch next to me and stretched out to stare at the ceiling, hoping its ancient water stains would show me a way forward. I'd tried and failed twice: to figure out where Jenny was, and to uncover who had written the book. Pathetic efforts at below-amateur-level detective work, but at least I'd done something. And something was more than I usually did.

Was it enough?

Could I let it all go now and forget that someone was trying to push my deepest, darkest buttons?

If ignoring touchy topics had been an Olympic sport, I'd have had a neck full of medals. But the imaginary ants crawling underneath my skin told me this time it was different. A fat joint and two hours of admiring the Rock's biceps weren't going to make *No One Suspected* fade away.

It was time (way past, if I was being honest) to face my demons. But there was no handbook for this sort of thing; no "So You're the Target of a Fictionalized Murder Book" article on the internet.

My phone rang. Like, a real phone call and not a text. I couldn't remember the last time I'd gotten one of those. I found the phone between my couch cushions, covered in unidentifiable crumbs. I thought maybe it was Gwen calling me back, but no.

"Uh, hello?"

"Is this Petal . . . Woznewski?"

The voice sounded female, and young.

"Who's asking?"

"I'm a writer. A blogger, actually. *I Like Big Books and I Cannot Lie* is the name of my blog. And I, well, I'm just going to come out and ask: Are you ME Littleton?"

"What the—Hell no! For the love of Sir Mix-a-Lot, why would you think that?"

"We thought—"

"Hold on, you said *we*. Who's we?"

"Oh. Me and some people on the boards. The, uh, message boards? The whole ME Littleton thing is a real mystery. One we'd like to solve. And, well, the name Petal didn't quite match the other character names in the book. It stands out, so we thought maybe it was supposed to mean something. We thought maybe it was a clue. Someone posted on the boards this morning that they'd found a real Petal Woznewski living in New York. Another poster paid for one of those online background check things and shared your cell number with all of us."

"I don't know what's worse: the actual book, or you book people."

I hung up. She tried calling back, and I blocked her. Then texts and calls started coming from other numbers. I blocked each one, but there seemed to be an endless supply of book monsters more than happy to ruin my day.

I shoved my phone back into the couch cushions and went for a walk. South this time, down Seventh until I hit Greenwich, then east on Eighth until I hit Tompkins Square Park. I grabbed an egg sandwich with scallion cream cheese from the nearest deli and looped back home again, eating as I walked. As I approached the door of my building, there was a slim young guy lurking outside. Tall, messy hair, with a copy of *No One Suspected* tucked under his arm.

"Dude. What the hell. You guys are stalking me at home now?"

"You're Petal?" he asked, eyeballs shiny with delight.

"Who I am is none of your business. I don't know anything about the book. I want to be left alone. Tell all the other . . . book . . . creatures I don't want anything to do with this. I don't know anything!"

"You are! I knew it. Here, will you sign my book?" He held out a Sharpie, face alive with dopey hope. I almost felt sorry for him.

Almost.

"Sure, kid." I took the marker, grabbed his book, and threw them into the street in opposite directions. I ran into my building and didn't look back until I was behind my own locked door.

My couch was ringing again.

I retrieved my phone and changed my Do Not Disturb settings to block everyone not in my contact list. I managed one relieved breath before my door buzzer started to ring.

"This is my nightmare."

I wasn't going to get any peace until I gave them something. Maybe everything. Signing one book or taking one phone call wouldn't be enough. They were chasing a mystery, like I was. I knew that hunger for answers. But they had each other, and message boards and blogs and Twitter and Reddit. My phone number was already posted on the internet. My address too, by now. Probably by the kid I'd pissed off downstairs.

I had to get out. Leave for a few days, until the book weirdos blogged themselves out and stopped harassing me. I could stay with Gus. He'd be goddamn thrilled. That would cause a whole new problem, pushing our relationship somewhere I wasn't ready to go.

Or I could . . .

Nope. There was no one else. My family began and ended with me. I solved my own problems, always had. And this time would be no different. I knew what I needed to do.

The only way out is through, I always say.

It was a slogan that belonged on one of those dumbass Successories posters, with DETERMINATION printed on top in large white letters on a black background. Maybe underneath, a glossy photograph of a tiny eagle chick ready to jump out of the nest. Cheesy as hell. But I'm from the don't-knock-it-till-ya-try-it school. And when nothing else worked for me, those words did. If I hit a wall, it was the nugget of wisdom I could always fall back on.

The only way out is through.

To find a way out of my tangle with ME Littleton, I had to go back to the beginning. Dig through the dirt. In Madison. And damned if that wasn't a punch in the metaphorical balls.

I made the arrangements fast, before I could chicken out.

I texted my boss: **Feeling better but my personal life is in the shit. Need a few days.**

I searched for flight deals and booked the cheapest last-minute ticket available, departing the next morning. I rarely spent money on anything but food, rent, beer, and pot, so I had a bit to spare. I found a vacancy at an Airbnb cottage in my aunt Shelly's old neighborhood near West High. It had no-contact check-in via a lockbox, just my speed. By the time I shut my laptop and went to pack, I had a travel itinerary but no plan—except to ignore the door buzzer and get to the airport early, then barrel into Madison, guns blazing, and see what ghosts I could raise.

Would Madison still feel the same as it had in high school—haunted and hostile?

I stretched out on my bed and tried to conjure a midwestern summer: sunbaked grass and encroaching thunderstorms and the smell of beer brats blackening on the grill. These sensory memories came too easily and hit me harder than I liked. When I pictured myself back there, it wasn't the adult me but the teenager. Older me didn't fit, somehow.

I stopped trying to shoehorn adulthood into my recollections and let my inner fourteen-year-old return. I slipped back in time, to the nights when all I wanted was to sneak out of aunt Shelly's house to stalk the shadowy streets, Megan and Jenny at my side, all of us putting mile after mile on our bright-white Keds as our restless feet gleamed like a constellation in the darkness.

Excerpt from
No One Suspected
1990

O N THE NIGHTS we planned to sneak out, we would sleep
over at Miri's. I loved spending time at her house, first
her and me, and then with Petal too. Why would we go anywhere else when Miri had everything? Her house was a castle,
built of dark wood and stone with a copper-capped turret on
the highest floor. Miri's bedroom was in the turret, a tower
fit for a princess. In the backyard, her parents had commis-
sioned a playhouse: a perfect miniature replica of the big
house. That's how her family referred to them: the Big House
and the Little House. I did, too, because I was "an honorary Rowley." That's what her family used to call me. I never
wanted to belong anywhere more than I did at their house.
Even though I loved my parents, sometimes I loved being
part of the Rowley family more. Life was easier there.

I had sleepovers at the Rowley Big House long before
Petal entered our lives, but when it was just Miri and me,
we never snuck out. We'd giggle over our old middle school
diary entries and play MASH and watch John Hughes movies
and listen to music on her giant boom box. After Petal joined
our sleepovers, those activities weren't enough anymore. Miri,
trying to impress her, suggested something "less childish,"

like sneaking out after dark. That's how it began. We would pretend to get ready to go to sleep. Miri, stretching out on her canopy bed, toes curling luxuriously into her duvet. Me, rolling out my tattered Rainbow Brite sleeping bag, turned inside out before I left home so Petal wouldn't notice and tease me about the cartoon character. Petal and I slept on the floor, on either side of Miri's bed. The carpet underneath me was soft as a cloud, and plusher than my sleeping bag—than anything I had ever or would ever own.

Squeals and protests echoed through the house, eventually making their way up the winding turret stairs. Miri had two younger siblings, and the au pair always had trouble wrestling them into bed. After Miri was born, the Rowleys had decided to try once more for a boy. They wanted to complete their matched set, Miri had told me once. It took a long time, and many doctor visits, before Mrs. Rowley was able to get pregnant. Miri was seven when her mother gave birth to twins, Mike and Beth; a different kind of matched set. Miri was wonderful with them, kissing scraped knees and reading bedtime stories and helping the au pair when she couldn't convince Beth to get in her car seat. She was a big sister in every sense of the word. But their parents treated the twins as unnecessary, like a second entrée they'd ordered but lost the appetite for before it reached their table.

The three of us whispered and giggled in the darkness of the turret as the house settled for the evening. I know I make it sound like Petal ruined everything, but there were good times too. She wasn't evil, just unwanted. She and Miri were too alike; I didn't need a second, lesser version of my best friend. But those sneak-out nights brought out the best in our friendship. Especially in the anticipatory hours before we left the house. We ate mini gummy bears and washed them down with Orchard Peach Clearly Canadian. We used flashlights to see our diaries as we scribbled pastel ink across the pages.

We twisted and braided each other's hair and made knotted crowns atop our heads, readying ourselves to rule the night.

Finally, the grandfather clock below us in the foyer chimed twelve.

"Not a single word until we get through the yard and out to the street. The neighbors are tattletales."

On nights like this, Miri spoke in orders that allowed no argument. We put on our shoes and snuck down the spiral stairs. Then it was a short walk down the rear hallway, behind the expansive kitchen, to reach the back door of the house. Once outside, we avoided the wide lawn of the front yard. It gave direct access to the street but was exposed on all sides and overlooked by the master bedroom and the au pair's room. The backyard provided the camouflage we needed for a clean escape. Not that the au pair could have done anything except tell Miri's parents about us sneaking out. But Miri loved to get away with something. With anything.

We were out in the crisp, early-fall night air in minutes, the lumpy stone wall of the Big House at our backs as we tiptoed toward freedom. Owls hooted from the trees, urgent and wary.

The girls, the girls, they're up to no good, they seemed to say.

We cut across the shaded backyard toward the side street. The property was canopied by tall oaks, but along the rear, a line of aspen trees stood sentinel. Their trunks were spindly and white, smooth except for the occasional black, scar-like marking. Their limbs, dripping with the golden leaves of October, stretched toward the house in a desperate, yearning way.

As we crossed the back patio and passed the Little House, Petal stopped to gather her unruly dark hair and secure it with a scrunchie. She was like that: never afraid to take her time, forcing us to stop and wait for her.

A soft murmur drifted across the backyard, filling my stomach with the mad flutter of a trapped moth. Not the owls this time. At first I thought it was the trees, their half-bare branches moaning in the wind. But then a pair of eyes flashed at me from the window of the Little House. I swallowed a yelp. Visions of Chucky dolls and *Children of the Corn* filled my head. I hated those movies, but Miri liked watching me squirm and often suggested we watch them. This was nothing out of a horror movie, though—only Miri's younger brother Mike, nose pressed against the leaded glass. His eyes were sliding back and forth, a metronome keeping time. And his lips were moving—repeating the chorus of a song or chanting a string of words, I wasn't certain.

I took a few steps closer to the Little House, trying to hear. The door was ajar.

"The skeleton trees have eyes, and they are watching."

He was trying to warn us, I think. That's why his eyes kept moving back and forth from us to the aspens. *Ticktock.* A moment ago I'd found the trees beautiful, white and black and golden, like they were dressed in finery for an autumn ball. When I looked again, I saw them through Mike's eyes. The black scars on the trunk repeated a pattern: two thin welts curved around a center knot. The markings were created when a lower, sun-starved branch fell off, I learned later. Together the ridged welts and the knot made the familiar almond shape of a staring eye. And the white trunks did indeed look like skeletons. Taken together, they were a legion of reedy wraiths with a thousand bottomless eyes: skeleton trees, watching.

"Miri . . ." Fear closed my throat. She heard me and turned, mouth twisted with annoyance. I'd done the forbidden: speak before we were safely away from the Big House. I pointed to Mike in the window, and her face softened.

"Oh, Mikey," she whispered, rolling her eyes. "He always does this. His idea of rebellion is sneaking out after the au pair goes to sleep. Then the trees freak him out and he's too scared to make it back inside by himself."

I couldn't blame Mikey. I too wanted nothing more than to be back indoors, cuddled inside my Rainbow Brite sleeping bag, eyes shut tight. But I didn't have the excuse of being seven years old. Miri and Petal would never let me forget it if I chickened out.

Petal and I waited while Miri crawled inside the playhouse to talk to her brother. His eyes disappeared from the window, and the plaid curtains he'd pushed aside fell back into place. I couldn't hear what they were saying over the rasp of tree branches, but Miri was able to soothe him. She emerged from the doorway, dusting off the knees of her ninety-dollar jeans. I'd been with her the day she bought them, from a trendy boutique downtown on State Street. All my clothes came from the clearance rack at Kohl's, and the bill for my meager back-to-school wardrobe that year hadn't reached the price of that single pair of jeans.

Mike followed his sister out of the playhouse, and Miri walked him to the back door of the Big House.

"Up to your room and be quiet. Flash the light once when you get there. I'll be watching. Go!"

He disappeared into the darkness of the house, and Miri inched the door shut. We all watched the second-story window that overlooked the backyard. Mike's room. All I could think about as we waited for the light to flash was that every time Mike looked out his window, his view would be full of the skeleton trees. Even inside, he couldn't escape them.

When the flash came, Miri led the way out of the yard, slipping between the aspen. Petal followed. I tried to scan the tree line for another way to get to the side street without having to pass between the bone-white trunks. The branches might bend to grab me, trap me against their spines, I thought. Make me one of them. But the rest of the yard was enclosed by thicker trees or blocked by other houses. There was no other way. I sucked in my breath, willed my feet to unfreeze, and ran after my friends.

The streets of Shorewood Hills didn't have sidewalks, though it never occurred to me back then to wonder why. There was so much about Miri's life that was out of my league. For all I knew, rich people hated sidewalks. Thinking about it now, I believe they shunned sidewalks because having them would encourage undesirables like me to walk there. It was a statement: *Shorewood Hills is different, somehow better, and we don't want you here.*

The three of us didn't care about sidewalks on those nights of freedom. Once we were a safe distance from the house, we marched right down the middle of the street like we owned it. If we saw a car coming, headlights sweeping along the blacktop, we'd jump behind a parked car or a tree or a garage. Shorewood Hills had their own police, who were known for being hard-asses. They'd once stopped me as I was Rollerblading over to Miri's house, pulling up behind me with lights twirling as I rocketed down a steep hill. When the hill bottomed out, I dragged myself to a stop and stood unsteadily to await my fate. They gave me a warning, told me to slow down. I had exceeded the twenty-mile-per-hour speed limit.

All the Shorewood police officers were men, which meant we had an advantage. Especially Miri. She could smile or cry her way out of almost anything. We made a game out of dodging them, and when we couldn't, she would turn on the tears. Boys were easy for Miri, no matter their age, and everything was a game to her. Even friendship. Petal and I played it according to her ever-changing rules. We had no choice—play or suffer the silent treatment. Most of the time I was grateful to be allowed into her orbit. But the more time Petal spent with us, expanding our duo into a trio, the less I felt like Miri's game was one I could win.

CHAPTER

5

My PLANE ENTERED Madison air space from the
south, banking northeast as it approached Dane
County Regional Airport. It felt like a low-key tourism
pitch to come at the city from its prettiest angle: over the
downtown isthmus between the city's two largest lakes.
The state capitol building stood tall at the city's center, a
white dome topped with a golden statue of a woman. Her
name was Wisconsin, I remembered from my fifth-grade
social studies paper. Regal, if you didn't look too closely. If
you did, you'd notice her accessories: a helmet with a badger crouched on top, and both corn cobs and cornucopias
on the sides.

The fall-themed food and glorified weasel I could
do without. The helmet, though. That was smart. Miz
Wisconsin knew how to protect herself. I had no idea if my
mental armor would cushion me from the impending colli-
sion with my past. Or if it could protect me from an attack
badger—much less likely, but I wasn't ruling anything out.
If you're not prepared, disasters will sneak up on you.

My last hit of pot had been hours ago, and my anxiety was spiking. I'd left my stash back in New York—a

possession arrest was the last thing I needed. The only thing staving off a panic attack as the airplane juddered to the ground—*bounce-lift-bounce*—was imagining myself as John Cusack in *Grosse Pointe Blank*. In that movie, he plays a hitman who returns to his hometown to do a job and attend his high school reunion on the side. He visits classmates and old haunts. People get shot. There are some laughs in between. I was hoping for the same on my visit home—minus the shooting. But again, not ruling anything out.

I rented a cheap car at the airport, thankful my ongoing paranoia had forced me to keep my driver's license current. But I hadn't been behind the wheel in years. And the last time I'd been in Madison was the day I graduated high school. After tossing my cap in the air, I hadn't even looked to see where it landed. I took off my gown, draped it over the cheap folding chair, and went home to my aunt's house to finish packing. I loaded two duffels' worth of worldly possessions into my old Mercury Tracer, bought with money earned slinging pies nights and weekends at Doc's Pizzeria. I said good-bye to aunt Shelly, got behind the wheel, and drove. First to Chicago, where I sold the car for rent money. Soon after, to New York, where I'd lived ever since.

Madison's population was somewhere around the quarter-million mark, but in many ways it was still a small town. A cold sensation washed over me the minute I walked out of the airport's automatic doors, despite the summer heat: I was on display. In Madison, it felt impossible to be inconspicuous or to blend in. My second-grade teacher, or the old pro who'd given me golf lessons at age ten, or Doc of Doc's Pizzeria—any of them might walk around the corner in the next minute, trapping me in a snarl of reminiscence.

Who was I kidding? All of those people had been old back when I knew them. That meant they were all dead by now.

The thought was comforting. My skin warmed. I went to find my rental car.

* * *

The Airbnb was listed as a "granny cottage." Cutesy code for a little house out back of a big house. Intended to contain a stray granny, I guess. The city layout came back to me as I steered the car west. I wondered if the cottage would feel anything like the old playhouse in Megan's backyard. Another Little House, behind a different Big House. I'd read that chapter on the plane, where her yard had been described in perfect, eerie detail. I'd had to flag down the flight attendant for a mini bottle of Jameson to get me through. But that had been hours ago. I turned off the AC and rolled the windows down, letting the humid midwestern air loosen my tensed muscles.

The cottage was located in aunt Shelly's old neighborhood, across Rowley Avenue and a block down from the house where we'd lived. Aunt Shelly had been a physics professor at the university. Her house was far enough from campus that she could get away from her students but close enough for her to walk to her office. Which she did, each weekday morning. In her clunky Reeboks, with low-heeled pumps waiting in her giant shoulder bag. She was built like a fire hydrant: solid and low to the ground. My father's older sister. She was gruff and strict, but she'd also taken me in with no fuss and given me a good home. Nothing about what happened to me was her fault. I hoped she knew I'd never blamed her.

Leaving town had meant leaving her behind too. I told myself now that she'd known why Madison was poison for me, and understood, and forgiven me. But she and I never talked about that stuff. I'd never know whether she felt abandoned, or thought I was an ungrateful brat. (I was. I am.) She died the year after I left, of a cancer she'd been battling since my senior year but never told me she had. She waited to start chemo until after my graduation, so I wouldn't have to watch her go through it. I found all this out when her lawyer mailed me her inheritance paperwork. She'd left me her investments and her house. I immediately cashed everything out over the phone from my apartment in Chicago. It financed my move to New York, allowed me to take my time finding a job and to avoid the grimiest, most roach-infested apartments. A few thousand of her money was still left—my emergency fund. I had a feeling it might come in handy soon.

I slowed to a roll as I passed her old house. Our old house, I guess. The current owners were power washing the brick. The vines and patina I remembered had been blasted away. Nothing had been renovated, but it didn't look like the same house anymore. This didn't make me sad. It proved I was right to have never come back until now, until I was forced. Madison wasn't my home. There was nothing for me here, except a mystery to solve and a past to bury, for good this time.

I pulled into the driveway of the Airbnb, parking off to the left as my reservation had instructed, and hauled my overstuffed backpack to the cottage.

It was nothing like the creepy Little House. It was adult sized, for one thing. The exterior was cream stucco with cornflower-blue trim. If I were the type to use a word like *charming*, that's what I would've called it. I punched the key code the owner had texted me into the digital door lock, which gave way with a soft beep and swung open. Inside were four neat rooms: kitchen, bathroom, and a living room/bedroom combo divided by French doors. The windowpanes of the doors were stained glass, and the midday light streaming through them pained the oak floors pink and orange.

I'd booked a week—at a hundred dollars a night for private accommodations, it was pennies by New York standards—though I wasn't sure how long I would actually stay. As long as I could stand it, probably. As long as it took, if I could manage it. My hidey-hole of an apartment in the big, anonymous city called to me every minute. The light in Madison was too bright, too insistent. It exposed everything I preferred to hide.

I muffled my homeward yearnings, pulled the window shades down, and focused on the unpleasant task in front of me.

Activate: Cusack Assassin Mode.

Memories needed to be jogged. Old ghosts needed to be raised.

First, a mental hit list, in no particular order:

Visit Megan's House
Visit Jenny's House
Visit the reservoir
Ask around about the book
Talk to Ben
Figure out what comes next ???

Ben was the only person from high school I could stomach getting back in touch with—not to mention the only person I'd call an old friend. We'd first met in the back of Mr. Sederquist's sophomore history class, whispering snarky comments to each other. Him from under a sheet of chestnut hair and me from behind a perpetual sneer. We were both on the slacker-yet-still-want-to-graduate, just-enough-to-get-by academic program. This put us in a lot of the same classes. Ours was the kind of vibe that might have evolved into a relationship if we'd made the effort to see each other outside school. I was a coward when it came to boys and relationships and feelings and dependencies. Thanks, Mom and Dad! I was still a coward when it came to men.

Exhibit A: Gus.

Probably for the best.

I'd found Ben's profile on Facebook before I left New York. He was still living in Madison and had a sign-making business and a pleasant-looking wife and two babies and a backyard with a swing set and a chicken coop. I figured it would be harder to blow me off if I was already in town, so I waited until I was settled in the cottage to send him a message.

I flopped onto the futon sofa in the living room and opened Facebook Messenger.

Hi Ben. It's Petta Woznewski. I don't know if you remember me from high school. I'm in town and wondered if you would meet me for a coffee. My treat. I know it's out of the blue but no weirdness, I promise. Just a few questions about West High, back in the day.

I hit send and checked the time. One o'clock had come and gone. My stomach took the opportunity to remind me I'd skipped lunch.

I sent Ben a quick follow-up, even though the app indicated he hadn't read the first message.

Or . . . any chance you're free for a late lunch?

I waited a few minutes, time slowing to an ooze as I stared at my phone screen. I gave up to rummage around the cottage's small galley kitchen. My hosts had left a welcome basket on the counter with a miniature bottle of white wine, a wedge of hard local cheese, and a small can of something called Nutkrack. I peeled open the lid of the can and tossed a few nuts into my mouth.

"Holy shit."

Pecans, covered in some sort of spicy, sweet glaze. They were goddamn amazing. I took the rest of the container with me back to the futon. When the nuts ran out, I hauled myself up to poke around the rest of the cottage. The bed had a blue velvet bedspread, so luxe I was afraid to touch it. But I did, and that was goddamn amazing too. A small grill full of charcoal waited outside the back door on a narrow porch, missing only the burgers and brats. Below the porch, a riot of low, leafy plants fought for space alongside tall flower stalks with blue-and-white petals. It was the dictionary definition of welcoming: quaint and lovely.

I fought the urge to leave and check into an anonymous chain hotel out by the Beltline where no one would make an effort and I would blend in with all the other sad sacks. But I forced myself to stay. Madison was showing off, hiding its underbelly with sunshine and velvet and flowers and welcome baskets.

Let it show off. I'd grown a tough hide in the last thirty years.

My cell phone buzzed. A message from Ben.

Hi. Petta! Wow! Long time. I'm at work now but can meet you at 4pm at the Barrique's on Monroe Street.

The meet was set, which meant now I'd actually have to face him after all these years. I'm not a great judge of these things, but something told me I hadn't aged that well.

I texted back but couldn't manage anything but a thumbs-up emoji.

I wanted to crawl under the blue blanket and ignore the reason I'd come back to town. Instead, I chugged the gift basket wine straight from the bottle. My fingers itched for a joint. Ben would have a local weed hookup, if he was still anything like his old self. And knowing I wouldn't have to survive the week without herbal assistance made the fog of anxiety lift.

I reviewed my mental hit list, deciding to visit Megan's old house next. I had enough time to fit it in before meeting Ben, so I drove over to Shorewood Hills, the phrase *old stomping grounds* dissolving on my tongue like a sugar-free cough drop. The medicinal kind, like the Sucrets my grandpa had kept in his bathroom cabinet. Bitter as hell.

It was a humid day in July, the temperature nearing ninety degrees. I found a shady spot inside the Shorewood village limits to park the car. I started walking, choosing a westward path, up a steep hill toward the country club. At the crest, I looked down over the pristine golf greens, huffing and puffing and sweating. New York walking hadn't conditioned me for hills. My Docs were lead blocks on my feet. The heat and the exertion and the repetitive motion of walking was like a sedative, rounding my edges and dulling my sharps. Until I caught sight of the lake, and the road that ran along it. Lake Mendota Drive, where Megan's house waited.

Just to be an asshole, I cut across the golf course to get down to the lakeside. A foursome playing nearby was already on the green, facing the pin. I wished one of them would turn and confront me. I could already see the brand of frown that would collapse their faces: superior and impatient. An argument would follow, delaying me from reaching the street and the house and the inevitable flood of memories.

But no one turned. I was deprived of my fight. I was a ghost to these people. No one saw me. No one cared.

Feet back on the pavement, I walked slowly. Up the middle of the street because there was no sidewalk, ears tuned for approaching cars. Megan's old place was several houses down from the golf course. I reached it before I was ready. The lawn was overgrown, a for-sale sign planted near the road. A neon-orange SOLD sticker was plastered over the Realtor's logo. The house itself sagged—an abandoned Eeyore of a building. Roof shingles were missing. The tawny stone walls were covered in moss—or was that mold? Paint had peeled off the wooden portions of the Tudor facade, a snake shedding its skin. The front bay window was cloudy with dirt but intact. I was tempted to walk across the lawn and peer inside, but fear kept my feet from touching the grass. I stopped just short of the property line. Megan's turret looked much the same, but its cone-shaped copper roof was darker, mottled dull shades of green and brown.

The inside of the house had smelled like pine. Or rosemary, I guess. The sound the stairs made as we sneaked down them after dark was like a piano long out of tune. A grandfather clock announced each hour. It all came back: the owl family that lived in the backyard, the way the aspens—

Dogs. Nearby. Their happy barking stole my attention, yanking me out of the nineties and bringing me back to the present. An older man leading a pair of golden retrievers down the other side of the road waited for a sleek black Tesla to pass. A chittering chipmunk dashed from oak to oak. The dogs had their eyes on it. The car stopped to let the man cross, but then honked to hurry him along. It startled me enough that my teeth clamped down on my tongue. Coppery blood mingled with the rush of saliva in my mouth. The dog owner wouldn't be hurried, took his time crossing. Good for him. The driver had his sun visor down. All I could see through the windshield was a stubble-studded chin and the popped collar of a glaring white polo shirt.

When the man reached my side of the road, he called out. I turned from the Tesla as it whirred past.

"You the one who bought that heap?" the man asked.

"The . . . oh, you mean the house? No way." I held up my hands to ward off the thought.

The man laughed as if I'd made a joke.

"I live up Sumac there." He waved vaguely to the street off to his left. "We've been waiting a long time for someone to do something with this place, and when I saw you standing here staring at it, I thought maybe you were the one. You had kind of a funny look on your face."

"No, that's just my face. Do you know who used to own it?"

"Oh, sure. The Hollister family. Owned it since the early eighties, maybe? They moved out after . . . well, I guess you'd say they suffered a personal tragedy. They left town after but never sold."

He paused, probably waiting for me to ask about the tragedy. I didn't. The goldens strained at their leashes, desperate to chase after the chipmunk, but the man was a talker. He switched the leash from one hand to the other, full bag of dog shit swinging from a small clip at the top near the handle. I could smell it.

"They left and started over fresh, up north somewhere. Never looked back. They rented the house once or twice. Difficult to find folks willing to pay Shorewood prices for a run-down rental, though. The village had to contact their lawyer to have someone come cut the grass once a season. Finally, a couple years ago, a moving company showed up and emptied the place. Shortly after, they put it up for sale."

The man chuckled before continuing. "Ever seen that old movie *The Money Pit*?"

I nodded. He laughed again and tilted his head toward the Hollister house.

"Whoever bought it has their work cut out for them."

The larger of the two dogs started pawing at the man's loafer.

"Okay, Huey, we'll go. I know, I know, I talk too much and it embarrasses you."

The man pointed to the dog. "Meet Huey. And that's Lewis. Let's go, boys."

"Did you leave the News at home?"

He didn't seem to get the reference. Or maybe he didn't hear me. He was already walking away.

"Nice chatting with you," he said, waving over his shoulder without turning.

"Yeah. Bye."

I checked my phone. I had to leave if I wanted to get back to my car and make it on time to meet with Ben. The shortest route was across the golf course the way I'd come. But when I started retracing my steps along Lake Mendota Drive, I noticed the Tesla again, idling a few houses down. It wasn't blocking my path, but I'd have to pass the car on my way. Same guy, same chin, same douchey shirt. NYC Petta would've marched right up and pounded on the window. Called him a douche to his face. But in Madison, my skin was thinner. I was more Petal than Petta.

I turned and walked the other way. If I looped around the country club, I'd end up back at my car. I still remembered the streets. I'd long outgrown my old Keds, both physically and stylistically, but the pavement felt familiar under my feet. I didn't check behind me until I was rounding a bend, nearly out of sight. The Tesla was gone. It hadn't driven past me; I would have seen it. It must have turned around and gone back the way it had come.

CHAPTER

6

AFTER SO MANY years, the meet-up with Ben was never going to be anything but awkward. I expected to recognize him, at least. But when I walked into the coffee shop, there were three brown-haired men sitting alone at tables, any of which could have been him. I waited for one of them to raise his head, to notice me. Would I look the same to him? High school Ben had favored army surplus clothes, avoided haircuts, and been generous with both his laugh and his weed. None of which helped me identify him now.

Someone tapped me on the shoulder, and I turned to see Ben's smiling face.

"You're bald." I wanted to snatch the words back.

He put me out of my misery by smiling. And there he was, my old pal Ben. History class confidant, lunchroom buddy, and the only high school friend I'd made after Megan died. In the wake of that terrible night, I'd avoided socializing. But Ben had managed to slip through the cracks in my hastily built wall.

He rubbed a hand over his hairless head.

"Yeah, well. The real estate up top started to shift quicker than . . . Let's just say I looked in the mirror one day, and my forehead had expanded north. I chucked it in years ago, shaved it all off. That way I can pretend it's a choice rather than an inevitability."

"Way to take charge of becoming an old fart. It suits you."

He laughed down at the toes of his beige Asics, thrilling the fragile, needy girl I kept buried inside. I remembered the way he used to dip his head that same way each time I made him laugh, long hair flopping down over his eyes. In high school, I didn't care if I learned how to write a thesis statement or titrate an acid. My only goal was to earn a laugh from Ben. It was a good sound: addictive and deep. He took his time with it. I should've made out with him back in high school when I had the chance. But our relationship hadn't been like that—I wouldn't let it be like that.

"You too. You look great, I mean. Same old Pet."

I was wearing my city uniform: navy Docs, darkest-blue jeans, and a gunmetal-gray T-shirt. My clothes were all the same—a Goth rainbow of dark neutrals. My fashion philosophy was half mix-and-match and half don't-give-a-shit. Comfort and camouflage beat all. In that respect, not much had changed since high school.

He gestured to a small table and we sat, him on the bench against the wall and me in the chair opposite. Neither one of us made a move to go to the counter for coffee.

"Never pegged you as the chicken coop type," I said, trying to find a way to bring the conversation into the present.

He narrowed his eyes at me and blinked, like I was a code he was trying to decipher.

"I saw—on Facebook. Your backyard with the chicken coop. Looks like a great house, a nice . . . coop." *A nice family*, I'd wanted to say, but couldn't. Even families who looked beautiful and happy from the outside were hiding things. I probably knew that better than anyone. "I'm not stalking you or anything. I think someone posted a photo of it and tagged you."

He smiled again, relieved. I expected him to say something else, respond or change the subject. He didn't.

"But you're good, right? You're happy here, it's a good life?"

"Shit, Petta. You jumped right to the big question, huh? I mean . . . yeah. I guess. As much as that's possible."

He didn't elaborate, not even with details about his kids. Didn't domesticated people get off on yapping about their offspring?

I wasn't about to share the details of my trash life. I didn't have a chicken coop. I didn't even have a backyard. But I'd called this meeting, and it was up to me to explain why we were staring at each other over a narrow wooden table after decades of silence.

He leaned forward to rest his chin in his hand, elbows on the table. His face was too close to mine. I could smell his aftershave. Had he taken the time to shave before coming here?

There wasn't enough oxygen in the room; Ben was hogging it all. I stood, and my chair scraped back across the floor. "Lemme get you a coffee. Uh, what's your poison?"

His gaze shifted toward the front counter to study the menu hanging overhead.

"I'll do a large cold brew. Thanks."

I gave him a thumbs-up, immediately regretted the cheesiness of the gesture, and hurried to the cashier to order our drinks.

Ben was looking at his phone when I returned, but the minute I sat he put it face down on the table. I set mine down the same way. Like we were representatives for rival factions, putting our weapons down to negotiate.

"So," I said. "I'm back in Madison for a bit."

"Yeah. What's up with that? If I remember right, you couldn't wait to leave town after graduation. Figured I'd never see you again. Your text was . . . a surprise."

"Accurate. A surprise for me too. Coming back wasn't my choice." I sipped my iced caramel latte, extra caramel. "Well, that's not quite true. I guess everything is ultimately a choice. But something happened that I couldn't ignore, and I'm back to figure out what's going on."

"Okay. Wow, cryptic. And have you?"

I shook my head and tipped my latte toward him. "That's where you come in."

"I guess I'm going to need some more information then." There was no trace of curiosity in his voice, making me wonder how much he already knew, or had guessed. The book wasn't exactly a secret.

"Right. I kinda wanted to avoid this part, but here it is. Have you read a book called *No One Suspected*?"

His eyebrows rose. A look flinched across his face. Surprise at the apparent change in subject, or something more sinister? Like maybe he was preparing himself to lie.

"No. Why?"

I told him about finding my name in the book, explaining that it was set during our high school years and the author wasn't exactly a big fan of mine. By the time I'd finished talking, Ben's cold brew was gone.

I'd avoided mentioning Megan, and he didn't show any sign that he suspected the book was inspired by her death. To Ben, Megan wouldn't have been anything more than a girl from his school who had died, perhaps killed herself, before our freshman year ended. That's all anyone knew, except me and Jenny. I hadn't met Ben until the second semester of sophomore year, nearly a year later. The hubbub over Megan's "accidental" death had dwindled by then. He and I had never discussed her death, or her life—I didn't do that with anyone except the psychiatrist aunt Shelly forced me to see for a while. But even with Dr. Sharma, I kept the truth to myself.

"I thought you promised no weirdness." Ben paused to wipe his mouth with the back of his hand. "In your text."

"I did, didn't I? Sorry, afraid it comes with the territory." I swirled a hand in front of my face, indicating I was the territory in question. "Actually, I meant I wasn't dragging you here to hit on you or anything."

"Well, shit. Now my ego is damaged beyond repair."

"Aw, you can take it."

"From you, yeah. Any day."

Silence stretched like a held breath, the delicious tension between us back in full force.

"So anyway," I continued, breaking it, "I'm trying to figure out who wrote the book and why my name's in it. I feel like . . ." I struggled with how to explain. He didn't need to know the truth—and I didn't want him to. "Whoever wrote the book might have known me in high school. There are some very accurate details in there that no one could have, you know, made up."

"Like what?"

"You want an example."

He grinned at me.

"Okay. Well, whoever wrote the book knew that Orchard Peach Clearly Canadian was my soda of choice freshman year."

I'd never been able to ingest peach-flavored anything after Megan died. Not without it coming right back up.

"Okay. But that could be a coincidence," Ben said. "What are you thinking? Someone we knew from high school used you as an inspiration for a character in their book? That's not so bad."

"Yeah, I guess. But the character isn't so flattering."

"Ooh! Now I definitely have to read this book."

Pins and needles prickled in my fingertips. I shoved my hands under my thighs, trapping them against the aluminum chair.

"Not worth your time. I called the publisher, but they wouldn't tell me who the author is. They're using a pen name."

"Could you get a lawyer to—"

"Yuck. No, no lawyers. I want to keep this on the DL. Apparently, the author lives here. I can't find any information about their identity online. Keep hitting dead ends. I thought there might be gossip around town about who wrote the book. It's a bestseller; they're adapting it into a movie and everything."

"Right, now I remember. I read in the *State Journal*—something about a local author getting a movie deal. Fincher, right? Rad."

"Yeah."

Fincher again? Was he, like, every dude's favorite director? *Alien 3* was pretty good, but his movies didn't have enough car chases. I'd take Michael Bay over Fincher any day.

"Here, let me look up the article."

He fiddled with his phone for a few minutes.

"Let me just . . ." He scrolled, skimming. "There's not much here. It's more about the plans for the movie and the deal itself, not the book. Wow! Two million! Here—it mentions the author, Littleton. Oh. It says they declined to comment for the story." He looked back up at me. "Nope, this was no help. I'm not sure who would know dirt on the author, if there is any dirt to find." He sounded skeptical, and I couldn't blame him. "Maybe, uh, try a bookstore or something? There's one right up the block." He pointed west. "Maybe they'd know?"

"That's a good idea." I added it to my mental to-do list. "What about other classmates? Who's still in Madison? You ever see anyone from West?"

I was hoping he would mention someone I could connect to Jenny or Megan. But they'd both been long gone from West before I met Ben. He was shaking his head before I even finished talking.

"Nah. Most of the people I used to hang with left town." He paused for a minute, thinking. "And none of them could've written that book."

"What about Jenny Isaacs? Do you remember her?" Saying her name out loud made my stomach clench, but I'd hit a dead end and I had to try.

"Nope, doesn't ring a bell."

He dragged a finger through the ring of condensation his glass had left on the table. "Did you message anyone else besides me when you got back to town?" The question was casual, but he wasn't meeting my eyes.

"Just you. You were the only one I could imagine seeing again without throwing up."

"Well, now you've made up for calling me bald." The old Ben was back, smiling again.

"You're welcome. I'm very good at compliments. It's my special skill."

"Clearly."

My phone buzzed. I peeked at the screen. Gus was texting again.

Everything OK?

I turned the phone back over.

"You could check on the Class of 94 Facebook group," Ben suggested.

"I glanced at it, but it wasn't much help."

"Yeah, I know what you mean. And the moderator gets kind of testy if you post about non-West stuff. I posted about a sale I was running at work and got suspended for a week." He shook his head. "I have a sign business. Cut vinyl graphics, large-format digital printing, that kind of thing. We do a lot of promotion on social media."

My attention was starting to drift. Ben wasn't turning out to be much help. I wondered how I might make a clean exit.

"There's an alt group, too, though," he continued. "It's private, but all you have to do is request access. It's run by Class of 94 people, not sure who. Things are loose, mostly tasteless jokes and nineties memes and hey-do-you-remember type stuff. Here, I'll message you the link." He picked up his phone, and shortly after, mine buzzed.

"Cool. Thanks. Well . . ."

Unable to figure out a smooth way to segue, I stuck to my standard blurt-and-see-what-happens method of conversation. "Got a local weed contact you could hook me up with?"

He laughed, and the years fell away again. "Yeah. Me."

We walked together to his truck, parked on a residential street behind the coffee shop. He pulled a wrinkled paper sack from underneath the driver's seat and gave me a baggie with a stash that would get me through the next few days.

"On me," he insisted, when I dug in my pocket for cash. "I hope you find those answers you're looking for."

"Thanks, Ben. It was surprisingly good to see you again."

"Farewell, my Pet. It was weird and wonderful. As always. Take care."

He opened the door of his Dodge pickup, and I turned to go. I'd made it a few steps up the sidewalk, mind already crossing him off my checklist, when a new question occurred to me. I swiveled back, but he was already in the car.

"Hey, sorry," I called out, waving my hand. He rolled down his window. "One more weird question: Did you ever go to the Madison School Forest when you were a kid?"

The School Forest was mentioned in the book, and returning memories of a place I hadn't thought of in years were ringing inside me like a bell.

He froze, looking at me like I'd asked him if he'd ever shot a man in Reno.

"Do you remember it? It's that piece of land outside town, owned by the school district. All the Madison schools used it for outdoor education and overnight field trips. I went with my sixth-grade class; we slept in big cabins. The area had hiking trails and a fire pit and stuff."

"Oh yeah," Ben said, confusion clearing. "Forgot all about that place. I think I did go, once. Why d'you ask?"

"I wondered if it was still a thing—if the district still owns it and kids still spend time out there."

"No idea, sorry. My kids are still too little for that stuff."

"Right. Okay, weirdness over. Sorry." I waved again.

He rolled up the window and started his truck, the engine growling. I didn't hear Ben drive away until I'd walked up the block and gotten behind the wheel of my own car.

Excerpt from
No One Suspected
1991

Like it or not, Petal had become part of our friend group. And for a while, she was tolerable. I tried to see her as Miri did: someone new and interesting. The three of us shared inside jokes and freshman year culture shock and, most of all, secret adventures. When we sneaked out of Miri's house on those late-night walks, the cool night air bonded us like nothing else could. I would make an effort to get along with Petal if it meant spending time with Miri.

But as I began to get comfortable with the expansion of our group, something changed. Petal had started out as the third wheel in my friendship with Miri. But at some point I became the third in theirs. Perhaps I should have realized this long before it became clear—that first day Miri invited her over, maybe, when I could hardly get a word between them. But I didn't, not until I found myself on the outside of their inside jokes.

Jokes that had originated when they spent time together without me.

"Hey, Petal: parachute!" Miri would say as we waited in the lunch line, and the two of them would dissolve into giggles.

"Fahrvergnügen," Petal would answer back, when she could breathe again. And the giggling would start anew.

When I asked them what they were talking about, they gave me variations on the same response:

"Nothing."

"Never mind."

"Forget it."

But I couldn't forget it, or let go of the implication that I wasn't worth the time it would take to explain. They'd work their secret code words into every conversation—to shove them in my face, I thought. How cruel.

In third-period history, the only class the three of us had together, we'd been learning about World War II and the Allied and Axis powers. That's when I began to think of our friendship in terms of shifting allegiances and enemy combatants and invading forces. Petal was an invasion, destroying Miri. I'd seen it from the beginning but had been powerless to stop what was coming. Mostly because Miri decided she wanted Petal as her friend, and Miri always got her way.

Threes are hard. In a friendship there's always an alpha, the one leading the way. That was Miri, obviously. An alpha requires a beta, someone who will admire and follow. I liked being Miri's beta. She needed an audience, and I liked being needed. Petal was an alpha at heart, even though losing her parents had knocked her down. She was off her game, masquerading as a beta that year. But the need to be the center of attention was still in her. I saw it lying in wait behind her eyes every time she looked at me. Miri never saw it, not until it was too late.

Our friendship dynamic needed a reset so I could get Miri back on my side. I waited, and recognized my chance when I saw it. For months, the three of us had been plotting a more daring outing than wandering the streets of Shorewood, hanging out at the reservoir near the lake, or sneaking lunch off campus (an upperclassmen-only privilege) to eat at Bagels Forever. Miri was the one always nudging us further: she wanted to take her parents' Lexus and drive somewhere. We were still a year away from getting our learner's permits, but she didn't care. She'd practiced in the family's Wagoneer when they were on vacation up north. And she was hungry to break new rules, to have a fresh adventure.

I wanted whatever Miri wanted.

"Did you ever go to the School Forest for an overnight when you were in middle school?" Petal asked over lunch one day, as we sat in the cafeteria picking at our doughy rectangles of hot-lunch pizza.

"Yeah," Miri laughed, peeling off a piece of pepperoni and popping it into her mouth. "Izzy found a tick in her hair and threw up in her sleeping bag, and her mom had to come pick her up. It was so gross!"

Miri poked a finger through my hair-sprayed wall of bangs and touched my scalp with her candy-colored fingernail, scratching the spot where the tick had burrowed. I swatted her hand away.

"What about driving there?" Petal continued. "It's not far. We could do whatever we want out there. In sixth grade, the chaperones took us into the woods at night, where it was super dark and scary. They gave us each a wintergreen Life Saver. We all got in a circle facing each other and chewed on them with our mouths open, and they made sparks against our teeth."

I rolled my eyes and waited for Miri to trash this idea, to tell her it was stupid, but she didn't.

"That's perfect. We wouldn't have to drive far, and like you said—we can do whatever we want out in the woods. That's it. That's our plan. When we talk about it, our code will be *Life Saver*."

I wish I'd spoken up then. If I could have made Miri see how awful the whole thing would be, with the bugs and the potential for bad weather and the danger of driving on those country roads, I might have stopped it. But it was impossible to say no to her, and she was already decided. It would be the School Forest, and there would be no talking her out of it.

I smiled and played along, pretending to be excited. After a while, my excitement became real: I tricked myself into going along with the Life Saver plan. It was easy after that, especially when I understood it would be my best opportunity to get Miri back. The night would be an inside joke we could all share. A secret code word I understood the meaning of, and a road back to how things used to be. The way things should be.

Two best friends, forever. Until the day we die.

I SAT, SWEATING IN my rented, pea-soup Kia Soul, unable to shake the memory of my sixth-grade trip to the School Forest. The chaperones—our teachers and a few parents—had made a big bonfire, and we sang camp songs and made s'mores. I'd never forget the surprising spark of Life Savers in the dark. That was years before my parents died. When I was living the carefree life of a rich girl—not a mean girl, but an oblivious and spoiled eleven-year-old raised with privilege.

In describing the School Forest plan, *No One Suspected* was eerily accurate once again. In real life, Megan, Jenny, and I had plotted to sneak away in her mother's Lexus and drive out there. But we never got the chance. Megan died before we could, and her death happened not on a risky adventure but somewhere we went all the time, only a fifteen-minute walk from her house. Playing it safe didn't keep us safe. That was a lesson I'd never forgotten.

The only people who knew about the forest plan were Megan, Jenny, and me. The day we cooked it up, the three of us made a pinkie swear chain: my little finger grasping Megan's, Megan's other pinkie holding on to Jenny's, as if Jenny and I might start a tug-of-war over her and split her like a wishbone. We promised the adventure would be secret, and ours alone.

If the intervening years had proved anything, it was that Jenny and I could keep a secret. No matter the cost.

Had she changed so much, gotten so desperate, that she'd decided to share our darkest moment with the world? It didn't make sense. Unless Megan's death wasn't her darkest moment anymore. Maybe things had gotten worse for her since high school, not better, and writing about Megan was her only way out.

Another thing about the book bugged me: it was clearly written by someone with talent, someone who could write. If Jenny had stayed on her path to juvenile delinquency, would she have been able to write a book like this, and get it published? Two things had put her at the top of my suspect list: the story was written from her point of view, and she was the only other person who shared my secret. But what if the author had deliberately chosen Jenny's point of view to make me suspect her?

I started the Kia, putting the air conditioning on blast and waiting for the prickly feeling of sweat drying on my skin to fade. I closed my eyes and relished the cold comfort pouring from the vents. When I opened them again, I saw something white peeking out from under my windshield wiper, half tucked into the hood of the car. Had it been there when I got in? I hadn't noticed it, but that didn't mean anything. I craned my neck, looking around to see if there was anyone on the sidewalks. There was a woman three houses down pulling weeds from her front garden bed, but otherwise the neighborhood was quiet.

I rolled the driver's side window down and pulled the white thing out from under the wiper, fingers scrabbling on the windshield glass as I pulled it toward me. It was a sheet of paper, the kind you'd find in any notebook. It was part of a sheet of paper, actually, one that had been torn in half so that I was left with about fifteen ruled lines. The writing was in sky-blue ink, the letters looping and feminine. As I read, I got a strange feeling, like an earthquake in my internal organs. Kind of like shivering but deeper. The feeling of too many coincidences, colliding.

Our plan will be called Life Saver, and it's because of something P. said. A story she told us about going out to that forest place with her class or whatever and eating those minty Life Savers that make sparks. I'm hoping we'll make sparks too. Only they'll be sparks of a different kind.

"What the actual hell?" I whispered.

I didn't know what I was holding. But I knew it was no fluke that I'd been reading about our Life Saver plan, and now here it was, left on my car, in someone's handwriting. But whose?

The page could be from an early draft of *No One Suspected*, maybe. Did writers do that, write things out by hand first, before a book became a printed document? I thought maybe they did.

The coincidence of it all made me feel as if one of those social media eavesdropper bots—the kind that made the targeted ads show up in your web browser or on your phone—had crawled out of the internet and into real life.

So who was my bot?

Who had stalked me here and left the paper for me to find? Ben was the only person who knew I was back in town.

I crumpled the paper into a ball, tossed it in the back seat, and put the Kia in drive.

On my way back to the cottage, I stopped at Taste of India for takeout tikka, extra spicy. While I waited for my food in their narrow, curtained entryway, my phone buzzed. Another text from Gus.

No pressure. I don't need details. Just want to make sure you're OK.

I started and deleted half a dozen different responses before sending two words.

I'm OK.

He didn't text back.

At the cottage's tiny kitchen table, I devoured my food straight from the cartons, alternating bites of cumin-seed-studded rice with hunks of spicy, saucy chicken. I flipped through the book as I ate, getting lost in the story, which was becoming less truthful with every page. But it got me thinking—about third wheels and pseudonyms, and the way memories play into the tug between fact and fiction.

I was at the center of it all.

Belly full, I retrieved my laptop from my backpack and looked up the private Facebook group Ben had told me about.

West High 1994: The Flipside.

The page content was barred to nonmembers, but I requested access and was let in. I studied the posts until my eyes blurred from looking at faces and places I'd tried so hard to forget. Megan's ghost lurked alongside me, but neither of us was learning anything new. The page was full of jokes and memes, complaints about old teachers and principals, and ribbing (not entirely good-natured) between members. They didn't seem to be strict on who they let in, and I didn't recognize half the members' names. Ben had posted a few things, promos for his business and a meme about trolling I didn't understand. No one had posted about the book.

Another dead end; another argument for deleting Facebook and never looking back.

Or maybe not.

Ben's meme gave me an idea. Some casual trolling might get me the wrong sort of attention, but from the right people.

I exited the private group page and made a new profile, this time for Megan Hollister. Was this creepy and wrong in several ways? Yes. Did I think Megan would have found it hilarious if she could see it? Also yes.

The admin admitted me to the group before I'd even decided on a plan of attack. Trolling was new to me—I was severely confrontation avoidant, even when hiding behind a screen. I dug out my travel pipe, disguised to look like a tube of lipstick, and smoked some of Ben's excellent weed. Three puffs later, I was ready.

What do you think, Megan? Is this a bad idea?

The only place she lived was in my head, but I asked her anyway.

My laptop didn't burst into flames, so I opened Google. I poked around and found an image of a white-sheeted ghost wearing neon-pink sunglasses to use as a profile picture. When I was done, "Megan Hollister" added a new post on The Flipside:

Due to recent events, the Ghost of Megan Hollister has risen. Who here remembers me? Oh, and has anyone read any good books lately?

I watched it take over the top spot on the page, usurping a Go Fund Me campaign for someone's graphic novel. The minutes ticked by. My post wasn't banned or attacked or trolled. No one noticed it at all.

Maybe I wasn't doing the whole trolling thing right.

I left Facebook and opened a browser window, looking for 1991 news coverage of Megan's death. It'd dominated the local newspapers and TV stations for a week back then, long enough that the Hollisters began to complain. I read an old *State Journal* article ("Missing Girl

Found Dead, No Sign of Foul Play"), and the bottled-up recollections exploded inside me like a warm Coke, shaken and uncapped. I couldn't stop the gush as my past returned.

Megan's parents had instituted a lockdown—on both statements to reporters and their own grief. When they were seen in public, they gave away nothing. I should have gone to see them, to tell them I was sorry about Megan. I didn't. I couldn't. Aunt Shelly went. She said it was the proper thing to do. She was big on proper. I couldn't tell her why I refused to go, and the look she gave me as she walked out the door was high-octane disappointment.

She was gone less than an hour. When she returned, she came up to my room and sat on the edge of my bed. I'd been listening to Alice in Chains on my Walkman and slid my headphones off my ears. All her disappointment had evaporated. The au pair had answered the door, she'd told me. Mrs. Hollister wasn't at home. The au pair left my aunt standing there to go chasing after the twins. Eventually, Mr. Hollister found aunt Shelly waiting there in the open doorway. No one had invited her in; no one had asked her to leave.

"He had no use for my condolences," she said. "It's odd, but he seemed ashamed, or like he was somehow undeserving of any kindness. I'm sorry I was short with you earlier about not going. I see now why you didn't want to."

"That's okay."

The apology, one I didn't deserve, stung much more than her earlier disappointment.

"I'd like to ask you something. And I want you to tell me the truth."

I nodded, heart beating so hard I could feel it on the roof of my mouth.

"Did Megan kill herself?"

It was not the question I'd expected, and it flustered me.

"No, I don't . . . I don't think she could have done that to herself. She wasn't like that, depressed or whatever."

"And you'd tell me the truth if she had those kinds of feelings?" She paused to swallow, and I could hear the click at the back of her dry throat. "Or if you did, or do?"

This time I didn't stumble. I didn't have any problem telling her this truth.

"I would tell you. But you don't have to worry about that with me. Not after . . ."

I couldn't finish the sentence. Aunt Shelly nodded. She stood, smoothing my bedspread, and left. We didn't talk about Megan again, but after that I started going to the therapist twice a week instead of once.

Everyone at school knew Jenny and I had been friends with Megan, and probably suspected we knew more than we were telling. But the newspapers never caught on. I don't know if it was because we were minors or because we were never official suspects, but the Hollisters kept a tight lid on the story and the police never gave our names to the press. I was thankful then that I didn't have reporters coming around asking questions. And I was even more thankful now. Because my name didn't appear in Google searches in connection to Megan's death. If it had, those book people who tracked me down would've had a lot more questions, and it would've been easy to connect the fictitious Miri to the real Megan.

Which still might happen. All it would take was for one person who remembered Megan, and remembered I had been her friend, to read the book and connect those dots. My plan was to find the author and let the truth out on my terms, to show that I wasn't what the book made me out to be. But if I didn't hurry up, someone would beat me to it and I'd lose all control.

The Hollisters hadn't had a funeral for Megan. One day her death was an active investigation and the next she was in the ground, a pink marble headstone marking the grave. The family escaped north to their lavish cabin in Eagle River and, as far as I knew, never returned to Madison.

At school, rumors flooded the halls in Megan's wake. It was common knowledge that the police had been under pressure from the family to wrap up the investigation, and that ruling it an "accident" was a kindness.

The most popular rumors:

One: Megan hadn't died but had been sleeping around and was secretly pregnant. The family had whisked her away to have the baby. (Yes, that old slut-shaming chestnut.)

Two: Her parents had sent her to a convent. (The school was doing *The Sound of Music* for the spring musical. How do you solve a problem like Megan?)

Three: She'd killed herself because she'd found out her parents had lost all their money, which was also why they left town afterward. (That one hit a little too close to home for me.)

West High's budding conspiracy theorists delighted in the mysterious nature of Megan's demise. But soon, even death got boring. Someone took a shit in the head of the Reggie the Regent mascot costume after a baseball game, and that became the new scandal everyone was talking about. Turned out it was the pitcher from the East High team. He'd sneaked into the locker room after the game and dropped a deuce, earning a weeklong suspension for his trouble. That kid became a state senator.

Jenny and I didn't get away completely clean. We'd been Megan's closest friends, so it was only a matter of time before we were interviewed by the police. I'd never found out what they asked Jenny, because we weren't speaking by that point, but an impatient male detective showed up on my doorstep the day after they found Megan. Aunt Shelly led him into the kitchen and sat next to me at the table. He asked his questions: had we gotten along (yes) and what was her state of mind (normal) and did she have a boyfriend (no) and had anything in her life or personality changed recently (no). I told him the truth as I knew it, and lied only once. The lie Jenny and I had agreed on. Because the truth wouldn't bring Megan back.

"When was the last time you saw Megan?" he asked.

I managed to keep my voice steady, but my words came out high and strained, like someone had their hand around my throat. "At school on Friday. During lunch. We were supposed to have a sleepover, but she canceled."

"Where were you that night?" he asked.

Aunt Shelly answered that one for me, saving me from another lie. "She was home. With me. She went to sleep early."

As far as she knew, that was the truth.

He looked at me for confirmation, and I nodded.

He scribbled something in his notebook and left. No one ever asked me about that night again.

I came out of the fog of the past slowly, refocusing on the laptop in front of me. One of the news articles I'd found online referred to the Hollister house as "a sprawling Tudor manse near the shores of Lake Mendota, a stone's-throw from Blackhawk Country Club." With eyes I could barely keep open, I looked up the property records. After my chat with Huey and Lewis's owner, I was curious about who in the family had owned it most recently, and who the recent buyer was.

Shortly after Megan's death, ownership of the house had transferred into something called the Hollister Family Trust. Some sort of tax shelter, it seemed. The house had remained in the trust until a month before I'd returned to Madison, when it was sold to a real estate developer for $400,000. I doubted any other house on the block had gone for less than a million in the last twenty years. According to a short article on the Village of Shorewood Hills web page, the very smug developer (sixty-something, based in Milwaukee, no apparent connection to the Hollisters) intended to restore the house and flip it for a profit. He was going to make a fortune, the bastard.

What were the chances he drove a black Tesla?

8

MY MORNING MOUTH tasted like tar and burnt milk. I staggered out of bed and popped a pod in the Keurig, glancing at my phone as I waited for my cup to fill.

Crap.

A flood of incoming notifications filled my screen: weather alerts, text messages, a missed call. I'd turned off my phone the night before, and this was my punishment for a decent night's sleep. Or perhaps the punishment was for breaking my personal code and joining Facebook.

I attempted triage.

Gus had sent three overprotective texts and had called once. No voice mail. That was bad; he was starting to panic and didn't want me to hear it in his voice. I sent a message that would hopefully turn off his watchdog mode.

Needed a break. I'm good. Talk soon.

The Facebook notifications had piled up too. People were reacting to my ghost post. It had gotten four thumbs-ups, three angry faces, and one comment. I clicked on the commenter's name and couldn't suppress a curse. It was Matt Hollister, Megan's younger brother. In the book, ME Littleton had named him Mike.

Who the hell is this? he'd written. *Your post and profile are in very poor taste. If you pull a stunt like this again I'm reporting you to the admin.*

What was little Matty Hollister doing in a Class of 94 group? If I'd known he would see the post, I never would have done something as tasteless as impersonating his dead sister. At least I didn't think I would.

Matt and his twin sister Bitty had been seven years old when I knew Megan. Matt followed Megan around like a stray puppy. Bitty was shy, and kept her head buried in the au pair's skirts when Megan had company. *No One Suspected* made "Mike" out to be a creepy, weird little kid. But maybe all kids were strange, and he wasn't any different. I didn't remember much about him. If Jenny had written the book—the only workable theory I had—her portrayal of Matt made sense. Jenny had never liked sharing Megan's attention and had resented it whenever Matt pulled her focus. I'd thought it was sweet, the gentle way Megan had with him, and with their sister when Bitty got over her shyness and joined us. No matter what we were doing, Megan would stop and help her siblings if they needed her—finding lost toys, handing out bowls full of Goldfish crackers. The way they adored her made me want a sibling. Orphanhood wouldn't have been as bad if I'd had a brother or a sister by my side.

I hadn't thought about Matt Hollister since I'd blocked all traces of Megan from my thoughts back in the nineties. I could see the round, big-eyed baby face I remembered in the man he had become. His profile picture was posed but casual. He looked happy and healthy and younger than thirty-something. He had the tan-but-not-too-tan look of someone who took care of themselves. A recent post included a collection of pictures with Bitty. They were on a Chicago River boat cruise, arms around each other in the sunshine.

It read: Three years since we lost Mom. Thinking of her today.

The twins weren't identical, of course, and looked nothing alike. Bitty was petite with long red hair, whereas Matt was brown haired and broad. Bitty had Megan's sky-blue eyes, and Matt had her smirking smile.

The Hollister parents used to travel a lot, for both work and pleasure. They breezed in and out of the house, often returning from a flight or a dinner late at night. The au pair, whom the twins called Mommy, was the only fix-ture of authority in the house, if you didn't count Megan. When we had sleepovers and sneaked out at night, more often than not it was the au pair we were afraid of waking, because the parents were absent.

The twins lived in downtown Chicago now, a few blocks away from each other. Seeing their faces again, rocketed through time from child to adult in the space of a mouse click, made me queasy. If I were one of those proper adults, like aunt Shelly had been, I would have mes-saged Matt immediately to apologize for my ghost post. But what could I say? How could I justify my clumsy troll-ing, if that was even the name for what I'd done? I would have to explain why I was back in Madison, and what I'd hoped to gain from the post.

No thanks.

He wouldn't even remember me, which would make everything all the more awkward. He'd been in kid-die playland while Megan, Jenny, and I were struggling through freshman year. It was like we'd lived on differ-ent planets back then—still did, judging by Matt's splashy Facebook page. He and his sister lived in gorgeous high-rise condos and went to pro sporting events and ate at Michelin-starred restaurants and traveled the world. They had expensive hobbies. Matt liked to scuba dive and collect cars. Bitty had her pilot's license and owned two horses. Matt was unmarried and went on double dates with other gorgeous couples. Bitty was a married mother of two. Her profile indicated she was active at her kids' (private, fancy, terrifying) school.

It's practically a crime, everything you can learn about someone on the internet, if that someone doesn't hole up and hide from life like I had. The twins were thriving—if their pictures were to be believed. They'd survived Megan's death much better than I had. I couldn't fault them for their happiness, or their wealth.

As I looked back at my shameful post and at Matt's comment underneath, self-hatred sinking into me like lotion on parched skin, three telltale bubbles appeared. Someone was writing a new comment. I braced myself for the worst, and it was beyond what even my tortured mind could conjure.

It was from someone labeling themselves *The Vengeful Ghost of Megan Hollister*.

Stop this now. I know who you are. I know what you're doing. You're not as clever as you think you are. Never have been. Go home while you can, before you get yourself into real trouble.

Saliva emptied from my mouth so quickly my tongue glued itself to my gums. I grabbed my coffee cup from the machine and attempted to scald away my panic but only succeeded in cauterizing my taste buds.

Someone was onto me. Could've been Matt again, but he didn't seem like the type to pick up and run with my tasteless joke. Ben knew I was in town and had pointed me toward the Facebook group. He had no reason to get defensive about my ghost post, though, and we'd parted on good terms.

Hadn't we?

That left Jenny, my scapegoat for everything so far. It was possible she'd found out I was poking around Madison, asking about the book. This could all be her doing.

Bing!

Another member of the Flipside group gave my ghost post a thumbs-up. (I was a terrible influence.) I still had a conscience—lying dormant somewhere under layers of fat and denial—but I didn't call on it much. Now it was telling me to delete the post, remove the fake Megan profile, and never open Facebook again.

But what if . . . , my inner selfishness whispered.

And Keanu help me, I listened.

What if this is the only way to smoke ME Littleton out?

I asked myself the hard questions: If my ghost post led to information about the book, was it worth the damage it could be doing to Megan's family? Was it worth the risk of another nasty comment from Vengeful that might further escalate things?

I knew the answer, even if I couldn't admit it to myself. Hell—I'd known it before I asked the question.

I left the post up but closed my laptop so I wouldn't have to look at it anymore.

I couldn't sit still inside the cottage's four walls for one more minute. Not if it meant being alone with myself. I downed the rest of my coffee in three gulps and shoved my laptop and the book into my backpack. I went out, to visit the bookstore Ben had told me about.

The place was appealing, if you went for that sort of thing. A cheery, colorful front window full of books and bookish things. The occasional comfy chair wedged between shelves and tables.

I saw *No One Suspected* as soon as I walked in the door. A table loaded with a pyramid of copies was arranged near the front window. My backpack sat heavy on my shoulders with the weight of my own copy, the thick hardback like a lead brick. I skirted the perimeter of the store, pretending to scan the shelves. I approached the table from behind, as if I might sneak up and surprise the books.

Local Author! a small table stand advertised.

Had Littleton stood in this spot, breathed this air, touched these books? I picked up the top copy and flipped through the opening pages. Would I find a signature scrawled across the title page?

The book was unsigned. I put it back on the table, tamping the urge to knock the pyramid over and stomp out the door.

There were no other customers in the bookstore at this hour, just after opening. I stood alone, conflicted. The woman working the register left her desk to come help me. She wore a short-sleeved dress with a long, flowy vest, both in shades of purple.

"Have you read it?" I asked, when she was within earshot. I was still staring at the table. There could be no mistaking which book I was talking about.

"Oh, yes. Very compelling. You?"

"I'm about halfway through. It takes place here in Madison, right?"

"Yes, it . . ."

She trailed off, distracted by a commotion outside the bookstore—an argument between parking enforcement and the owner of a motorcycle.

"Sometimes authors are inspired by real events," I said, trying to nudge her. I wanted to know what local people were saying about the book, how they were reacting—and if anyone had made enough connections to set their sights on me. "Do you think that might have happened with this book?"

Her eyes lit up. "Now that you mention it, someone in one of our book clubs was saying she'd Googled the character from the inscription—Petal. Not much came up about her, except that her parents committed suicide. Which also happens in the book—oh, I hope I'm not spoiling anything."

"Nope." I tried for a smile, but I could tell it came out sour. "I'm past that part. But it says on the back flap the author is local. Have you met her? Or him? ME Littleton?"

"No. Unfortunately not. I'd hoped to do an author event here in the store, but I haven't gotten anywhere with my inquiries."

Me neither, I wanted to say. "ME Littleton sounds like a pen name, don't you think?"

"Do you know?" She leaned in a bit closer, like we were old friends sharing a secret. "That's exactly what I thought."

"Any gossip about who might have written it?"

Her mouth twitched, like she wanted to say something but held back.

"Not that I've heard. There is a network of local authors here in town. They're very active and supportive of the local bookstores. But I don't think this author is involved with them." Her tone made it obvious she was not a fan of ME Littleton—probably because of her failure to lure the elusive author to the store.

"Is it odd for a new author to be so . . . ?"

I left it open. She could fill in whatever adjective suited her.

"Not unheard of. But unusual, yes. These days, both authors and booksellers need all the help we can get. But this title is selling so well, they don't need to chase publicity. And the author's hidden identity won't hurt. Any mystery surrounding this type of novel only keeps people talking."

That's what I had hoped, but whoever was talking, it wasn't to me.

"Right. Thanks."

I moved away from the table and continued browsing. At the register, I grabbed a copy of *The Master Cheesemakers of Wisconsin* from a small display of locally themed gift books. A single purchase wouldn't keep the store afloat, but at least I could pay for the bookseller's time. The only thing I'd learned was that I wasn't the only one who'd butted up against the secrecy surrounding *No One Suspected*. It wasn't the answer I'd come for, but it was the only one I was going to find at the bookstore.

I wouldn't have stopped there if Ben hadn't suggested it. Had he known more than he was telling when he'd sent me there on a wild-author chase?

I hiked up Monroe Street toward Michael's Frozen Custard, dropping the cheese book I'd just bought in a Little Free Library along the way. I could count the things I missed about Madison on one hand. Michael's was one of them. Even the worst days could be improved by frozen custard—that had been one of aunt Shelly's life lessons. She wasn't wrong. Eating a Michael's turtle sundae wouldn't solve my problems, but it could bury them under hot fudge, caramel, and pecans for a while.

Aunt Shelly and I ate a lot of frozen custard in the four years I lived with her. Departmental squabbles and the politics of tenure at the university were the banes of her job, but she endured them so she could do what she loved: teaching. We'd sit together at one of the red-and-white fiberglass tables, letting the cool, soft custard soothe our overwhelmed hearts. By the time our plastic spoons scraped the bottom of the dishes, her department chair's voice had faded and the ghosts that plagued me had gone fuzzy.

My mouth began to water when I was still a block away. But when I got there, the Michael's parking lot was roped off and the boxy white building was dark. Tall weeds bobbed up through the cracks in the pavement.

"Well, shit."

The red-and-white tables were still there, now sad and empty. I went to sit and feel sorry for myself—but mostly I was pissed. Michael's was magic, and Madison had let it die. The day was hot and bright and perfect for eating custard. I leaned back into a sliver of shade. The unrelenting summer sunshine made everything too sharp. I had to close my eyes against the glare.

When I began to sweat, I ducked inside the tavern next door. In the comforting, stale-beer-scented darkness, I checked my phone. No new messages from Gus, a small mercy. On Facebook, Matt Hollister had checked in for lunch at some trendy restaurant in downtown Chicago, all heavy draperies and reclaimed wood. My stomach growled, chastising me for skipping both breakfast and lunch. It had been denied the frozen custard it was due, and it was angry.

"A little longer. I'll make it up to you soon." I was talking out loud to my stomach, the sort of thing that had started to feel alarmingly sane.

I wondered if anyone on the Flipside had chimed in on either of the ghost posts. The need to know was a chicken-pox-level itch. Social media was addictive, just like everyone said.

I caved and opened the app. Several other group members had supported both Matt's response and Vengeful's warning; they each tore me a new one in a different, crude way. Which I deserved. I didn't recognize any of their names. One of them was in Australia, which reminded me that any of these people could be anywhere or anyone—even the opposite of who they claimed to be. This actually made me feel better and took a bit of the sting from Vengeful's threat.

I was about to put my phone away and belly up to the bar for a burger when a new comment popped up on my ghost post. It was from Ben.

No words, just a GIF of a clenched cartoon fist, vibrating with anger.

Did this make it more or less likely that Ben might be Vengeful? I was too hungry to guess. I took a deep dive into his profile to see what I could find out.

What I saw there made my insides clench: Ben was Facebook friends with Matt Hollister. There was no reason they should know each other—Matt had moved away from Madison before his high school years. According to his profile, he'd attended St. John's Northwestern Military Academy. So how had they met, and why was Matt posting in a West High Facebook group?

Megan.

She was the answer to both questions, the crux of everything. The rope in more than one game of tug-of-war.

I scrolled back through the Flipside posts so fast my fingers cramped against the phone screen. I didn't know what I was looking for, but when I found it, those fingers convulsed into a fist.

A post from Ben, on the anniversary of Megan's death. Two years ago.

RIP Megan, gone too soon. You were my first love.

A hundred people had given it a thumbs-up, including Matt.

Thanks man, he'd commented. I remember you always being good to her when you were over at the house.

I dropped my phone onto the tavern's scarred wooden tabletop. It made a clatter like falling dominoes. Ben had been in love with Megan? When? How could I not have known about this?

Until that moment, I hadn't seriously thought Ben could be involved with any of it—not the book, not the Vengeful post, nothing. The cute high school version of Ben, the person I thought I knew, had taken up residence in my brain so long ago I couldn't evict him.

But if he could hide the fact that my dead best friend had been his first love, what else was he capable of? Wanting to get back at the person responsible for Megan's death certainly gave him a motive for coming after me with the book. And being chummy with Megan's brother was another nail in the coffin of my old assumptions.

I closed my eyes against the jittery neon lights in the bar—*Go Pack Go, Schlitz: The beer that made Milwaukee famous*—but Ben's vibrating-fist GIF was printed on the insides of my eyelids like an afterimage. There was anger there, and it was directed at me.

I'd thought I'd known Megan. I'd thought I knew Ben. I'd been wrong, on both counts.

No One Suspected was accurate when it came to those last weeks Megan was alive. She had been distracted and distant. The book version of Jenny seemed to think Miri and Petal were sneaking off to hang out on their own. But in the real world, Megan had been ditching me too. Sometimes she and I would wander the makeup counters at Marshall Field's or go see a movie without telling Jenny. But in the weeks before she died, Megan was mostly absent. When I did see her, she never told me how she spent her free time. I knew she was hiding something, but I didn't think she and Jenny were going places without me. Things between them had gotten tense. I was too self-involved to see (or care about) much more than that.

I'd suspected she might be seeing someone, but Megan never said who. Only her diary knew that secret. She'd acquired a certain sparkle, though. None of us were dating

back then, but we talked about boys a lot. To my recollec-
tion she'd never mentioned Ben, and I hadn't met him yet;
Mr. Sederquist's history class was still in my future. Megan
hated being prodded about personal stuff, so I was careful
not to ask too many questions or tease her. That was the
quickest way to earn the cold shoulder—and Megan's was
legendary. It could kill you dead where you stood. Just ask
Jenny.

Nauseous, I dashed for the bar's exit. The world blurred
and spun. The hell with social media and damn me double
for getting sucked in by it. Sites like Facebook lured people
into living their whole lives in their heads, without any
real-world awareness. I stuffed my phone in my pocket and
leaned against the front window of the tavern. Its awning
kept me shaded, and the breeze off nearby Lake Wingra
blew my clamminess away.

I shambled back up the street to my car. Stomach still
empty, I was running on rage and bitterness.

The hell with you too, Ben.

I had so many fond memories of him. We'd had . . .
something. A friendship on the verge of more. He wasn't
the one who got away. But he was the one who might have
been, if high school me had been different. Or if Megan
had lived—but no. If Megan had lived, I would've found
out they were together. And I never would have known
him as anyone other than her boyfriend.

Could I trust anything he'd told me—back in high
school, or during our coffee shop chat?

Ben was my Madison touchstone, the only memory of
high school that was good. And now it was ruined. He was
ruined. I tried to go easy on him in my head, manufactur-
ing excuses and wondering if maybe he'd tried to talk to
me about Megan back when we first met. I would have
shut him down. That's what I did to anyone who uttered

her name back then: teachers, classmates, aunt Shelly. My therapist was the only one who hadn't let me get away with it.

Navigating high school is an exercise in self-preservation, and teenagers get good at hiding things. It's the period in life when you begin to wonder if all those crazy thoughts you're having aren't quite normal, if you might be the weird kid and no one else will understand what you're going through, so you keep it all inside. You're too young yet to realize that weird is good—that all the weirdos become the most interesting adults.

I considered the possibility that Ben had sat across from me in that coffee shop and lied to my face for an hour.

Did he know I'd been friends with Megan? Had she told him things about me? Had she mentioned our planned forest adventure? Maybe that was why he'd been so freaked out when I mentioned the School Forest.

I pointed my sweltering rental car toward the closest Culver's drive-through. I ordered a Double ButterBurger Deluxe with fried cheese curds and a large Mountain Dew. The first three curds burned the roof of my mouth, but oh Keanu were they good. I sucked down Mountain Dew to calm the sting. By the time I'd let go of a long burp, my stomach had stopped eating itself. I pointed the car south, toward the Beltline and the city of Verona. Fifteen minutes later, a sign for the Olson Oak Woods State Natural Area flashed past the car. I took the next left.

The cornfields were endless, but then I saw it—a familiar strip of gravel road leading to the Madison School Forest.

Excerpt from
No One Suspected
1991

M IRI EXPLAINED THE Life Saver plan again, even though she'd already told us a hundred times. For weeks it was all we talked about. After her house was asleep, she'd steal the spare set of keys to the Lexus and drive to my house to pick me up. Then we'd go get Petal.

It worked just as she'd said. She parked a block away from our houses, and we slipped out to meet her. Once we were all in the car, backpacks stuffed with contraband, we drove southwest out of Madison toward the School Forest.

We'd never talked much about what we were going to do when we got there. Our focus had been on the plan, the logistics, the thrill. Forbidden adventure. *We can do anything we want out there*, Miri kept saying. It was something Petal had said first and then Miri stole and repeated until it was like it'd been hers all along.

The day before our adventure, Miri had announced she was bringing vodka and bottle rockets and we should find our own contraband to bring. She meant that whatever we brought better be good, better impress her and at least be as interesting as alcohol and fireworks. Disappointing her was the last thing I wanted to do.

Before I left that night, I filled my backpack with every naughty thing I could find, without pausing to consider the wisdom of each item: my mom's cigarettes, my dad's *Penthouse*, a few cans of Busch Light from the back of our garage fridge, and a hunting knife. I don't know why I brought the knife. I might whittle with it, I considered, fleetingly. That's what people did to pass time out in the woods, right? My dad had told me never to touch his knife without supervision, but I wasn't thinking about him as I reached for it. It hung near our back door on a special peg. Dad used it for skinning the rabbits and gutting the pheasants he shot. As I walked out the door, past its place of honor, I lifted the knife off its peg. Because it was a night for doing forbidden things.

The three of us were quiet for most of the drive. Miri said she needed to concentrate; she had exaggerated her comfort behind the wheel, and I suspected she'd never driven in the dark before, or on a highway. The initial excitement of sneaking out had burned off. We kept our eyes on the road, on the place where the reassuring glow of the Lexus's headlights dissolved into black against the pavement.

The forest's gravel access road was blocked with a chain. We idled in front of it for a long time before Miri turned around and glared at me. She was waiting for me to get out and move the chain. I was in the back seat—riding bitch, they called it. We had never been alone in a car before, the three of us. I had never been the bitch. Not officially.

I got out of the car and unhooked the chain. It was easy, almost as if no one much cared about keeping us out.

We drove up the gravel road, the crunch of our tires the only sound. The road came to an end at a small parking lot. A series of wooden utility buildings, worn gray with time, stood just beyond it. They edged the bottom of a wide, oval grass clearing. Miri nosed the Lexus up against one of the large rocks separating the gravel from the grass. At the opposite end of the clearing was a fire circle with wooden benches. On the left side, a row of three bunkhouses. On the right, a picnic shelter with a large stone fireplace inside. A thick stand of trees bordered the entire oval, holding everything, including us, inside.

Miri turned off the engine, and I took that as my sign to get out of the car.

The moon was bright that night, and I felt exposed standing there in the parking lot. I'd envisioned a shadowy, secret cubby in the woods where we could convene like witches over a cauldron. Mischief waiting to be conjured. But the School Forest was run by the school district, and its institutional presence was everywhere. Signs forbidding the dumping of trash were posted near the woods, alongside others detailing the proper use of the shelter's fireplace. The largest utility building had a metal door with a hefty padlock and a row of dumpsters out back. Peeking in the window, I saw stainless-steel countertops and an industrial-sized refrigerator. A motion light clicked on as we passed, and suddenly we were well-lit actors striding upstage. And, as if we all had stage fright, we froze.

No one moved for a long time, as we waited for the light to click back off. These were the moments I needed Miri most: to cure my indecision, to tell me what came next now that the hard part of getting here was over. We'd snuck away from our normal lives and entered the forest as we had planned. But the tree-hugged clearing held its breath, and the stars seemed to form a giant question mark across the inky sky. Miri was waiting too, I could feel it. Waiting for her courage to kick in or for inspiration to strike or to torture us, I wasn't sure. But then she glanced at me, and I knew why she was waiting. Her normally bright, clever eyes were in shadow, her brows heavy in the harsh spotlight. The night had let her down: it wasn't turning out the way she wanted. She didn't know what should come next, maybe for the first time since I'd known her.

A craving for the old days filled me, for the way it used to be between us, and I saw a way to get it back. My thoughts were already skipping ahead to the moment I would save the swiftly deteriorating night and she would shine her gratitude on me. I knew what we had to do. And what's more, I knew it would fix things between us. I cleared my throat.

The fire circle. I was going to announce it like Miri would, like it was already decided and there was no room for argument. We'd sit together under the bright, round moon. We could howl and share forbidden thoughts. Warm vodka and juicy secrets. Bad beer and the sparks of fledgling witchcraft all teenage girls possess.

But then.

Oh, the many hours I have killed wondering how the night might have gone had I spoken sooner, before the dreaded *but then*.

But then—the motion light clicked back off, throwing us into darkness. It startled me, and I hesitated.

Petal spoke first, before I could utter a word.

"C'mon, over here. I see a way up."

I looked at Miri.

Up where? I wanted her to ask.

I waited for Miri to say no. To wrestle control back from Petal—surely she could see this was not how the night should go. But she didn't. Petal began to walk, and we followed. Even Miri, who was accustomed to blazing the trail.

Petal stopped when she reached the farthest bunkhouse. Neat pyramids of firewood, piled against the wall of the building, were sheltered by the overhang from the roof. Petal secured her backpack on both shoulders and began climbing the woodpile. She approached it from the end, using the outermost stack like a staircase. Once she was high enough, she slung an arm and leg onto the roof and pulled herself up. She made it look easy.

Miri climbed up next, following the path Petal had set. Together they spread the quilt Petal pulled from her backpack across the pebbly shingles. The roof slope was gentle, and there was little danger of tumbling off. They stretched out on the blanket with twin sighs of satisfaction.

"You coming?" Miri called, eyes on the stars, as if just realizing I hadn't followed them.

I was petrified of heights, and this was no secret to Miri. She was my best friend. Of course she knew. And it was common knowledge at school; I had a note from my doctor, excusing me from climbing the rope in gym class and breeding envy in my classmates. Petal knew this as well. But that night, they either forgot or didn't care. She and Miri were already rooting through each other's backpacks, taking inventory of their loot.

I had no choice. I couldn't stay there on the ground; I couldn't go home. I had to follow.

I managed the ascent by not looking down. Instead, I focused on reaching Miri, making her my finish line. But not watching my step was a mistake. I put my weight on the wrong log and the pile shifted, several pieces of wood tumbling to the ground. I squawked in panic, a mortifying, birdlike sound. My so-called friends sniggered, the first sips of alcohol already hitting their bloodstreams. My legs had spread into a painful split and I caught myself by pitching forward onto the pile. Sharp edges of wood bit into my palms, tore at my jeans. When I was certain no more logs were going to tumble away beneath me, I continued to climb in careful increments. I threw myself, bitter and battered, onto the roof, pulling a splinter the thickness of a toothpick from the pad of my left thumb.

Miri and Petal were hogging the blanket; only a thin strip was left for me. It wasn't worth complaining about, or risking

Miri calling me a whiner. I hurried to sit and unzip my JanSport. I dumped everything I'd brought, all my desperate attempts at belonging, onto the edge of the blanket in front of my friends. Miri grabbed a cigarette from my mom's pack of Merit Ultra Lights, lighting it with the kitchen matches she'd brought for the bottle rockets. It stayed there between her pursed lips, but she didn't inhale. She grimaced, and at first I thought it was the smoke getting in her eyes, but it was the *Penthouse*. She picked it up by the bottom corner like it was soiled.

"Ew. Gross, Izzy." She tossed it off the roof. The magazine fell open, pages fluttering in the moonlight. For a moment, it was flying. "Like, totally perverted."

I shrugged to show her I didn't care, but I was embarrassed I'd gotten this wrong. I was mad too. Because if Petal had been the one to bring the dirty magazine, Miri would've laughed and thought it was great fun to flip through the pages and gawk at the fake boobs. Our access to naked female bodies, to seeing versions of what we each might look like when we finished growing, was limited to glimpses of our mothers or dramatically lit movie scenes. I was curious, but had never been brave enough to look at my dad's *Penthouse* at home. That's why I'd brought it. I knew the other girls were curious too. We talked about it sometimes. But not that night. Miri had decided mine wasn't the right kind of contraband.

Petal hadn't brought anything interesting: a half-empty bottle of oversweet Boone's Farm wine and a bunch of stinky permanent markers in case we wanted to do graffiti. *Graffiti? Who even does that?* I wanted to ask. But I was still stinging over my *Penthouse* mistake. I didn't want to do or say something else wrong and have to listen to more silence as they ignored me. I stared at the moon, shining down on the rooftop, and waited for my time-out to be over.

Miri drank her vodka, I choked down a beer, and Petal sipped her wine. We all consumed at about the same rate, but as the teacher liked to drill into us in health class—drinking a few ounces of wine or beer is not the same as drinking the same amount of hard alcohol. Miri got drunk much faster than Petal and I did, but I didn't notice at first. None of us were experienced drinkers, and I didn't know what drunk Miri was like. Not yet, anyway.

We kept having to get down off the roof to pee in the woods. No one had thought to bring toilet paper, and the latrine building was locked. Our adventure became less fun each time I trudged into the trees. By the time the moon had inched higher in the sky, we were getting cold and all three of us had to pee but no one wanted to make the effort to climb down again. I zipped my hoodie up to my chin and tried to ignore my multiple discomforts. Petal was getting snappy. Miri was getting sloppy. Bored, she began digging through our belongings again, looking for a distraction.

Petal was absorbed with her own project, scribbling on the outside of her backpack with a marker, drawing a big, smiling moon. Underneath it, a simple sketch of the bunkhouse. She dated it and signed her name underneath before handing the marker to Miri.

"Here. Sign. That way we'll have a souvenir of the night."

Miri took the marker and made an unintelligible scrawl, right across Petal's moon drawing. Petal's face pinched into a grimace, but she didn't say anything.

"Oops," Miri giggled. "Don't be mad, Petal-Wetal." She tilted her head, studying what she'd written. "I think I made it better, actually." She still had the marker in her hand and leaned toward Petal. "Here, lemme make you better too. Lemme turn that frownish upside-downish."

Miri stuck the marker in Petal's face but Petal recoiled, overbalancing and falling back against the roof. She banged her head on Miri's half-empty vodka bottle. It tipped over and rolled off the roof, smashing on the ground below.

"What the hell, Miri?" Petal was mad, two spots of red high on her cheeks. Her hand was cupped gingerly over the back of her head where her skull had struck the bottle.

Miri didn't hear, deep in a fit of giggles.

"Frownish upside-downish," she said again, when she could gather enough air to speak, delighted by her own word-play. The laughter was coming hard, tears leaking from her eyes.

The look on Petal's face was pure rage. She didn't like being laughed at, being the butt of the joke. Her anger was thrilling, filling me with steely satisfaction.

Not so fun when it's you, is it?

Miri staggered to her feet, holding the marker in front of her like a sword. She was still deep in the throes of drunken giggle mania and took a wobbly fencer's pose. We'd watched *The Princess Bride* together many times, and I could see Inigo Montoya in the way she held the marker. It made me smile.

I attempted to play along. I didn't see the harm in it at the time. "*My name is Inigo Montoya*," I said.

"You killed my buzz," Miri finished. "*Prepare to die.*"

It was bullheaded of her, still trying to turn the whole thing into a joke. Petal was the only one of us not laughing. I watched her as she sat on the blanket, looking up at Miri with a hate in her eyes I'd never seen before. Something my dad had said once came back to me then. *Some people are mean drunks*, he had told me. *Alcohol turns on their nasty switch.* He'd warned me to give them a wide berth.

I hadn't understood what he was talking about, or what something like that would look like. But as I watched Petal, I saw it. Her switch had flipped.

She stood to meet Miri's challenge. It wasn't until she'd steadied herself against the shallow slope of the roof that I saw she held my dad's hunting knife. I'd forgotten all about it, buried under the other items I'd dumped out of my back-pack. My hand tingled—I knew the feel of the knife against my own palm from the few times my dad had let me hold it on camping trips. Its timeworn bone handle was soft as vel-vet. Petal took a step forward, and the silver blade caught the moonlight. Time slowed as Miri looked down at Petal's hand, and we all finally scented the danger in the air.

Miri's laugh cut off like someone had found her mute button. A breath later, one final, high-pitched giggle escaped. I heard the panic there and knew it had been involuntary, like a hiccup. It turned out to be one too many for Petal.

"Stop! Laughing! At me!" Petal screamed.

She didn't raise the knife but took a step closer to Miri. The force of her footfall was a mini earthquake along the roof underneath us. I was still seated, wanting to either cower or stand up and get between them. I did neither, frozen in place. Miri retreated a step, and Petal's eyebrows rose. Nei-ther of us was used to Miri giving any ground. The whites of Petal's eyes gleamed in the ghostly light. She advanced another step. They moved past me, horns locked, nearing the edge of the roof.

I could've broken the dark spell of anger that had woven itself between them. It was within my power to dis-tract Petal from her anger and Miri from her fear. If I'd been a better friend to Miri, less afraid of Petal, and more confident in my actions, I would've said something clever and shattered the moment wide open. Me, the heroine who brought all of us back to ourselves. But I didn't. I was cocooned in shock as Miri backed toward the edge of the roof. Petal advanced on her, an arm's length away. Then they both stopped moving.

Petal raised the knife in agonizing slow motion. The hilt was gripped in her fist, the blade thrusting upward. Her arm was tensed, the elbow locked. If she'd kept her arm on its current trajectory, the knife would have sunk into the soft underside of Miri's chin. Into the dandelion spot, where Miri and I had rubbed the fuzzy yellow flower heads when we were little girls.

Your chin turned yellow; you must like butter.

When this moment returns to haunt my dreams, nothing about Petal's movements is slow. She pinwheels her arm up and the knife goes in, hitting a dandelion-yellow mark like it's a bull's-eye. There is blood then. All of us screaming. Underneath, a deadly giggle.

But that version is all in my head; I'll never know what Petal intended by picking up that knife.

The blade, still inching upward, was halfway to Miri when Petal opened her mouth to speak, her eyes wide. She managed only a single syllable, a stuttering *duh* sound falling softly from her lips. Miri flinched. In anticipation of what was coming, I suppose, though none of us got to hear what Petal was going to say. Miri's shoulders hunched and she recoiled, her back foot lifting off the roof. And that was it; that was enough. She'd been terrified to take her eyes off Petal and had no idea how close to the edge she stood. She put her foot back down, onto nothing. And my Miri fell.

If I close my eyes, I can still see the blinding white of her Hard Rock Cafe Acapulco T-shirt against the inky backdrop of night. She was there with us one minute, glowing, and gone the next.

Crunch.

That was the sound Miri made as she hit the ground. Like someone had collapsed a folding chair. Breaking bones and crumpling cartilage. Death sounds. It had happened too quickly for her to cry out. Through the thick quiet of the rooftop, I fixated on the spot where Miri had stood. Time stretched, turning into a formless puddle around me. Until Petal's sobs wrenched me back to reality.

I looked around. I could hear Petal crying but couldn't see her.

I began humming to myself, loud and tuneless, to drown out Petal's keening. I got down off the roof, half falling but thankful to have the nerve-racking descent to focus on. Petal was kneeling on the ground beside the broken body that had once belonged to my best friend.

Miri had fallen backward and was splayed on the ground like a stringless marionette. Her limbs were a loose jumble, legs going in directions no living person could manage without terrible pain. The permanent marker was still in her hand.

I focused on the marker. I studied the black cap and the gray barrel and the way it tapered slightly at each end. I kept my eyes on that damned marker until my insides stopped imploding, until my lungs ceased convulsing in gasps and I could breathe again.

Petal's crying had stopped. A rustle behind me, and she materialized at my side. I couldn't look at Miri—never, ever again, because what I'd already seen of her ruined body would haunt me forever—but in my peripheral vision Petal bent to slip the marker from her still-tight fist. I sidled away, and my foot brushed against my backpack. Petal had gathered our belongings, mine and hers, from the roof. Anything belonging to Miri she left behind. Miri's backpack gaped open from the rooftop, bottle rockets littering the shingles. Shards from the vodka bottle glinted in the grass near the woodpile.

I cursed the overbright moon, shedding too much light on our tragedy. Illuminating our terrible mistakes.

"If we start walking now and hurry, we'll maybe make it home by dawn," Petal said.

"We can't! What about—" I couldn't bring myself to say her name.

"Nothing we can do. It was an accident. She fell."

My whole body flushed, skin hot with anger and the shame of my relief. "Well, I mean, it wasn't totally—"

Petal zipped her backpack, the sound tearing a hole in the night. She stalked over to me, thrusting her face uncomfortably close, eyes boring into mine.

"It. Was. An. Accident. Nothing I can do. Nothing you can do. She wasn't looking—*Izzy!*"

My gaze had begun to drift, panic encroaching and drawing me into myself. She gripped my upper arm like a vise and I gasped, forcing myself to look at her. The pain helped. The pain made everything but Petal go away.

"We're in this together. We're going to leave the car here and walk home. We are never going to say a word about this. Ever. Not even to each other. If anyone finds out, there will be questions, and our lives will be ruined. You could get taken away from your family, sent somewhere. Miri's parents will hate us forever, and everyone in school will see us as criminals. *Izzy!*"

She shook me, hard, and my head snapped back.

"You were the one who brought the knife. This never would have happened if you hadn't been so fucking stupid. But I'll help you. One mistake doesn't have to ruin your life."

Petal was right. My knife. I shared in the blame. We all did, because Miri wasn't innocent either. She had been teasing, the way she always did. This time she had picked the wrong person to tease at the wrong moment, and now she was dead. All because I'd grabbed that damned knife on my way out the door.

"Okay." To let the word out was a relief. A frantic bird, uncaged. I allowed myself to believe. I could deny what had happened, lock it away forever. The events of that night would be buried there in the forest, never to intrude on my real life.

"Our secret, right? I need you to say it." Petal's voice had gone soft, wheedling.

"Right. Our secret. We won't talk about it. We won't tell anyone."

Petal nodded encouragingly. I was a toddler finally learning my ABCs.

"We were never here," she said, almost singing the words. "We were home in bed. We didn't know Miri was coming here tonight. She'd been acting weird lately. She was distant." Her voice was silky. "Say it."

I looked into Petal's eyes. They were hard and dark and mean.

"We were never here," I repeated. "We were home in bed. We didn't know Miri was coming here. She'd been weird lately, and distant."

Neither of us said another word the entire five-hour walk back to town. Petal peeled off toward her aunt's house when we were halfway up Midvale Boulevard, but I kept going, until the street ended near Shorewood Hills. I tried not to think about what was going on in Miri's house, about the twins or her parents or the empty turret bedroom that I would never, ever get to sleep in again.

I turned right, away from Shorewood and toward home. When the familiar slump of my duplex came into view, I cried with relief. My feet were blistered, raw and aching. I composed myself, and when I knew I could remain quiet, I eased the back door open. The dread didn't settle in my stomach until I'd replaced the hunting knife in its slot by the back door.

I crept down the hall, stepping lightly to avoid the spots I knew would creak, and crawled into my pullout bed in the living room. Ten minutes later I heard the bedroom door open. My mom was up. She made coffee, clinking and clanking in the kitchen. Outside the living room window, dawn stained the sky.

I rose and went to join my mom in the kitchen. I couldn't sleep, and I didn't want to be alone. I asked her if I could have a cup of coffee, my first ever. I thought she was going to say no, but she paused to study my face first. I don't know what she saw there. She reached into the cupboard for a second mug.

CHAPTER

9

IT HAD BEEN a mistake to drive out to the School Forest. Regret congealed inside me as soon as I saw the place. It was the latest in an impressive string of screw-ups that echoed throughout my life. Somewhere along the line I'd started to believe mistakes and bad choices were all I was capable of making. And I hadn't proved myself wrong yet.

But I couldn't stop now. Just like I couldn't stop reading the book, no matter how much I wanted to. I'd been dosing myself with the chapters like they were penicillin, one bitter swallow at a time as I made my way to the end. Hoping for a cure.

I pulled to a stop in the same parking spot described in the book, my Kia nosed up against the boulders that formed the border between gravel and grass. My pulse throbbed in my fingertips. Sweat stood out on my forehead in fat droplets. I retrieved the book from my backpack and read through Miri's death chapter again.

No One Suspected trapped both truth and fiction between its covers. The way the two rubbed against each other, mixing and mingling on the page, made my head feel soft. Last autumn's apple left to rot on the ground.

I rolled down the windows and let the summer breeze harden my resolve.

Memory is a tricky bitch, but I was certain of two things.

One: Megan, Jenny, and I had never seen our Life Saver plan through. We'd never come to this forest together.

Two: On the night of Megan's death, there had been no knife.

So why write it that way instead of using the sad, simple truth?

Assuming Jenny was the author, it made a certain type of sense to blame me—no one liked to claim the worst thing they'd ever done. But why make up an entirely different version of events? If the book had stuck closer to the truth, people would have connected Miri to Megan, and her novelized death to the real one. It would have been a short leap for the cops—or Google-addicted book club ladies and rabid book bloggers—to reopen the case and start looking right at me. Which, I realized, could still happen. There was a reason I hadn't unblocked unknown callers on my phone.

If destroying me was the point, the author wasn't doing a very efficient job.

Maybe it made more sense that the author was someone who didn't know the whole truth. They could have concocted a scenario from the bits of the story they'd gathered. But who would do that?

And why a novel at all? Why not go balls-to-the-wall nonfiction? Dispense with pseudonyms and put everyone's true self on the page?

Unless the author didn't want their true self anywhere near the pages of *No One Suspected*.

I found an old ballpoint pen at the bottom of my backpack. The cap was missing, and the ink had leaked inside the plastic barrel. But it still worked. I scrawled my biggest remaining question across the inside front cover of the book.

What _does_ the author want?

Ink had splattered across the pad of my thumb and the nail of my middle finger. I threw the pen out the window, wiping my hand on my jeans. I wrenched open the door of the Kia and walked into the clearing.

Even through ME Littleton's fictions, the book had revived the sharp, ammonia stink of panic and desperation I'd felt the night Megan died. After I realized she was dead, I'd only wanted one thing: to rewind the night, to make different choices, to nudge fate in a different direction. The force of instantaneous regret had almost crushed me. And that load hadn't gotten any lighter in the last thirty years. I'd just gotten better at distributing the weight.

The grass in the clearing was tall, matted in some places and wild in others. I knew my destination but wouldn't let myself look at it, circling the open field as I kept its gray bulk in my peripheral. Stalking my prey but never acknowledging it. Every inch of me was clenched or tensed. Ready for anything.

But then Mother Nature did her work. The swish of the wind through the trees loosened my lungs. I could breathe again. The ashy, ancient smell of the shelter's stone fireplace brought my shoulders down. The wads of pink-purple bubblegum lined up along the edge of a weather-beaten picnic table made me smile as I passed.

This was the place where Life Savers had sparked in the dark between my classmates' molars and I'd learned my sixth-grade crush snored like a warthog. A place for kids and campfires, nature hikes and scout patches. Not death. It was not the fearscape the book made it out to be. I knew that like I knew my own name. I was not scared.

Until.

In Wisconsin, they have a saying: *If you don't like the weather, wait five minutes.*

That's about how long my moment of calm lasted. Then my internal weather changed. A storm blew in. The cabin— the reason I'd come—stood in front of me. I wouldn't be able to shake my ominous feelings until I faced it.

There was no woodpile stacked against the outer wall—that was the first thing I noticed. The grass there was sparse and matted, yellow, not green. Like something had sat there, and recently. The roof was broad and mostly flat with black shingles, a thick layer of pine needles carpeting it. No sign anyone had been up there. The cabin was sad and old, beaten up by the many school and scout groups that had passed through it.

Weirdly, I was disappointed. I think I'd been expecting to find something here. An answer, or a new question.

Like what, dumbass? ME Littleton, hiding in the cabin, hunched over a typewriter?

The breeze ruffled my hair, bringing the smell of fresh manure from a nearby farm. A low-hanging tree branch scraped across the back side of the cabin. Nails on a chalkboard.

Something shiny glinted at me from the cabin entrance. Inviting me closer. A large metal padlock secured the door. As the trees swayed in the windy afternoon, dapples of sunlight hit its stainless-steel casing, causing the glint. The door itself was wood, weathered and infested by some type of wood rot—a pulp-eating worm, maybe, wiggling its way across the surface. I stepped closer to inspect. The dark squiggles on the surface of the door transformed as I got closer, from insect trails to letters. From letters into words. Words into messages. They crawled across the face of the door, written in black permanent marker.

Miri.

Over and over, the name jumped out at me.

In big, ballooning letters or tiny, cramped scrawls, the sentiment was always the same.

Justice for Miri.

Miri we miss you.

Miri, you are gone but not forgotten.

The messages made it seem like Miri had been a real girl. As if Megan had never existed and Miri had taken her place. In the minds of the book's readers, that was the truth.

My name was there too, of course.

I know what you did, Petal Woznewski.

It was all Petal's fault.

Petal deserves to die.

The door was a shrine to the book and its characters. I had to keep reminding myself they were talking about book Petal and not the real me. The locations described in *No One Suspected* were real, though, and readers had clearly found their way out here. They'd assumed the forest location used in the story was real and the death was fake. Joke's on them—it was the other way around.

There was one more message. I nearly missed it, placed vertically in the ditch between the door hinges. Featureless block letters in the same black marker. The kind of black permanent marker Miri had died holding.

W
E
L
C
O
M
E

H
O
M
E

P
E
T
T
A

Not *Petal* but *Petta*. This wasn't just some reader. This
person knew me.

I ran. Fast and clumsy, like the devil was nibbling my
ass. Unable to tamp the panic until I was locked inside my
rental car. I wanted to crank the engine and get the hell out
of Dodge. Go, go, go. Every heartbeat screamed *run*, but I
couldn't drive yet. I'd crash and splatter my brains all over
the gravel. Damned if I'd give the asshole the satisfaction.

Loud music helped; I fumbled for the local classic rock
station and cranked Van Halen as far as the volume knob
would allow. When my hands stopped shaking, I started
the car and headed back to the cottage. It was time to hide,
preferably on the other side of a locked door and through a
cloud of pot smoke and behind a Netflix screen and under
a pile of blankets. But until then, I ran snarky Deadpool
quotes through my head to keep the bad stuff out.

I flicked a glance at the rearview mirror. The book was
lying faceup in the back seat where I'd tossed it before I'd
gotten out of the car. The cabin on the cover looked nothing like the real thing. Not that it mattered. They were one
and the same. Dead gray wood was all I could see.

ME Littleton and whoever had written my name on the
cabin door—maybe one and the same, maybe not—were

screwing with me. Every instinct in my arsenal told me this was not something Jenny would ever do. Even though she was the only other person who had witnessed Megan's death. The Jenny I knew would never write a book about that terrible night. The Jenny I knew wouldn't waste her time taunting me with messages.

The only person I knew capable of those taunts and cruelties had been dead for thirty years.

What if it is her? What if she's not . . .

The thought rose inside me like a bubble of acid reflux. A surge of nausea followed.

"Nope. No. Not happening. Not possible." My words were drowned out by a loud Metallica riff.

Megan was dead. Jenny and I had kept the secret. Ghosts weren't real. The end.

But The Ghost of Megan Hollister haunted me. And not just on Facebook.

Was I actually entertaining the idea that a dead girl had written a book to torture me? Around the bend toward batshit—that's where I was heading. And I wasn't sure how to slow my roll.

"Facts," I reminded myself. "Reality. Get a grip, Woznewski."

I turned onto Regent Street and drove past West High School. It still looked the same, a stately pile of bricks that I'd been desperate to put in my rearview.

The book was real. Not everything in its pages, but its very existence—that was indisputable. Someone had written it. Someone had named me. Someone had left me a message in permanent marker. Had one someone done all of those things, or did they have help? I couldn't be sure.

Did the message on the cabin door mean I was on the right track, or stumbling into danger?

I pulled to a stop at a red light a few blocks from the cottage. It would take me maybe two minutes, in traffic. I could hold my shit together for two more minutes.

The only way out is through. It was branded on my brain. I wanted to scream the words out loud, feel them tear out of my throat. If I closed my eyes, I could see my hard-won mantra printed on a strip of white paper in tiny type. Like a fortune from the world's most depressing cookie. I forced my eyes open again, crossing my arms against my chest to help contain my hammering heart.

The book, the piece of paper left on my windshield, and the message on the cabin door. The message, the paper, and the book. Those were the cards I held, and I shuffled them around as if it would help me see my next play.

The cabin door message could have been written by anyone who knew me and had connected me to the book, guessing it would lead me out to the forest. Jenny could have written the message. Even Ben could have, especially given what I'd learned about him and Megan. But could either of them have written the book?

The person who'd left the paper on my windshield was likely the author of the book, because who else would have an early, handwritten draft of the story?

The light turned green, and I drove.

Miri's death scene felt like an ending, but it happened halfway through the book. Her fictitious fall from the cabin roof had spooked me, and driving out to the School Forest had only made things worse. And not only because of the message. There was something else, a splinter under my skin I couldn't tweeze out. Until I did, I wouldn't be able to concentrate on finishing the book or finding its mysterious author. I wouldn't be able to answer any of my burning questions or go home to Gus or get on with my life.

What was I missing?

Part Two of the book, which began after Miri's death scene, jumped ahead in time to present day. I didn't mind admitting I was afraid of what I would find there. I wasn't ready to face it. I told myself the answers I needed lived in the past. So that's where I stayed. At least its horrors were familiar.

At the next intersection, I turned and parked. I needed to make a pit stop at the neighborhood market. I'd been inside countless times, back in the day. It was halfway on my walk from aunt Shelly's to West High. Gum, soda, chips, candy, chocolate milk. Whatever my jones, the market had my fix. Since then, the small grocery had absorbed the liquor store next door. I loaded up on Coors, a spiral notebook, and a fresh pack of pens. Before I got back in the car, I called in a delivery for a large meat lover's pie, extra onions. One plus to Gus being hundreds of miles away: there was no one to complain about onion breath or pizza farts.

I unpacked my purchases at the cottage's kitchen table. The delivery guy arrived at the door three beers later. I downed a few slices and another beer in quick succession. An idea brewing, I cracked the notebook and uncapped a pen. I put *No One Suspected* on the table nearby, open to the first page. For a few minutes all I did was stare down at them, waiting as my idea baked from batter to brownie. (It should come as no surprise that I've made a few pans of brownies in my day. The special kind, of course.)

A chain of events emerged from the haze. None of it was new information, but I started to see how one occurrence followed the next.

First event: I'd read the book's death scene and noticed (impossible not to) that the location of Megan's actual death and the location of Miri's written death were different.

Second event: That difference, along with the paper left on my car, had drawn me out to the School Forest.

Third event: I'd found the message written to me on the cabin door.

Had that been the intent of setting the death at the forest all along? To get me out there?

That sounded farfetched, even to me. But it was plausible that someone had guessed I'd go out there after I read the book. What did it mean that the piece of the story that had led me there was fictional? There were many fictions in *No One Suspected*—many times the author had embroidered their inventions into the blanket of truth. What if all those fictions meant something, or pointed somewhere? What if they were intentional signposts instead of random acts of imagination, and the author had intended for me to find them?

Maybe that was the piece I'd been missing.

I picked up my pen and let it hover over the paper for a minute while I decided how to get my ideas out. I drew a line down the center of the notebook page, writing TRUTH above the left-hand column and FICTION above the right. I made a note of every difference I could recall between what had happened to Megan, Jenny, and me in real life, and to Miri, Izzy, and Petal in the book. Then I went through the first half of the book, looking for any fictional details I'd missed. It was painstaking work, combing through two overlapping versions of my past.

If only I could find Jenny and talk to her about all this, have someone to share my recollections with. But my detective work had hit a dead end and I didn't know what else to do to find her.

Memory is unreliable—sand through the hourglass and all that. I couldn't be certain of my own recall or trust the author's. Was either of us telling the whole truth? No way. I was confident I was getting the big things right. But the little things, like Megan's favorite order at Big Mike's Super Subs (skinny turkey with mayo?) or the fake-sounding reason she'd canceled our last sleepover (menstrual cramps, or had she been grounded?) were slippery in my mind. In the notebook, I recorded any deviations from the truth that were significant. Since there was no one else I could compare notes with, I used my gut as a gauge.

I smoked a bowl and attacked the leftover pizza as soon as I finished my list. The THC and the cheese did their job. My body stopped humming with anxiety. I tilted back in the kitchen chair, put my feet up on the table. The book was splayed facedown near the heel of my boot. I resisted the urge to give it a kick, to listen to it fall onto the tile floor with a satisfying clunk. I stayed that way for a while, riding a warm, loose, disconnected wave. It was a gift. One that didn't last.

The book nagged, begging me to finish it.

Night had already fallen, and a wall of rain came with it. Thunder rumbled like a hungry stomach. I opened the windows and let the humid smells of wet earth and ozone blow through the cottage. Then I picked up the book, flipped to Part Two, and began to read. I kept at it late into the night.

After I turned the last page, I came back to myself. The story had cast a spell over me.

Was that what reading did, if you let it? Did you get so consumed by the story that the world fell away? I'd felt that way with a movie before, or a video game, but never a book. Too bad it had to be this book, but still. I thought I might get the whole reading thing now.

My hands shook, from sleeplessness and dread. The book had left me hungover. Not because the present-day events mirrored my own life; they didn't—the author had known a lot about me as a kid but almost nothing about me as an adult. The so-called novel had crossed over fully into fiction, and the story had become all Izzy's.

What got my teeth chattering and my eyes burning was ME Littleton. The author's hatred of me was soaked into every page. Whoever had written this wanted to bring me down, or worse. I was powerless to stop it, unless I could figure out who'd written the book and expose them first.

The shaking finally stopped, but I had nothing left in my tank. It didn't matter that my mind was still clicking. My body was screaming for rest, and it won.

I went to lie down. The futon was closer, so I took it instead of the bed. The velvet blanket was still there. I fell into sleep like a dead body down a well. Hard, and fast.

* * *

The *Mission: Impossible* theme woke me after one AM. It took me a minute to register my ringtone. I'd turned my ringer back on after successfully blocking all the book weirdos (and who knew what other random calls). Maybe that had been a mistake. I answered before I was fully awake, before I could decide whether it was a call I wanted to take. But Gus knew me. He'd timed his call after my bedtime on purpose.

"Mmm . . . yah?"

"Petta. You answered." I could hear the shit-eating grin in his voice. "How are you?"

"Hi." My brains were still sleep scrambled. I didn't know how to answer. But I did know it was good to hear his voice. "I'm okay. You woke me."

"I did. Sorry." He didn't sound sorry. "I was worried."

"I'm still hunkered down. Just need some alone time. You know how it is."

"I do. I know."

Neither of us said anything for a while. I could hear Gus breathing. Talking to him made me miss my life in New York. My real home, not this poor, haunted substitute. I regretted ever leaving. Would it have been so bad to turn my back on the book, ignore the obsessive readers showing up on my doorstep, and let sleeping murders lie?

Another day or two, I told myself, *and I'll be done with Madison forever*. I could go back home and crawl into Gus's bed, let him worry and fuss over me in person.

Maybe it was Gus I missed, and not the city at all.

I coughed, as if I could dislodge the idea. But it only burrowed deeper. "Should be back in fighting shape in a couple days. I'll text you."

"Will you?"

He was challenging me more than usual. Pushing, and I couldn't figure out why. In fact, he wasn't acting like himself at all. He hadn't offered to come over or cook me dinner or have my favorite pierogi delivered. He was distant. He wasn't bombarding me with questions. And the bastard was *smug*. There was only one explanation that made sense: he wasn't asking questions because he knew the answers. *He knew I'd left New York.*

I let him hear my I-give-up sigh. "When did you figure it out?"

He laughed. "I've known the whole time. You never turned off Find My Friends."

When Gus and I first got together, I'd agreed to keep the Find My Friends phone app turned on. He wanted to be able to find me if I got myself in trouble. He didn't like that I walked by myself at night. He worried when I disappeared. And because I'm an asshole, I used that. When we were in our "off" periods, I punished him by making myself invisible in the app. He didn't like it but respected my need to not be looked after occasionally. I needed untethered time to indulge my lone-wolf tendencies. And to my knowledge, he'd never used the app to track me down—until now. But the last time we'd been together I'd rushed out of his apartment, still thinking I could outrun the book. I'd forgotten to shut off the app's ability to track me.

"Crap. You're right." It was reassuring, though. Someone knew where I was. In case.

"You only talked about where you grew up that one time, when we caught the end of a Packers game on TV. Then you run out of my place with no explanation and go back there, even though I'm pretty sure you hate it. Did somebody die?"

Now it was my turn to laugh. "Yeah. Megan. And my loose grip on sanity." I sounded crazy, even to my own ears.

"Not exactly calming my fears here, P."

"No, it's not . . . like that. I'm not . . . I'm in the middle of something, and it's thrown off my normal, uh—"

"Groove?" Gus loved *The Emperor's New Groove*. He'd made me watch it once. It was adorable. I hated it.

"Yeah. Something like that."

The need to tell another human what I was going through was a tear-filled ache at the back of my throat. We needed each other, Gus and me. It was annoying that he'd been right about that all along. We were friends, and more than friends, and something more special than either of those things. I didn't know how I'd gotten there, but I was at the point where it would hurt like hell to lose him.

"Oh, Gus. Shit. Hold on." I put the phone down, got off the futon, and walked. I circled the living room three times, then came back. I put the phone on speaker so I could talk while I stared at the picture of him I had saved in my phone. The only one I'd allowed myself to take. In the photo, we were at his apartment. He was offering me a soup dumpling with a pair of chopsticks. There had been five in the order, and we'd each eaten two. He'd given me the last one. I didn't even have to ask.

"I'm back," I said.

"Tell me. Whatever it is. It'll be okay."

I did. I started with the moment I'd rushed out of his apartment that night. I told him my friend had died when I was fourteen, though I didn't tell him how. And that I'd lied to the police about not being there when it happened. I told him about Jenny and how we'd never spoken again. And now there was this book, the one he'd tried to show me, and the mystery of its author. Maybe Jenny had written it—to punish me, or absolve herself, or make money, or all of the above. Maybe ME Littleton was someone else. I wasn't sure of anything anymore.

"I came back to Madison because I think this is the only way to end it. I got good at pretending Megan's death didn't happen. But now the past won't stay quiet. I came back because it's time. I might be the only person left who can tell the truth. And I will, if it comes to that."

"Then why wait?" Gus made it sound simple. "Go to the police and tell them what you know, what happened to your friend. And about the book. Who cares who wrote it? Get everything out in the open. You'll feel better. Ghosts can't haunt you when they're exposed to the light."

"That's some deep-ass stuff, Gus. But I'm not ready."

I was on a path. I needed to follow it to the end. And I couldn't bear the thought of a stone-faced cop letting me spin my whole tale only to dismiss me. Writing out that list of truths and fictions had convinced me the book was trying to tell me something. That was my next move; the list would lead me to answers. Then I'd take everything to the police—when I knew what was going on. Red bow, silver platter, everything. I could walk away clean. Or as clean as I'd ever be.

"I could go with you." Gus was trying to make me see that going to the police was the right thing to do. But it wasn't the Petta thing to do. If I was going to do this, it would be my way.

"No, but thanks. I'm not ready to tell anyone else yet. There are still a few things I have to figure out first. Okay? When it makes sense, I'll go to the police. I promise. And I'll call if I need you."

"You better."

"Um, Gus?"

"Yeah?"

"Thanks for calling. I needed . . . someone."

"Thanks for letting me be the someone."

"You're it, Gus. You're the only someone I want."

I hung up, too chickenshit to wait for what he might say back.

CHAPTER

10

I DRAGGED MYSELF OFF the futon at dawn. At the kitchen table, I curled around a mug of coffee and stared down at my notebook. It was still open to the list of truths and fictions I'd made the night before. At the top was the first lie, apparent from page one of *No One Suspected*.

TRUTH	FICTION
Megan Hollister	Miriam Rowley
Jenny Isaacs	Izzy Jacobs

Names and lies, lies and names.

I'd noticed the moment I read the blurb on the back of the book that mine was the only real name used. Maybe it was seeing the other names in my own handwriting, or side by side in the notebook, that allowed me to see them in a new way. If the point of using my real name was to get my attention, there might be a point to the fake names too.

When I'd first noticed that Miri had been given the last name Rowley, I'd assumed it was another dig at me.

Aunt Shelly's house had been on Rowley Avenue, and the comforting memories of her had drawn me to the Airbnb cottage on that same street. It was where I'd lived when I knew Megan and Jenny. One more connection to the past. My past. The overlap of street name and character name could be as simple as that. But my gut didn't think so.

I drained my coffee and picked up a pen.

Hollister, I wrote on a new page. *Rowley.*

I turned the two names over in my head. I filled my mug at the tap and chugged the coffee-tinged water.

Rowley. Hollister.

The two names were linked in my mind, and not because of the book. The connection was older than that, fogged by the decades I'd spent trying to forget Madison and everyone in it. I stared out the window over the sink, watching a female cardinal nibble at the bird feeder hanging behind the cottage. This neighborhood was a coveted area of Madison, close enough to the isthmus that you could still feel the city's pulse but with a more discreet brand of charm than the chaos of downtown. The houses were well made, well kept, and eclectic. The trees were tall and the streets were quiet.

The answer clicked into place: this neighborhood. These streets.

Hollister Avenue—another street in this same neighborhood, not far from where I sat.

Was I reading too much meaning into the names? Probably. But that didn't stop me. The Rowley-Hollister connection was a stray thread, and I would pull it until the whole thing unraveled. Even if the "whole thing" turned out to be me.

I brought up a local map on my phone to remind my middle-aged brain of the street layout. Hollister Avenue was three blocks long, running parallel to Rowley Avenue.

Megan and Miri: parallel girls with parallel deaths.

Hollister and Rowley: parallel streets.

It had to mean something. But I didn't know what.

I shushed my angry stomach and assessed the clothes I'd fallen asleep in. I had others in my backpack, unwrinkled and without pizza grease stains, but it would take time to dig them out. My hair, wild on a good day and savage after a bad night's sleep, would have to wait until later for a shower. I pulled it into a snarl of a bun with the black hairband that lived around my wrist.

I noticed a small card on the front porch next to the doormat as I stepped outside. A business card—from a cop. Detective Samantha Gull, Madison Police. On the back, she'd scrawled two words: *Call me.* She must've dropped it off while I was gone—maybe the day before, when I was out at the School Forest. I'd been freaked out enough when I returned that I could've easily missed it if it was stuck in the front door. I heard Gus's voice in my head, urging me to go to the police for help.

But I wasn't ready. A visit from a cop probably should've spooked me, but I was too wrapped up in the Hollister thing to care much about what the detective wanted. That was a problem for future Petta. I tucked the card in my back pocket for later.

I could see the Airbnb's owners shuffling around their kitchen, wearing matching robes and flipping something in a pan on their stove. Sunday pancakes. It made my mouth water. I put my head down, avoiding the windows as I walked up the driveway past the main house. Out on the street, I looked up and down Rowley Avenue. I was alone. No cops, no mysterious message writers.

Across the street sat the familiar craftsman where the history professor, one of aunt Shelly's occasional dinner companions, had lived. Maybe he still did. The longer I stood there, the more the neighborhood came back to me. The gentle downhill slope where Rowley met the nearest cross street was deceptive. Late one March when I was fifteen, I'd skidded on some road grime and fallen off my bike there, scraping the skin clean off my elbow. I still had the scar.

My fingers found the pebbled skin. The neighborhood held scars both real and imagined. If it held anything else, I'd find it—or wear out my Docs trying.

I took off at my usual NYC pace to see about Hollister. I started where the street did, branching off Commonwealth Avenue at a triangle-shaped green space facing Blessed Sacrament Church. My steps slowed as I walked up the block, on the church side of the street. Outside the safe confines of the cottage, all my suspicions and conclusions felt silly.

What the hell was I hoping to find? *Anything that doesn't belong*, I reminded myself. (Not including me.)

Midwestern normalcy conspired against my search for the unusual. Two neighbors chatted to each other over an actual white picket fence. Somewhere a basketball bounced, giving my morning a backbeat. A lawn mower roared to life.

Fool's errand. A term I'd never considered but now understood.

"Idiot. It's a street. Avenue. Whatever. Nothing more."

But I knew myself: I wouldn't be able to let go of the Hollister idea until I'd walked all three of its blocks.

The houses were well kept and the street was lined with decades-old trees, forming a canopy overhead. Their shade dappled the sidewalk—nature's Jackson Pollock. Each driveway had a tan garbage bin at the curb, soldiers at attention awaiting their next command.

I'd walked this street during my high school years. I knew that not because I had a specific memory but because

I'd walked them all, roaming the neighborhood on foot or by bike when I was bored. I'd make my way down Commonwealth and across the bridge and down to the railroad tracks and back up to street level before heading home. I closed my eyes and kept walking. In spring these streets would smell like lilacs and rain. In fall, crisp leaves and rotten crab apples. Today it was mown grass and the metallic tang of hose water.

When I reopened my eyes, none of the houses looked familiar, but nothing seemed out of place. Nothing jumped out at me. I'd hoped my gaze would land somewhere, that instinct would tell me what I was looking for. But I was throwing wild darts at the board, hitting nothing. Hollister could have been any street, in any midwestern city. It wasn't special, and neither was I. I had not decoded some secret message in the book. It was all a coincidence, and I was an idiot.

But I kept going anyway, trying to walk off the buzz of anxiety inside me.

I reached the street's end and turned around, crossing so I could walk back on the opposite side. I paused to let a car pass when I reached the next intersection and spied a poster stapled to a nearby telephone pole. It looked familiar, like maybe I'd seen a few others in the neighborhood without registering what they were. *LOST CAT* were the only words I could read from where I stood.

Most of the poster was taken up by a grainy picture of a fat black cat, I saw when I got closer. The paper was rain blurred and torn at the edges, like it'd been there a while, waiting for me to find it. Underneath the photo, in smaller letters, was info on the cat and how to reach the owner, which my eyes scanned but did not register. My attention had already moved on, a train bound for the next station. I hadn't stopped walking and was almost past the telephone pole when a single word jumped out at me.

Izzy.

I stopped so hard I tripped over my own feet. I whirled, my eyes found the poster, and I read.

She's a skittish little thing. Answers to Izzy or Jenny. Likes to go on midnight walks. Last seen: 1991.

There was a cell number below, with instructions: *Text for more info. If you have the guts.*

Izzy or Jenny. "Holy. Shitballs."

Paranoid I was being watched, I looked around, trying not to show that my panic levels were redlining. But not even the squirrel hopping across the road was paying attention to me. I snapped a photo of the poster and took off, heart pounding, craving the four solid walls of the cottage.

I debated the wisdom of texting the cell number. If I decided to do it, what would I say? I hurried down the sidewalk, holding myself back from breaking into a run. I saw two more *LOST CAT* posters on the way, one on the back of a *No Parking* sign, the other half torn from a maple tree. There were a couple on Rowley too, one right in front of aunt Shelly's old house. That stopped me in my tracks. If I'd been more observant, I would have seen the poster right away. It was as weathered as the rest.

Safe inside and huddled on the futon, I draped the velvet bedspread over my legs even though I was sweaty from my speed-walk back to the cottage. I set my phone in my lap and waited for my heart rate to slow. I was going to text—of course I was. The poster's message was too intriguing not to investigate, even if it was framed as a taunt. Somewhere inside, a voice that sounded a lot like Gus whispered about curiosity and cats. It told me to call the detective instead of texting the mystery number.

I didn't listen.

Who are you? I typed into my message app, and pressed send. It was eight o'clock in the morning, maybe too early for a response.

While I waited, I looked up the number online. It was registered to an anonymous cell owner in Thief River Falls, Minnesota. I'd never heard of the place and had to look at a map. Northwest corner of the state, not far from the Minnesota–North Dakota border. It sounded like a fictional town, something from an old Western. Or *Little House on the Prairie.*

A headache bloomed behind my right eye. Fact sounded like fiction. Fiction mirrored my past. And I was chasing ghosts. It was hard to know what to believe. I had only my own memory and my gut to use as a gauge. And I wasn't sure I could trust myself anymore. Especially not after the revelations about Ben had thrown my whole high school experience into question.

My phone buzzed, the vibration a Taser zapping my hand. I switched back to the message app.

I am the owner of this number. Who is this and how did you get my number?

I hadn't been expecting that. If the point of the poster was to get me to send a text, why was the person on the other end so defensive?

This is Petta Woznewski, I wrote, in no mood to mess around. Maybe you know me as Petal.

Three maddening dots. They disappeared. That was all for almost ten minutes.

Then finally:

Stop this. Leave me alone.

Another surprise. I took a risk and countered: Tell me why you wrote the book and I might.

Three dots again. It was longer than ten minutes this time. I waited them out, worrying the edge of the blue velvet blanket with nervous fingers.

I don't know how you got this number. I don't want any part of the book. I made a mistake talking, and saying what I said, but it's too late now. Petal, or whoever you are, leave me alone.

Before I could digest all that, another text fired off:
Not safe. Goodbye.

I shot off an answer:
What isn't safe? Who am I talking to?

No more dots. No more anything. My last message sat, waiting to be *Read*, but remained only *Delivered*.

The exchange had given me chills, even under the heavy blanket. I threw it off and stood, not wanting to touch or be touched, or have any sense that I was stuck under or inside anything—and that included my body. The crap that came with being flesh and blood was too much sometimes. I smoked a bowl. I paced the living room. I walked to the market and loaded up on as much beer and junk food as I could carry back with me. When I was floating and my stomach was full, I let myself think about the posters again. And the text messages.

I sat at the kitchen table and turned to a fresh page in my notebook, jotting ideas as I reasoned through the last couple of hours. The purpose of the Hollister-Rowley name parallel was to get me to pay attention to the neighborhood and find the posters. The purpose of the posters was to get me to text the number. But who was on the other end? Were they in Madison, or somewhere else? It was a cell number, so the user could've been anywhere. But it had originated in northern Minnesota. I didn't know anyone who lived up there or anywhere close.

I got back on my laptop, smearing the keys with Cool Ranch dust but too lazy to do anything about it. I scrolled through Facebook, checking the West High pages, the Hollister twins' pages, and Ben's page for any mention of the Thief River Falls area. Nothing.

I checked to see how everyone was spending their day.

Matt Hollister was in Chicago. His Facebook was clogged with posts; he seemed unable to go anywhere or do anything without bragging about it. An hour before, when I'd been texting with the mystery number, he'd been leaving for a charity brunch for scleroderma research. Photos showed him at the podium giving a speech and posing for a photo op with Bitty and some old dude in what looked like a very expensive suit.

I looked up Ben's whereabouts next. I didn't want to believe he could have anything to do with the book or the posters or the whole mess. But he had a strong connection to Megan. One she'd never told me about, and one he might be trying to keep hidden from me. I couldn't rule him out. He was one of the only people who knew I was in town.

His Facebook page gave me nothing. He'd made a few comments on other people's posts but rarely put anything on his own page. He could be anywhere, doing anything. Like texting me. Like writing graffiti on the cabin door. Like leaving the paper on my car before coming into the coffee shop to meet me. My mind spun further: maybe he was behind the Vengeful posts, maybe he was telling Matt horrible things about me, maybe he'd told the cop I was here, sent her after me.

I had to admit to myself—forcing the idea into my head like one of those baby watermelons in Japan, trapped inside boxes so they'd grow unnaturally into a cube—that Ben was looking more suspicious all the time. He wasn't the person I'd thought he was.

But where is Jenny? my inner voice screamed. Finding her would solve so many problems. But I had no idea how to find someone who seemed to want to disappear.

Nothing I could recall about her was helping me figure out where she'd gone. I remembered her sly jealousy, the way she always hung back and waited for things to play out before acting. If she'd done all this—which seemed out of character—the question remained: Why?

I was being epically trolled, but I couldn't figure out the motive. Was I blind? I wasn't in on the joke, but the joke was on me. And I deserved it. I knew I deserved it, and maybe that was why I'd come back to Madison, choosing to stay in my old neighborhood and driving out to the School Forest and texting the cat poster number. Rather than going to the cops and letting them handle everything, I was punishing myself, letting the zombies of my past rise from their graves. I hadn't even put up much of a fight.

Most people think the passage of years can dissolve this stuff—the guilt and fear and anger and shame. The same way the ocean will swallow a broken bottle and, with the battering of thousands of waves, dull its edges and turn it into something beautiful, like sea glass. Time is supposed to soften us, give us distance from the people we wronged and the deeds we regret.

But it doesn't.

I was living proof. I was suffering proof. I was living-dead-on-my-feet, hard-ass evidence.

If what you're trying to bury is bad enough, it never sinks, never fades.

It returns. It rises.

CHAPTER

11

I SCRIBBLED EVERYTHING I was feeling down in my note-book, confessions and suspicions and fears. I'd never kept a journal (barf) but I'd started to understand why people did. I wrote until my hand cramped up on me, and when I was done, it felt like a mental zit had been popped.

My mistake was reading back over my scrawls. I had to stop myself from taking the notebook out back and setting fire to it. Instead, I hid it under my laptop and got into bed—not the futon but the real bed this time.

Staring at the wood-beamed ceiling, I put Jenny, Ben, the whole Hollister family (both dead and alive), and the mysterious texter into my mental blender, where they spun for several sleepless hours. They formed a poisonous puree of doubt and speculation, Megan's ghost floating to the top. Then she took over. I imagined Megan dumping this puree in the trash, smashing the blender on the floor, and pointing one long, Tiffany blue fingernail at me. She was trying to tell me something, but I didn't know what.

Trust my instincts?

Call it instinct or something else, obsession or com-pulsion maybe, but I couldn't get Jenny out of my mind.

My not being able to find her or track her down online was making her into something of a ghost as well.

Back in 1991, she'd lived with her parents on Harvey Street in an old brick duplex. They'd owned the building, living in one half while renting the other. I knew this because sometimes Jenny would bail on us to help them clean out between tenants. She always bitched about it. Rightly so—their renters constantly screwed them over. One family disappeared in the night, leaving all their stuff behind and owing months in rent. Another time, Jenny was helping her dad carry an old, stained mattress out to the curb when a mummified cat fell out of it. Megan had loved to hear Jenny tell these stories, about the weirdos and transients that passed through the rental. It was like poverty porn, a world Megan couldn't fathom and couldn't get enough of.

I gave up on sleep and dragged myself to the kitchen. Breakfast was Funyuns and assorted Takis, a salt bomb on my exhausted, sober taste buds. I packed a fresh bowl but put it aside. Maybe, for once, a clear head would help.

I cracked my laptop to look up a recent Google map image of Jenny's old neighborhood. The duplex wasn't there anymore. It'd been razed, along with the other homes on the block, and a mixed-use building had been constructed in their place. Condos on top, retail on the ground floor. Those buildings were everywhere in town, an invasive species—taking over the old Ken Kopps grocery on Monroe Street, and the liquor store on University Avenue where the high school kids always tried to buy beer. More expensive housing, more chain stores. It seemed I was the only person who wanted out of Madison, not in.

So Jenny's duplex was a dead end when it came to tracking her down. But she had a big family. Both of her parents had multiple siblings, all of them in or around

Madison. Aunts and uncles and cousins were always over at her house. Her cousin Ericka was the only one I'd ever met—the one who'd gone to West with us. Ericka would drive us around sometimes, without comment or complaint, but then ignore us in the hallways. She was older and therefore superior—typical upperclassmen stuff. But my impression of her, overall, was positive. She was always there for Jenny, ready with a free ride or lunch money or a death glare for Megan. Those two did not get along. I wouldn't go so far as to say Ericka hated Megan. Not until The Sweater Incident, at least.

Be good, Jennifer. Be careful. This family is vulgar. I'd once heard Ericka say that to Jenny after dropping us all off at Megan's house. She whispered it but didn't try very hard to make sure no one else heard.

Ericka had hung around us enough to know certain things, though probably not enough to write the book herself. But if anyone could've gotten the whole story out of Jenny, it would be Ericka. Maybe they'd written the book together. They'd have been a good team.

I reached back in time for Ericka's last name but couldn't come up with it. It wasn't Isaacs. Ericka was from Jenny's mom's side of the family. The Mormon side. They'd lived on the far east edge of town, attended the Mormon church there. Maybe they still did. I'd never been clear on why Ericka went to West High, except that her home life seemed rocky and they often had trouble making rent. She stayed with Jenny a lot, so maybe that was her official residence.

Despite the warmth of the summer morning, I felt a chilly anticipation at the thought I might be closer than ever to unmasking ME Littleton. Ericka and Jenny working together made a new kind of sense, one I hadn't felt so far in my clumsy investigations.

Ericka's church was easy enough to find online, but the website didn't have photos of its members. I followed a link to their Facebook page and scrolled through the list of their followers. Near the bottom, I found her. *Ericka Udall.*

Her face was broader and her eyes more sunken, but I recognized her stern features. The posts on her profile were mostly about the church. She was active in the choir and led youth activities. She was married to a boring-looking guy named Doug but didn't seem to have children of her own. In one photo, a perfect circle of kindergarteners sat on a manicured, too-green lawn. Ericka stood in the middle, smiling down at the kids, who all wore black dress pants and white shirts. A large white building with twin columns loomed behind them—a fancy event venue or country club, I thought. But after more scrolling, I discovered the white building was her house.

Wow—Ericka had come a long way since the days when her family had been forced to crash at Jenny's duplex. Sifting through the pictures of her lavish home, I noticed it was located in Maple Bluff, a few streets over from where I'd lived with my parents. That was an area of Madison I'd avoided visiting, or even thinking about, since I'd come back to town. I could stomach the other haunts. Aunt Shelly's neighborhood? Easy. The old Hollister house? No problem. The reservoir? I'd get there eventually. But I didn't want to go anywhere near Maple Bluff. It was beautiful to look at, but all it had given me was death.

The only way out is through. That might be true. But the only way to survive a trip down bad-memory lane was to focus on one tragedy at a time. And, mostly because of the book's sudden intrusion, Megan's tragedy had won.

Ericka. Back to Ericka. It doesn't matter where her house is; the point is that it's an expensive pile of bricks.

Had she married into money?

Or maybe the cash had come from somewhere else. Like, say, writing a bestselling book. A Mormon woman might use a pseudonym to write something like *No One Suspected* if she didn't want her church finding out.

But my follow-the-cash theory died a quick death. The pictures of her house went back years, long before the book was published. She hadn't gotten rich from the book. But I still believed she could fit into the Jenny-Megan puzzle in some way.

I followed the church's Facebook page and Ericka's personal page and texted a quick DM to Ericka. Maybe she had information on her cousin's whereabouts she'd be willing to share or, if she'd talk to me, would let something incriminating slip.

Hello Ericka. Maybe you remember me. My name is Petal and I was friends with your cousin Jenny a long time ago, in high school. Do you have a number or an email address for her? I'd like to get back in touch. Thanks.

I pushed my computer aside and picked up my phone, considered texting Ben. He'd taken up residence in my head. The more I thought about him and Megan sneaking around together, the more that mental image made me want to throw up. What I wanted to do was drive over to his perfect house, grab him by the ears, scream in his face, and shake him until his head snapped back and he gave up the answers to all my nagging questions.

Why did you never tell me you went out with Megan?
Did you know Jenny too?
Do you spend time with Matt Hollister?
What do you know about the book?

On the few occasions when I'd thought about Ben over the years, a distant warmth had gathered inside me, like the memory of a sunny beach in the dead of winter.

But that was gone. Now he conjured an overwhelming wrongness. I'd lost something good, and I didn't have too many nice memories to cling to—especially not from high school. Starting from the day I became an orphan, my whole life had split off on a new path. One I had no choice but to go down. And it hadn't led anywhere good.

When Ben had met me at the coffee shop, he'd known more than he was telling. I could feel it, now that I wasn't drugged by my old fondness for him. But more about what exactly? I thought back over our conversation, trying to remember if I'd mentioned Megan. I was pretty sure I hadn't—I'd been focused on the book, and Littleton, and the local angle, and his laugh.

I put my phone back down.

I would not text Ben.

Don't do it, Petta! Leave it alone!

I wanted to know what he knew, but facing him after what I'd learned would be messy.

I would not look up his address. I would not drive to his house and yell at him on his own front porch. I'd avoid him, ignore his existence if I could. Seeing him would only screw things up. And by things, I meant me. Concentrating on finding Jenny was simpler—it was cleaner and far more plausible that she (and maybe Ericka) might be Littleton.

I scrolled through both West High Facebook groups again, even though I'd already searched for any mention of her. She was probably married, no longer Jenny Isaacs, instead Jenny Something-Else. I had no idea how to go about tracking her down if I didn't know her name. My limited repertoire of detective skills and tricks—procrastinating, Googling, smoking pot, trawling Facebook, finding nothing, and then giving up—had been exhausted.

And so was I.

The gummy lump of breakfast junk food was a rock in my stomach. My head ached and my energy was waning. I hadn't been awake for long, but it felt like a decade. I needed a steadier routine. I needed more sleep. I needed Gus. I needed to eat a vegetable. At the moment, only one of those things was in my grasp. I packed my backpack with necessities and drove aimlessly until I spotted a restaurant that looked like it would sell rabbit food. I asked for a table in the corner. I ordered a coffee and an ice water and a giant salad with blackened chicken on top.

Scrolling the categories on Netflix for a bit while I waited on my food, I settled on *Speed*. It was no *John Wick*, but it was one of my comfort watches—it'd gotten me through that first lonely, pot-hazed Chicago year after I left aunt Shelly's. That was the year she got truly sick, the year she switched from fighting the cancer to actively dying from it. Not that I knew any of that was happening at the time. She didn't want me to. Before I left town, she'd given me a small, white TV/VCR combo unit. A graduation present. I was a movie addict even then, and she knew me. Probably the only one who did. In those pre-cheap-laptop, Blockbuster-video, no-Netflix days, it was the perfect gift. And *Speed* was one of the few VHS tapes I'd owned. I wore the damn thing out. I could quote every line, and rewatches never got old. The movie had convinced me that if I could find my own lazily smiling, buzz-cut Keanu (the best Keanu, obviously) to stand by my side through the crazy shit life threw, I could survive anything.

As Netflix loaded the movie, I thought about Gus. I tried to stop him from intruding; I wanted to concentrate on green vegetables and unattainable movie stars. Not on my reality, not on "The Deal with Gus," as my internal monologue labeled it. But he snuck in while I wasn't paying attention (his MO) and was hard to ignore.

He was broad and strong and nicely padded. When we met, he'd had a thatch of short, dark curls shot through with gray. When his hair got longer, he'd keep it out of his eyes by pushing a pair of wraparound sunglasses up onto his head. (Blue, mirrored, dorky.) Each time he did this, clumps of curls would hang down on either side of his face like long, silky dog ears. I started calling him Puppy. Then one day, he showed up to work with a fresh buzz cut. He'd kept it high and tight ever since. For me, I knew, though he never said. I never called him Puppy again.

The waitress approached with my food, and I put in my earbuds and pressed play.

I watched buses explode, ate my salad, envied Sandra Bullock (not for the first time), and downed two cups of coffee and three tall glasses of ice water. By the time *Speed* was over, my bladder was bursting, but I was human again. Like maybe my internal organs weren't going to shut down in protest. I packed up my things and rushed to the bathroom.

Outside the restaurant, the sun was bright. Glaring, the way it does when you come out of a matinee in a dark theater. I took the long way back to the cottage, diverting down side streets, blasting music, and trying not to think about all the heavy stuff I should be thinking about—like how Ericka had not responded to my message.

Nestled back on the futon, my new favorite blanket piled on top of my restless feet, I was about to continue avoiding my impending doom by queueing up another Netflix distraction when there was a knock on the door.

Crap.

Hardly anyone knew I was in Madison, and no one knew where I was staying.

Did they?

Probably the owners from the main house wanting to check in. Or worse, chat.

Double crap.

Or what if it was the person on the other end of those mystery texts? I wanted to know who they were, but not, like, face-to-face. Not in my safe space.

I ducked under the blanket. When the knock came again, sharp and impatient, hiding started to feel stupid. Grown-ass woman, big-girl pants, and all that. I got off the futon and wrenched the door open, bracing myself to face my tormenter.

But it was a harmless stranger. A woman. She didn't look like she'd come to dismember me. Medium height, shiny auburn hair slicked back into a low ponytail. She wore fancy jeans and a tailored suit jacket. An I'm-here-on-official-business vibe hung around her like a cloud of bad perfume.

"Petal Woznewski?" She put a hand on her hip. Her jacket shifted to expose the badge glinting from her belt. And a lump under her arm I thought might be a gun.

Detective Samantha Gull, I presume.

"Uh. Yeah. That's me." Movement over her right shoulder—the curtains in the main house, twitching closed. "You want to come in?" No need to put on a show.

She didn't answer but stepped over the threshold, boots clicking on the floor like she was wearing spurs. Her vibe was aspiring gunslinger with a side of *I'm too old for this shit.*

In the movies—*Lethal Weapon*, for instance—detectives always came in pairs. Where was the Riggs to her Murtaugh?

"Detective Samantha Gull, Madison Police." The words were clipped. From nerves or hostility? Her tight-ass-cop intensity was turned up to eleven. It made me want to know what had gotten her all fired up and brought her to my door.

She reached up to tuck a stray hair behind her ear, and I saw her nails. Bitten down to the quick. Hmm. Maybe she was a Riggs, not a Murtaugh.

"Mind if I see your ID?" I asked. "No offense."

On closer inspection the badge was legit, and she handed over her ID without complaint. Everything checked out.

"None taken. Would it be okay if I asked you a few questions?"

I swung the door closed behind her and led the way into the small kitchen.

"Yeah, sure. Coffee?" It was the only thing I had to offer besides Funyuns dust and pot. And I needed to keep my hands busy, so she wouldn't notice the nervous twitch in my fingers.

"Black. Thanks."

I laid out the Keurig pods and mugs and turned on the machine, getting the first brew started. I pulled my Cinnamon Toast Crunch–flavored Coffee Mate out of the fridge.

The detective lowered herself into the nearest chair with a two-weeks-out-from-retirement sigh, despite the fact that she looked to be a healthy woman in her prime. It was as if she'd learned to be a cop on TV and relished a good cliché. When it was time for her to leave, I fully expected her to pull a Columbo. I'd always liked Peter Falk's TV detective. His interrogations only seemed clumsy until he hit the suspect with a banger on his way out the door.

I handed her the first mug of coffee and started my own, putting the creamer in first, the way I liked it.

"So. Woznewski. When did you get back into town?"

"Couple days ago," I said, though if she was any kind of detective, she knew that already. She was testing me. She'd said *back* into town. Neither of us mentioned the business card she'd left at the cottage. I sipped at the edge of my cup. The sweetness hit me like a sunbeam.

"What brought you back to Madison?" She got out a tiny notepad and a stumpy green pencil. *Vitense Golfland* was written on the side.

"It's kind of a long story."

I hadn't told her anything yet, but she started writing anyway.

"I've got time," she said, head still bent over her notepad.

"I'm trying to track down an old high school . . . friend." It wasn't a lie to call Jenny a friend. We had been, once, if only briefly. If only because of Megan.

"And have you found your old . . . friend?" She mimicked my awkward pause. Her left hand spun the mug of coffee around on the table, like it was a prop rather than something she was supposed to drink. It was still steaming, still full. Some of it slopped onto the table. I waited for her to apologize for the spill, but she didn't.

"I haven't. Not much luck at all, actually. I should probably go home."

It was good to say it, and good to believe for a second that I could give up and go home. But I was too far in to walk away clean, and in too deep to escape. I was trapped in quicksand of my own making, but that didn't make it any less dangerous.

"Giving up so soon? That would be a shame."

"Would it?"

I hated this dance we were doing, reciting lines and avoiding truths and pitting ourselves against each other even though we were most likely on the same side. But

Detective Gull annoyed me. I didn't want to be on any side with her. I wanted her to drink her bitter coffee and go the hell away.

The detective must have sensed she wasn't getting anywhere with the tough act. She put down her pencil and tipped her head toward the kitchen counter where I was leaning. Under a pile of empty fruit roll-up wrappers sat my copy of *No One Suspected*.

"Your visit have anything to do with that, by chance?"

I swallowed back an automatic no.

Lying was one of my main defense mechanisms, but it wouldn't pay off here. I knew she knew the truth. And she knew I knew it. I took another sip of coffee.

"A bit, yeah."

"There's something strange about that book. Don't you think?"

Now we were getting somewhere interesting.

"What, like it's supposedly fictional but my real name is in it and the author made up a whole School Forest death scenario and is making me out to be a heartless killer, which I am not?"

Gull's face cracked into a smile for the first time.

"Noted." She didn't write anything down, but she stopped spinning her mug, leaning forward in the chair. Her posture sent a clear message: *This is what I really came here to ask you.* The other questions had been a formality, the opening act. The main event was about to begin.

"Have you received any strange letters, or other communications? About the book or otherwise?"

I wasn't ready to tell her about the graffiti or the poster or anything, not yet. I had no idea if I could trust this person. She was like a pet peeve in human form.

"No letters."

She watched me for a long moment, probably wondering how truthful I was being. She didn't know me well enough to know I was only as truthful as I could stomach, and not a bit more.

"I've gotten some letters," she said. "Addressed to me, at the station."

"From who?" I was too curious to keep my cool.

"Anonymous, but with a local postmark. Plain white envelopes containing book passages copied longhand from *No One Suspected*. Blue ink. Your name was there, like in the book. But the other characters, Miri and Izzy, had their names crossed out. Other names were written in red ink above them. Can you guess what those other names were?"

I didn't say anything but nodded, too afraid to open my mouth.

"I ran those names, along with yours, and something interesting came up."

"I'll bet. Jenny—did you talk to her?"

Gull shook her head, and my hopes died. "Not yet. My sergeant isn't convinced there's anything to the letters, so I haven't been able to officially do much. But I'm working on it. On my own time. Have you been in touch with her?"

I saw no reason to lie. "No, I can't find her. But you believe there is something to the letters, and the book?" I wanted her to say no, to calm my fears and tell me it was okay to go back to New York. I wanted her permission to give up. But I knew she wouldn't give it.

"I do. There's the detective character in the book. Samson Bull. Call me crazy . . ."

It was tempting to do exactly that, but I squashed the impulse. Detective Gull wouldn't like being called crazy any more than I would.

I guessed this was why she'd come to my door solo—dragging a partner along would've meant having to attempt an explanation for something she didn't yet understand, and didn't have permission to investigate.

". . . but that name sounds a heck of a lot like Samantha Gull. Ever since those letters started arriving, one every week for a month, I've been asking myself: *Sammy, how much is too much of a coincidence?* And I decided this is it." She pressed a finger into the kitchen table until the nail bed turned white. "This is what too much of a coincidence looks like. The book, those letters, and you, back in town. If I wasn't worried about sounding like a lunatic, I'd say the letters were a small part of a big plan. I'd say I was chosen, before that book was even published, when the author made up the name Samson Bull, to be the eventual recipient of those letters."

I knew exactly how she felt. We'd both been chosen. But that didn't make me feel any better.

Gull tilted her head, studying me. Trying to figure out why I wasn't saying anything, maybe. She talked enough for the both of us, though I noticed she didn't ask me if I'd written the book or sent the letters. Whether it was because she knew I hadn't or she didn't think I'd tell the truth, I wasn't sure.

"Is there anything you'd like to tell me, Petal? Now's the time. If you tell me now, I can help you. Later, no promises."

"Call me Petta."

"Petta. I've got a bad feeling about what's going on here, and you can help me. I don't think it's going to stop with the letters."

I've got a bad feeling about this.

Han Solo's lazy drawl echoed in my head. I gave Harrison Ford a mental shove and tried to concentrate on the real live person in front of me. We stared at each other. Slowly she stood up, not breaking our visual standoff. I was either going to spill my guts or keep my mouth shut but couldn't get my inner voices to stop with the movie quotations long enough to decide.

Paranoia pounced like a needy house cat. I looked away, scanning the kitchen for anything Gull might notice and use against me. My notebook, its strange lists and incoherent scribbles. My cell, with texts to the mystery number. My pot pipe, sitting full on the windowsill over the kitchen sink. But she wasn't looking at any of it. She was looking at me.

The detective inhaled, her lips pursing around whatever she was about to say. I didn't wait to find out.

"Actually," I said, cutting her off. "I don't feel good. Can we do this another time?"

It wasn't a lie. My stomach was a hurricane. I regretted everything I'd ever eaten.

Detective Gull's hand moved to the inside of her jacket. I turned to toss my coffee dregs into the sink with a wet splat.

When I turned back, she was holding one of her business cards. I declined to tell her I already had one.

"Here's the address of the station and my cell number. Will you come down tomorrow? Or I can meet you, anywhere you like. This is not an interrogation. I need you to tell me what you know about them. About Megan and Jenny. And what really happened that night."

Their names sounded wrong in Gull's mouth.

"Yes, yes. Okay. Tomorrow, I . . . I'll come down."

"Ten o'clock?"

"Ten tomorrow."

I wanted her gone. I wanted to stop feeling like I was trapped inside a straitjacket. I wanted to go home.

The detective waited one more beat, as if I might change my mind. I closed my eyes, willed my stomach to settle, and waited until I heard the reassuring sound of her spurs jangling back across the living room floor. Halfway to the front door, they stopped.

Here we go.

I braced myself.

"Oh, one more thing before I go."

Boom: the Columbo.

"Do you know anyone who drives a black Tesla? Minnesota plates."

It was the last thing I'd expected her to ask. I opened my eyes. Gull waited.

I'd noticed only one black Tesla since returning to Madison, outside the Hollister house. But I hadn't clocked the plates.

"No. No one with a Tesla. I might have seen one around town, but I don't know who was driving."

"If you suddenly remember who was driving, or if there's anything else you want to tell me before tomorrow morning, you've got my number," Gull said before slipping out the door.

When it closed behind her, I collapsed against the kitchen counter. My elbow bumped my empty coffee mug, sending it flying. It hit the floor and shattered, shards of cobalt pottery exploding in every direction.

I took my time picking them up. If I focused on not slicing my fingers, I could avoid thinking about what came next—about what Littleton had in store for me.

It wouldn't be a few letters, like the ones Gull had been sent. I wasn't getting off that easy.

Excerpt from
No One Suspected
2021

IT HAS TAKEN me many years to comprehend and account for the mistakes I made that night. The mistakes that ruined my life and ended Megan's. First, there was the knife, of course. But worse than that—my real mistake—was allowing Petal to get away with murder. The image of Miri, crumpled on the ground, has lived on in my head for thirty years. Frozen in a nightmarish snow globe, swirling with moonlight and terror.

My penance: a life that has been one long, agonizing downward spiral. There was a time when I vowed I would have a better life than my parents had. A real house, not a duplex. A life like the Rowleys had. I wanted to live up to the name they'd given me—an honorary Rowley. But when Miri died, so did my vow.

I dropped out of high school, moved away from Madison. I'd return every few years, after my parents forgave me for dropping out, to visit them while they were still alive. Then when they died, not at all. Why would I want to go back to the scene of my torment? I waitressed, I managed a smoothie shop, I took the graveyard shift at a twenty-four-hour gym. Mindless jobs that would pay the bills. It was survival, not a real life.

Cousin Ella—my favorite of my aunt and uncle's kids, the one who had been at West High with Petal, Miri, and me—checked up on me sometimes. Cosigning a lease when I was in a bind, helping me pay off the car I needed to get to work. She understood I wasn't ready to be saved, but she wouldn't let me drown either.

I kept my promise to Petal; I never told Ella, or anyone else, what had happened at the School Forest. But Ella knew Miri's death had wrecked me, and that was enough to keep her worrying about me for years. She considered it a sort of religious duty. The church she was born into, the one my mother had left behind when she married my father, was intense: missions and dramatic baptisms and three-times-weekly meetings. Her life and work became fully entwined with the church, and she made it her personal mission to keep me from killing myself with drugs and alcohol. But I kept using. It was the only thing I was good at, and the only thing that helped me forget. Eventually, I succeeded in pushing her away, and even she gave up.

For most of my adult life, what happened to Miri was something I could keep in the background, buried under antidepressants and alcohol. But then something changed. Maybe it was turning forty, or finally trying AA, or my third divorce. The guilt over my role in Miri's death began to feel uncontainable. If I lost concentration, even for a moment, everything would explode.

I couldn't sleep. I lost my job at the gym. I stopped going to AA because I was still keeping secret the one thing that was driving me to drink. The past would kill me if I continued to keep it inside. So I went back to Madison to face it.

My motives were selfish. I comprehended that but decided I didn't care. I wanted to be able to sleep again, to live without a bomb inside me. And that leads me to the rest of the story. This is the point where it becomes, to my shame,

less about Miri and more about me. But most of all, it's about
the truth. It was long past time that I faced it.

But I couldn't do it alone.

Samson Bull, the detective who had investigated Miri's
death, was the person I had in mind to help me. If he was still
alive. What I remembered most about him were his eerie blue
eyes. I'd been convinced they could see right through me. He
had come to my house to ask me about her, about Miri, the
day after they found her body. I'd braced myself for a stern
interrogation, but he was soft-spoken and only asked a few
standard questions.

How well did you know the deceased, Miriam Rowley?
Was she troubled about anything?
Was she acting differently in the days before she died?

I'd told him the truth about everything he asked. I'd steeled
myself to lie, but he never asked where I had been that awful
night, or when I'd last seen Miri. I wasn't a suspect. He had only
come to learn more about Miri. He visited Petal's house too, I
heard, and talked to a few teachers at school. The investigation
was completed quickly. Her death was ruled an accident, under
pressure from her parents, it was said. The s-word was never
mentioned in any official capacity, though many speculated.

The eight-hour drive back to Madison from my home in
northern Minnesota drained the nervous, chaotic energy that
danced under my skin, my hands tense on the steering wheel
the whole time. I hadn't had a drink in twenty-four hours,
and my body was punishing me. I pulled into a Kwik Trip on
the outskirts of Madison and used the bathroom. When I felt
well enough to leave the safety of the stall, I returned to my
car and tried to decide what to do first. Instead of calling Ella
to tell her I was in town or checking into a hotel so I could
shower off my panic sweat, I called the Madison Police.

I was insistent as they passed me from department to
department, and eventually I found someone who'd known

Bull. He was still alive and long retired. They wouldn't give me his contact information, but after a quick internet search I found him. One of his old coworkers had gone to visit him at Meadowridge Bluff Senior Living and posted a picture on his Instagram that had both Bull's name in the caption and the Meadowridge sign in the background.

I called ahead to Meadowridge, and they gave me their visiting hours. The on-duty nurse asked me to wait in the common area, and it was half an hour before he shuffled into the room. My stomach clenched at the sight of him—so diminished. How could this husk of a man possibly help me? He was stooped, and grouchy, and stingy with his words. But he remembered us. And those eyes, so blue, were the same. The minute I said the name Miriam Rowley, his face came alive. The fire that blazed inside me burned in him: the need for the truth. The desire to set it free.

After securing permission from the nurse, I drove us to a nearby Perkins. In a corner booth, under a stained-glass pendant light that cast a jaundiced glow, we ordered coffee and eggs. He waited until his midafternoon breakfast was on the table before he started talking.

"Never did feel good about the way the Rowley case wrapped up"—he sipped delicately at his coffee—"back then."

"What made—or makes—you feel that way?"

"Hell, if I knew the answer to that, I woulda solved it." He was growling. I must have hit a nerve.

He continued. "We looked at the boyfriend pretty hard, but then the mother . . ." His eyes went vacant as he stared at something over my head. A shiver whispered through me at the word *boyfriend*.

Miri had mentioned dozens of crushes and flirtations but never a boyfriend. She'd never had one, as far as I knew. She was only fourteen when she died.

Bull was talking again.

"Doesn't matter anyway. He had an alibi and zero motive. At least none we could find. We didn't find much of anything. Did a full sweep of the girl's bedroom, but nothing gave me what I was looking for. I still don't know what happened that night, though I've thought back on it now and again over the years. Never been able to get free of the idea that we had it wrong. I thought maybe . . . I've seen my share of suicides, and the markers weren't there. Accidental death was as close to an answer as I could get, with the family breathing down my neck. But it didn't ring true then. Still doesn't."

"What was the boyfriend's name?"

His rheumy stare found mine.

"You don't know? Thought she was your friend."

"She kept him a secret, I guess." I made sure my voice was light, but this new information was not what I had expected to get out of our conversation. Even all these years later, it was a blow to find out Miri had been keeping another secret from me.

He stabbed at a loose cube of ham that had fallen from his omelet. The meat was perfectly square, like it had been extruded by a machine.

"Some kid from the high school. Don't remember the name." He sighed. "That happens more than I'd like these days. My memory's gone slippery. I remember he smelled like sweat socks and pencil shavings."

"Do you remember coming to talk to me? After Miri died?"

"I talked to a few of her friends. But it was routine, and all those interviews blur together now. Nothing came of them anyway. So no, I don't specifically remember our conversation. Sorry if that upsets you."

"It doesn't. I wasn't very memorable. I certainly wasn't helpful. But there were things I didn't say. Secrets I kept."

Bull finished his coffee. I refilled it from the orange carafe of decaf our waitress had left on the table. I'd expected a reaction from him at my confession, but he was impassive. As if I'd said exactly what he'd expected me to say.

"That's why you've come back. Why we're here. So you can say those things to me now."

"Yes. If you'll listen."

"I'll listen. I'll do more than listen." He pointed his fork at me, yellow bits of egg dangling from the tines. "If someone's still to blame for that girl's death, you can bet your ass I'll do everything I can to take them down."

I wasn't sure what he would be able to accomplish, frail as he was, but I was grateful for the sentiment. And relieved I wasn't going to have to walk the road back in time alone. I opened my mouth to start my story, but Bull wasn't done.

"I'll make the guilty party pay. Even if it's you."

12

THE BOOK'S PRESENT-DAY chapters read like a halluci-nation in word form. Or maybe hypnosis was closer to the truth, because as I read through them for the second time, they lulled me, pulling me into a dark fairy tale. Izzy the Brave going after Petal the Wicked Witch, Samson the Bull at her side.

Being painted a villain didn't bug me anymore. But something about these new chapters did—they ate away at me, for a reason I couldn't figure. A termite nibbling along my brain stem.

I took a long drag off my pipe. I'd retrieved it from the windowsill as soon as I heard Gull start her car and drive away from the cottage. I was sprawled on the futon, staring off into space and holding the smoke in my lungs until I felt the familiar, tight yearning to breathe. I let it go with a grunt.

"Once upon a time," I whispered to the plume of smoke snaking out of my pipe, "a beautiful princess named Megan lived a charmed life in a city hugged by lakes. She was beloved by all who knew her. Until the day she met Petal. Who was not a princess. She was a troll. Disguised as an ogre. Pretending to be a witch."

Sometimes the stories we tell ourselves become more real than the truth.

"Holy crap." I dropped the pipe, pawing at the living room rug to find it before I burned a hole in the soft, butter-colored shag.

I'd figured out what bothered me about the present-day book chapters. They read, if not like a fairy tale, at least like some kind of tale. A story one person would spin for another over a campfire, or while bellied up to a bar, beer in hand. A version of the truth, carefully crafted.

"*Jenny didn't write the book*." Hearing it out loud made it finally real. Two ideas had been fighting inside me for days: no one else knew enough to write it, but the Jenny I knew never would have publicly aired our secret—not any more than I could have. But she might have confessed the truth to someone, if she trusted them.

So who would Jenny trust?

Ericka seemed the most likely. They'd always been close. And if *No One Suspected* was to be believed (that was a big *if*), she would have been there waiting to help if Jenny asked. I checked my phone, but she still hadn't responded to my message.

Then there was Ben. I could imagine a scenario where Jenny might have reached out to him, if she'd ever found out about him and Megan. Maybe they'd bonded and she'd told him a version of the truth that didn't make her look bad—making me look bad instead. And Ben was so mad he wrote the book to punish me.

No matter the *who*, the underlying premise felt solid: Jenny had told someone else what happened to Megan. The version of events she wanted them to hear. And with that information, and maybe her help, they'd written the book. That's how Littleton knew so many details, and at the same time had never quite squared with the Jenny I remembered.

Littleton, who are you?

"Who? Are? You?" I asked, trying (failing) to blow smoke rings like the Caterpillar from *Alice in Wonderland*.

It could also be someone else entirely. A stranger, someone I'd never met. But if so, what skin did they have in this game?

My body was tight as a fist. I was short of breath, nauseous. A headache loomed. I willed the pot in my system to soften all my hard edges, but for once, it didn't work. I spent the rest of the afternoon lying down and drinking water. As if I could flush the past and its bad karma out of my system.

At some point, I slept. Not a fall into oblivion but a slow slide into the blue haze that danced behind my eyelids. The Caterpillar lived there. He taunted me, blowing smoke rings with his hookah, until I couldn't even be sure of my own name.

*   *   *

When I woke, it was dark. Not the half-assed dark of dusk or dawn but the deep, sticky, tarry stuff. I remembered my promise to Gull, the impending visit to the station. My dread—about the visit but also about facing my whole situation—hung inside the cottage like a thundercloud. I was not fond of cops. Ever since the day my parents died and the police treated me like a lost teddy bear on its way to St. Vinnie's, I hadn't had much use for them. Gull wasn't that bad, just full of herself in a very punchable way. I didn't want to talk to her. Not because I wanted to hold on to my secrets, but because I needed more answers before I'd be ready to let them go.

The only way out is through.

It was time to move past secrets and stop lying to myself. Finding my way out wouldn't be pretty, but facing the truth rarely was. My parents had taught me that.

Involving the police in my business went against my fly-under-the-radar instincts. I wasn't going to be like Izzy in the book, teaming up with a cop to reveal the truth. But if Gull was getting mysterious letters, my future did seem to involve her. The book was a tether between us, and the only way to break it was to unmask its author. And she might be able to help me do that.

I had no appetite, even though I'd slept through dinnertime hours ago. I opened my laptop and checked my email (none) and looked at the weather in New York (overcast all week), wishing I were there. I picked up my phone to text Gus but put it back down, thinking better of it. He'd only ask questions I wasn't ready to answer. Like when I was coming home, or if I'd talked to the police. Instead, I texted my boss, telling her I'd need to dip into my unpaid vacation days.

The web browser was still open on my laptop from the day before, a messy scatter of tabs left over from recent searches. Facebook was one of them. The groups icon at the top of the page indicated there was a new post on one of the three pages I had followed—both of the West High pages and Ericka's church.

Something cool breezed through the room. I looked over my shoulder to see if I'd left a window open, but the cottage was locked tight and the air conditioning had shut off at dusk. There was a smell too. Sweet, almost powdery.

I clicked on the groups icon, half expecting a new Vengeful post to attack me.

But the notification was from the official West reunion page. A classmate I didn't remember, someone named Jackie, had posted: **Didn't someone just ask about her the other day?** She ended her post with a sad-face emoji and attached a breaking story from WDAZ, the ABC affiliate in Grand Forks. A body had been found the day before, over the Minnesota border in the Red Lake River. Just inside the Thief River Falls city limits.

I squeezed my eyes shut and knuckled my lids until miniature fireflies danced across my vision. I didn't want to click on the link, didn't want to see who had washed up on the banks of the river. But I knew. Just like I recognized the smell wafting on the phantom breeze: Final Net hair spray and Dr Pepper Lip Smackers. Megan's smells.

I shivered, unsure what this sensory hallucination was trying to tell me. It was a scolding, maybe, a punishment for my stupidity. Or—more likely—a warning.

Hands shaking, I opened the news article. I forced myself to read the whole thing.

The victim has been identified as Jennifer (Isaacs) Cushman of Thief River Falls.

There was no information on her cause of death. It was too early yet. And also too late.

Eating was the last thing I wanted to do, but I'd become very aware of the emptiness in my stomach. I was wrung out, hollow. I wanted to cry, but there was no substance left inside me to call up any tears. I hadn't moved from the comfort of the futon since waking, but as the reality of Jenny's death sunk in, I ran for the bathroom. There was nothing to throw up, but I sat on the toilet, rocking. The pain in my stomach was roiling and sharp, like a hailstorm.

I was scared, for myself and (much too late) for whatever had happened to Jenny. But there was something else too. Something more selfish, more muddy than the icy crispness of fear.

I'd been expecting, from the moment I read the opening lines of *No One Suspected*, to get one last face-to-face with Jenny Isaacs. A meeting thirty years in the making. Something we both were owed, for different reasons. We'd each held on to a portion of Megan's death, splitting the horror between us like a pair of Best Friends necklaces. The only way to make us whole again would be to bring our two fragmented souls together and confront what happened.

We'd never get that now. I'd be stuck with my half of the secret. Maybe forever.

I was the only one left who knew the truth.

Wasn't I?

On shaky legs, I shuffled back to the futon. The last place I should've been in my fragile state was on social media, but once the shock began to recede—and my trusty defense mechanisms kicked in—it registered that the news article had given me a key piece of information I'd been missing. Jenny's last name. After that, it was easy to find her Facebook profile.

A few life events were listed, moves and jobs and marriages, but only from the last decade, and there was no mention of her maiden name or her connections to Madison. She and her cousin Ericka weren't even Facebook friends. There was a smiling photo at the Minnesota State Fair, a white plastic bucket of chocolate chip cookies held up to the camera. Behind the smile her eyes were empty, and her skin hung on her bones like an oversized suit. She lacked the healthy padding so many people gained in middle age. She was gaunt, looked haunted.

A panoramic photo was the last thing she'd posted, two months ago. A rainbow arcing over a sparkling lake, disappearing into the trees.

The fact of Jenny's death—not the emotions surrounding it, which I'd unpack later—took me a while to digest. Like a snake swallowing a goat, I consumed the idea whole, in one long gulp. But that didn't mean I was ready to move past it. Jenny was a painful lump, her death stretching my insides to uncomfortable dimensions.

I read back over the article with a keener eye. New details jumped out, and I thought back over my last forty-eight hours. Jenny's approximate time of death was one PM on Sunday. Yesterday. Early that same morning, I'd had a text exchange with someone from Thief River Falls.

Not safe, one of the texts had said. The texter was Jenny—had to be. She'd been warning me. And then she died.

"Jesus, Jenny. Fuck."

A dry heat washed over me. I couldn't manage a full breath. The grief and guilt were like waves crashing against me, and I couldn't muster the strength to rise above them. I thought, for the first time in a very long time, that I might drown.

But I survived, like I always do. I let the feelings have their moment, and then I tucked them away. Not because I was going to ignore them, but because I needed a clear head if I was going to figure out who had done this horrible thing.

When the grief dulled, there was a hot ball of terror inside me. I tilted my head back and stared at the ceiling until I could face the computer screen again.

No one on the reunion page had commented on the news story. The post was only a few minutes old, and the hour was late. Most people probably hadn't seen it yet. I went to the Flipside group to see if anyone was talking about Jenny's death there, but there were no new posts since my last visit. It felt like I was the only one in the world bearing witness to her death—her murder?

I didn't know who might be capable of such a thing—not just logistically, but mentally and physically. Or who might have known Jenny's recent whereabouts.

The latter was easier to wrap my head around. When I'd asked myself who Jenny would trust, who she might be comfortable telling her story to, her cousin Ericka was the first person who came to mind.

I checked Ericka's Facebook page again, and her church's page, but there was nothing new. It was logistically possible for her to have been involved, but murder didn't fit what I knew about her.

The Hollister twins were also on my list of ME Littleton suspects, because it made sense that they might want to avenge the death of their sister by exposing the truth about who'd caused it. Could either of them have gotten the story out of Jenny, written the book, and then killed her? According to Facebook, the twins had been together in Chicago on Sunday. Hundreds of miles away from where Jenny died. Bitty had hosted a birthday party for her youngest son that evening, with a home-baked Batman cake that probably would have cost a couple hundred dollars at a fancy bakery. Matt had given the birthday boy a miniature battery-powered Mercedes. Neither of them fit my idea of a murderer either.

And then there was Ben. He was connected to Megan and by extension to Matt, but I couldn't see any link to Jenny. My suspicion of him was something I didn't want to have inside me but couldn't expel. He still hadn't posted anything on his Facebook page. But I noticed something there I'd missed before: a link to his business page. I clicked on it.

The Quick Signz page was active, with pictures of their products and giveaways, and workshop videos of their sign-making process. On Sunday they'd launched a new promotion with every tent rental. The tents were the giant kind, red-and-white striped or plain white, for big events like weddings. Ben had gone live on Facebook at 1:17 PM, explaining the promotion and inviting people to his shop on the far west side of Madison. He'd also uploaded a photo of himself, grinning and leaning against a sign that read FREE SIGN WITH TENT RENTAL! The midday sun glinted off his bald head.

I closed the laptop with relief. Ben was in the clear, but that was about the only good news I had to focus on. I was no closer to unmasking ME Littleton, who I now suspected of also being Jenny's murderer.

What was I missing?

Maybe I had it all wrong. Jenny's death could have been accidental, I reasoned. Or unconnected to our shared past. Or a suicide.

Bzzzt! Nope. Thought you were done lying to yourself, Petta.

The person who texted me hadn't been suicidal. They'd been scared, because something was "not safe."

I thought about texting Gus again. And again, I stopped myself. I didn't like being the needy one in our relationship. I didn't like that I'd started thinking about our arrangement as a relationship. And I didn't want him to know how deep my reliance on him had grown. For a long time, I hadn't let myself see it either. I'd tell him, sooner or later. But not today.

I looked back over the texts I'd sent to the phantom number from the cat poster.

Jenny, is this you? I sent.

It couldn't hurt. If I got a response, I'd know the number wasn't Jenny's and I'd feel one degree better. If I didn't, I'd be right back where I started. And I couldn't feel any worse than I already did.

I stared at the phone for ten minutes. *Delivered* never turned to *Read*.

I tried a movie, but even Sigourney Weaver kicking *Alien* ass couldn't distract me. Since my fingers seemed desperate to text someone, I found the chain I'd exchanged with Ben the day I arrived in town. I glanced at the time, saw it wasn't quite one AM, and sent a new message—too blunt to be ignored.

Did you only want to be friends with me because I knew Megan?

He read it immediately, but it took a long time for the telltale three dots to appear.

My intestines cramped with nervous indigestion. I curled into a ball on the futon, trying to will the pain away.

My phone buzzed with an incoming text.

Only at first. I was so wrecked after she died. And so were you, I could tell. I thought we could share that, maybe. Get through it together. But then you never mentioned her. I didn't either. After a while, it seemed like it was too late.

I got up and paced the living room, trying to decide what to say back. Then I wrote:

She kept you a secret. And I wanted to forget what happened to her. That's why I never said anything.

The three dots hovered on my screen for a long time before disappearing for good.

I needed more from him. Probably too much. And I didn't know how to ask for it. I fell asleep with my phone in my hand, waiting for a text that never came.

*　*　*

I woke the next morning with that feeling again—the one I called The Itch. The walls of the cottage were closing in and my skin crawled with ants and my brain was on fire. I had to get out, blast the bad thoughts from my head. Jeans, T-shirt, socks, boots: I pulled them on, not caring how I looked. I stuffed my laptop in my backpack and my phone in my pocket, unsure when I'd be able to stand being indoors again. I needed loud music. Rushing wind. Spicy food to punish my tongue. Anything to elicit a physical reaction. But my first stop would be Quick Signz. It was time to settle The Ben Question once and for all.

When I pulled into the parking lot, it was empty. The shop was dark. There was a lime-green bench next to the front door, so I sat there until Ben's truck pulled into the lot twenty minutes later. I checked my phone. It was 9:57; his shop opened at ten. I'd be late for my meeting with Gull, but this was more important.

He didn't notice me until he started walking up the grassy rise in front of the building. When my presence registered, he stopped, body sagging. He glanced around, like he was checking for witnesses. I stood up to meet him, eye to eye.

"Just you and me, old pal."

"Aw, Pet." He shook his head. "What are you doing?"

I'd thought he was going to ask, *What are you doing here?* But he didn't. His question was bigger than that. "We need to talk."

"I'm not sure what to say to you. Or what you want from me. You've come back here and stirred up nothing but trouble."

After that accusation, it took me a minute to find my voice. "Me? I'm the trouble?"

"Yeah, Miss Facebook Ghost of Megan or whatever."

Well, he had me there.

"Oh. Right. That. Not my finest hour, I'll admit. But I had to do something. I was getting nowhere."

He looked at me with real anger for the first time, and I knew then that he was Vengeful—in more ways than one. He put his hands on his hips, and I got a glimpse of what his kids would see if they ever pissed him off. I took a step back.

"By exploiting the memory of your dead friend? Real fucking nice, Petta."

"I know! Okay? I know. I'm sorry. I just . . . I'm lost. I've always been lost. I'm no good at this stuff. Not the emotions or the confrontations or the detective work. I thought talking to you that day over coffee would give me some answers. But it didn't." I took a minute to catch my breath, and the next question came not from me but from high school Petta, who had a crush on the boy in her history class. "Was it all a lie?"

He shook his head again, and I noticed how deep the bags under his eyes were. "I never lied to—"

"So when I showed up back in town, you had no idea why, and you've never read the book?"

"I knew about it. But I haven't read it. No, really. But from what I've seen and heard . . ."

I stiffened, every Spidey sense I had trained on his next words. He looked disappointed as he said them.

". . . the most likely author is you, Pet."

That shut me up, for a whole fifteen seconds. "Trust me, I didn't write it."

"Yeah, trust you. Sure."

Ben crossed and uncrossed his arms, like he'd rather be anywhere but here. He wasn't meeting my eyes, instead looking at his watch and the shop door behind me and the bright blue sky. But not at me.

There were more questions I wanted to ask. It still felt like he was holding things back. Maybe even lying. But I wasn't smart or emotionally tuned enough to ask in a way that wouldn't piss him off.

I wanted to know if he knew Jenny was dead. I wanted to know if he'd talked to her. But her death was still too raw for me to find the right words. I didn't think he was Littleton, and I didn't think he'd killed Jenny. But that didn't mean he wasn't somehow involved in both.

In my experience, when death comes for someone important to you, it's a fist to your gut. Jenny and I hadn't been close, but we were viscerally connected, and that's almost the same thing. It was still a gut punch to know she was gone. It always went the same way for me, with death—after my parents, then Megan, and aunt Shelly. Now Jenny. Her death would sit inside me for a while, a rock in my hollow belly. Then it would be like someone dropped a Mentos into a Diet Coke. The emotions—sorrow, anger, dread, fear—would gush like a geyser, up into my chest cavity to surround my heart until I became all fizz and no self. Eventually, the fizzing would stop. The bubbles would settle. I could go on with my life, promising I'd never let anyone get close enough to hurt me that way again.

Then, mostly, it'd be okay. Until, without warning, one of those little grief bubbles would dislodge. Never can tell what's going to set them off. But it would rise, up from where it was hiding in my chest, into my head, where it would form a permanent scar. Not a memory of the person who had lived but of the grief they'd left behind.

Some days I wondered how much of me was still me and how much had been taken over by little bubbles of death. Jenny being gone tipped my scales a few more degrees toward the death bubbles. Because I was sad, yes. But I was also partly responsible for what had happened to her.

"So where does that leave us?" was all I could manage with all that turmoil inside me.

Ben took a moment to answer. "It leaves us alone, I guess. Me in my life and you in yours. The way it's always been."

"Well, that's a *Get lost* if I've ever heard one."

He didn't disagree.

I wasn't bitter, and he was right. Whether I'd understood it at the time or not, Megan's death had bonded us. He'd been damaged by it, just like me. Only he'd gotten over it enough to build a life. And I . . . well, I'd survived.

"Bye, Ben. I promise to conclude my business here in a more polite manner going forward. I shall not bother you again."

I turned up the theatrics to cover my pain, waving wildly and calling out to him as I walked backward toward my car. "Unless, of course, I find out you've been lying to me about the book. Or about anything else. Because now that Jenny's dead, all bets are off."

He turned his back on me, too quickly for me to see his reaction, and made busywork of unlocking the shop door. He didn't ask *Jenny who*, so that answered one question. He disappeared inside, and I heard the lock click behind him.

I wanted to never have to see him again.

*　　*　　*

On the way back to the cottage, I pulled into a fast-food joint I didn't see the name of and ate a burger and fries I couldn't taste. I was still coming down from the morning's revelations and found myself back on the cottage's front porch without quite knowing how I got there. I stepped up to the door's keypad to punch in the code and kicked something across the porch.

It tumbled off into the grass with a plasticky clatter.

"Shit!"

I thought at first it was my phone, or maybe my laptop charger had fallen out of my backpack. But no, both were safe.

I was in no mood to go hunting around the lawn for who knew what, but it took only a moment to locate it. I could see it from the stairs—a rectangular black box with a frail rubber band looped around it. I picked it up. It was an old mini-cassette recorder. I popped it open to see if there was a tape inside. There was, but before I could play it, the rubber band snapped. Something grazed my leg on its tumble toward the ground. A white plastic card with a photo. An ID. I bent to retrieve it, and a face came into focus: pinched, and aged beyond her years.

I was holding Jennifer Cushman's Minnesota driver's license.

I started humming, low in my throat, to block the scream.

Petta Woznewski, you are too cool to scream bloody murder in public.

I walked carefully back up the porch steps, worried I'd fall if I ran, punched in the door code, and closed myself inside the cottage. I heard it latch and flipped the dead bolt before leaning against the door. My backpack slid off my shoulder. At some point, I'd had a cup of Coke in my hand, the one I'd gotten at the drive-through. I had no idea what had happened to it. The cottage gave me shelter, but nowhere felt safe. Not my rental car, not my Airbnb, not my body, not my head.

When I'd gathered enough nerve, I hit play on the tape recorder. I didn't think my life could get any worse, but then I heard her voice. Cigarette-smoker deep and full of anger. It wasn't familiar, but I knew who it was all the same.

"I was Megan's best friend. I can't tell the rest without getting that out first, even though it says more about me than it does about her. We were each other's number-one person, even if she didn't act like it all the time. She had her moods; anyone who knew her would tell you the same. But Megan was mine, and I was hers. We were the perfect pair. Friends since we were little. Until freshman year of high school when Petal Woznewski transferred to West."

13

I RAN INTO THE kitchen, yanked open the closest drawer, and threw the tape recorder and license inside. My panic sweat started to cool the minute I slammed the drawer shut. I was shivering, but that was an improvement.

"Okay. Okay. Okay."

I circled the living room until I was dizzy, trying to calm myself. Arms pumping like a speed walker on coke. I started sweating again.

"Okay. Okay. Okay."

By the time I collapsed onto the futon, exhausted, I'd formulated a new mental list.

THE STUFF I KNOW:

One: My hunch was right. Jenny didn't write the book. She probably told someone her version of how Megan died, and that person used it to write the book.

Two: Jenny died shortly after our text exchange, which can't be a coincidence. Someone taunted me into texting Jenny, but then . . . what? Didn't want us communicating more, so they killed her? Or maybe Jenny had just outlived her usefulness.

Fuck.

Three: Someone is messing with me. First, they left a weird note on my car. They hoped I'd go out to the School Forest and see the graffiti on the cabin door, which I did. They used the poster to get me to text Jenny. They wanted me to feel responsible for Jenny's death. It worked.

Four: ME Littleton is behind it all. And they're not done with me.

I needed to see Detective Gull. I was stubborn, but I wasn't stupid. The time for being squeamish about the police had passed one dead woman's driver's license ago. I checked the clock on my phone: deep into the lunch hour. I was hours late for the appointment I hadn't intended to keep. Digging Gull's card out from under the mess of chip bags, empty beer cans, and dirty dishes on the kitchen table, I sent her a text.

This is Petta. Woznewski. I'm coming in now.

I pushed send and wondered if the police in Minnesota had found Jenny's phone along with her body. If so, they'd likely seen my texts—and my name—in her phone. I'd be a suspect. I collapsed into the nearest kitchen chair. The bottoms of my feet still throbbed from the stress of me stomping across the living room floor.

My phone buzzed with the detective's response.

I guess you heard about Jennifer Cushman. Wrapping up an appointment. Heading back to the station in 5.

Had Gull already known Jenny was dead when she sat here in the kitchen and quizzed me? The thought made me want to throw up. I put my head between my knees. She'd said she hadn't talked to Jenny, which probably wasn't a lie. But it wasn't close to telling the whole truth either.

When the nausea subsided, I looked up the quickest route to the station on my phone. A Facebook notification blipped onto the screen, blocking the map. Another group post—from Ericka's church page this time.

The church had added a new photo. It was slow to load on my phone. At first, all I could see was a wide expanse of blue sky with palm trees peeking into the frame. I read the caption while I waited, pacing around the tiny kitchen.

Our dedicated group of elders and sisters arrived in Vanuatu two days ago, ready to start building a new school. Our presence here is more vital than ever. More photos to come soon. Everyone is already hard at work.

The group of pale white people in the photo wore big grins and even bigger sun hats. There were eleven of them, nine men and two women, the women in modest, flowered dresses and the men in dark pants, white shirts, and ties. Everyone wore clunky hiking shoes. Not exactly island wear.

Ericka was easy to spot, one of only two women. She stood, straight backed, the tallest of all the missionaries. Looking at the clear, saintly determination shining from her eyes, I found it hard to believe she could have done any of the things I suspected of ME Littleton. And the fact that she'd been halfway across the world when Jenny was killed proved she hadn't hurt her cousin or left the recorder and license for me to find.

I looked at her smiling face again, wondering how long it would take for news of Jenny's death to make it all the way out to that tiny island.

I didn't feel safe, alone in the cottage. Whoever had killed Jenny knew where I was staying. I had to get out. I had to tell Gull what I knew.

Grabbing my backpack from where I'd flung it onto the floor, I opened the cottage door. I was still bent over my phone screen as I walked out onto the porch, studying the directions to the police station. I didn't get very far, slamming headfirst into what felt like a brick wall.

"Whoa, Petta! Are you okay?"

The words didn't register, just the deep male voice. I pushed hard against the solid barrier of his chest, trying to back away. Arms grabbed me. I couldn't move.

"Let me go!" I was sure the scream would bring the owners from the main house, but it dissolved into the summer air like vapor.

The arms released me, as requested. I fell backward onto the porch floor. It wasn't until I'd crab-walked back a safe distance into the house that I looked up at the giant looming over me. He was outlined by the morning sun; it gave him a halo.

"Dammit, Gus! You scared the crap out of me."

"Uh . . . surprise?"

I curled forward into a ball and rested my forehead on my knees, willing my body to switch off fight-or-flight. As soon as his wide, warm hand came to rest along my spine, my adrenaline stopped pumping. I stood up and he gave me a hug, wrapping his arms all the way around. He was like a walking weighted blanket, able to soothe away my anxiety. A stuffed animal in human form.

"I'm glad you're here." My voice was muffled, face pressed into his chest. His heart beat steadily against my right cheek. He smelled like a grandpa, old leather and clean laundry and spearmint sucking candy. But I liked it.

He leaned back and looked down at me like I'd sprouted horns. "You are?"

"Is that okay, Mr. Drop-In-Out-of-the-Blue?"

"It's not like you to admit it, that's all. But I'm happy you did." He smiled, as if to prove it.

"Yeah, well. It's true. Asshole."

My grumpiness only made his smile bigger. "I'm sorry for the surprise. But I had to come. When you first left the city, I figured you'd be back in a day. Two, tops. Then when you kept avoiding my texts—don't try and tell me you weren't—I got worried and booked a ticket. I didn't tell you I was coming because I knew you'd tell me not to."

He was right. I would've. I thought I had, at one point. But he'd come anyway. I stepped back, trying to decide if that annoyed me or not. I'd left a wet spot on the front of his T-shirt. Tears, snot, or drool, I wasn't sure. I rubbed a knuckle across my nose, and it came away wet.

"My flight got in late last night," he explained. "But I didn't want to freak you out by showing up here unannounced, after dark. So I waited till today, but I guess I freaked you out anyway. Sorry. Where you off to in such a hurry?"

"Long story."

He sat down on the front porch steps and looked back through the still-open door at me, waiting for me to sit down and tell him.

"No. Not here. In the car. I can't be here anymore."

Gus didn't ask any questions but led the way to his rental car, parked out on the street. I plugged my phone into the car's USB port, and the directions to the police station popped up on the navigation screen. If Gus was surprised at our destination, he didn't show it.

"A detective came to visit me yesterday, but I wasn't ready to tell her anything. I am now. Some of what I need to say is bad, and it will be hard."

"Hard to say or hard to hear?" he asked.

"Both. I only want to do it once. You can come with me when I talk to her if you want. I'd like you to be there, and to hear the truth. About me. And about . . . everything."

He nodded, eyes on the road.

"Yeah, I'll come." Like I was asking him to come along on a snack run. As if me offering to flay myself alive, to show him my wet, nasty insides, was an everyday occurrence.

I flipped through the songs on my phone and chose a banger by the Foo Fighters. Gus rolled all the windows down. My hair whipped across my face, stinging my cheeks. For a moment, I was okay. I told myself it was the drive and the wind and the music that calmed me. But it wasn't. It was Gus.

Needing another person was weak. That was what I'd always told myself. Whatever I needed could be found within, because when you counted on other people, they either died or let you down. Sometimes both. I was independent to a fault—a lone hunter, the star of my own action movie, the female Wolverine. But the last few days had taught me a lot. Too much, if you asked me. I'd learned I didn't need to be a loner to be strong. I could be strong and still need other people. As long as they were the right people. The ones who got me and stuck with me through the bad. Like Gus and aunt Shelly. Not the ones who bailed, who left me alone when I needed them most. Like my parents.

My palms were sweating. I wiped them on my jeans.

At the station, the front desk officer led us directly to Detective Gull's office. I'd pictured spilling my guts to her in a claustrophobic, windowless interrogation room. I was grateful for her peach walls and dark-wood trim. She had photos of her parents on her desk and a row of community service awards on the shelves behind her. I might have been in any office, anywhere. In New York, even. Picturing myself there was soothing.

I introduced Gus as we sat in the two wooden chairs facing the desk. Gull didn't want him there, but I insisted. I wouldn't talk without him, so she caved.

I gripped my hands together to stop them from shaking.

"Feeling better?" Gull asked me.

Her visit to the cottage seemed so long ago. I had to call it up from the depths. Right: I'd told her I was sick to get her out of my face.

"Not really. But that doesn't matter anymore."

"If you're sick, Petta, we can . . . ," Gus began. But Gull and I both scowled at him. He let it go.

She settled back into her chair, waiting for what I'd come to say. But I needed to know something first.

"Why did you come to talk to me yesterday?"

Gull frowned and glanced at Gus, then back at me. She didn't like being questioned in her own office. Well, too bad.

"You already know the answer to that. It was because of the letters. And Jennifer Cushman, who turned up dead. Right after exchanging a few text messages with you."

"You knew she was dead when you came to see me." It wasn't a question.

Gus tensed, but I put a hand on his arm.

"I did. She still has some next of kin around here, and we were helping track them down for the notification." *Ericka*, I thought. *Have they told her?* "I couldn't say anything to you about it until that process was complete. But now it is, and now you know. So what did you come here to tell me?"

I put my feet flat on the floor and sat up straight, not letting my back touch the chair. I wedged my hands between my knees and squeezed my legs together, trying not to let my inner quaking show. Gus put a hand on my back, moving it in slow circles.

"There's . . ." My voice faltered. I had to wait until my throat unclenched to continue. "I didn't bring it with me, but someone left something on my doorstep today. I couldn't . . . Shit. I feel stupid now for not bringing it, but I couldn't . . . I didn't want to look at it, or touch it, ever again. It was a recorder, one of those mini cassettes? And it had Jenny's voice on it. Also, Jenny's driver's license. Attached to the outside. I don't know who left it, but they wanted me to find it."

Detective Gull held up a finger and gave curt instructions to someone on the other end of her desk phone to go retrieve the recorder and license. She quizzed me on the entry door code and the location of the kitchen drawer where I'd stashed them, relayed the information, and hung up.

"We'll find them. While we wait, I think it's long past time you tell me your story. And I want every detail. Even if it doesn't seem important."

"Is this going to be an official statement?" Gus asked.

"It can be whatever you want," she said to me, ignoring him. "As long as you start talking."

Official transcript of Petal Woznewski's statement to MPD Detective Samantha Gull regarding the 1991 death of Megan Hollister. Gus Johnson also present.

DETECTIVE SAMANTHA GULL: Go ahead, when you're ready.

PETAL WOZNEWSKI: I'm not sure where to start. I . . . You've read the whole book?

GULL: Yes.

GUS JOHNSON: Yes.

WOZNEWSKI: You did?

JOHNSON: It had your name in it. And that made you mad. Of course I did.

WOZNEWSKI: Right. Well, anyway, you both know how the book describes what happened to Megan—or to Miri, I guess. That it blames me for her death.

GULL: Yes. And without protecting your identity with a pseudonym.

WOZNEWSKI: Yeah. Pretty pointed, isn't it? I still don't understand why the book is aimed at me. But a lot of what's written in it is true. The stuff leading up to Megan's death was accurate. The way we all met. The feel of our friendship. And so many details I thought I'd forgotten until the book brought them back. Like what kind of bagels we each preferred, or my favorite

soda flavor. Jenny's sensitivity about her family having less money, and Megan always passing the time
by writing in her diary. The way the Hollister house
smelled.

[throat clearing]

Sorry, I . . . Sorry.

[muffled sound]

When I heard Jenny's voice on the recorder today, some of
the things I'd been trying to figure out finally made sense.
I think, at some point, she told someone a version of what
happened to Megan, and that's what is on the tape. That
someone, ME Littleton, adapted it into the book. I still
don't know who they are or why they did it. But I want to
say on the record, before I get into that night, that I am not
a murderer. Or a manslaughterer, whatever you'd call it.
The death in *No One Suspected*, at the School Forest where
Petal forces Miri off the roof of the cabin—that's not how
it happened. That's not even where it happened. Petal
might have been to blame for Miri's death in the book version, but I did not kill Megan. I couldn't have and I
wouldn't have. I didn't.

GULL: No one is accusing you of anything. And I'd like
    to hear your version.
WOZNEWSKI: It's not my version. It's the truth.
JOHNSON: I think what the detective means—
GULL: Don't put words in my mouth.
WOZNEWSKI: It's okay, Gus. I get what she means. I
    didn't mean to be bitchy about it. I'll tell you. I'm just
    not sure where to start.
GULL: Why don't you start first thing that morning. The
    day Megan died. What was that day like for you?

WOZNEWSKI: It was a Friday, so I had school. I don't
   remember much about my classes. At lunch, I got my
   food and went to our normal table, but Megan wasn't
   there. Only Jenny, looking miserable. We were supposed to meet up and talk about our weekend plans,
   but Megan had ditched us. She'd been doing that a
   lot lately. I guess maybe she had a boyfriend, but she
   didn't tell me anything about him. Megan liked her
   secrets.

GULL: Do you have any idea who that boyfriend was?

WOZNEWSKI: No. I—no, I didn't have a clue back then.
   Now, I could make an educated guess at who she was
   off seeing instead of hanging out with us. His name is
   Ben. But he has nothing to do with how she died. It
   wasn't a boy thing, it was a girl thing. Megan liked to
   know everything about her friends, the more embar-
   rassing the better, but she never shared her own stuff.
   She saved that for her diary, and maybe Ben, I guess.
   I was too wrapped up in my own internal shit to pay
   much attention to hers.

GULL: In the book, the Izzy character thinks Petal and
   Miri are spending a lot of time together without her.
   Was that true of you and Megan?

WOZNEWSKI: No. A few times, maybe. We went to the
   mall together, and down to State Street. Our friendship was complicated, but it didn't feel deliberately
   cliquey like that, like in the book. At least not to me.
   Megan and I weren't ganging up on Jenny or icing
   her out. But there was . . . something. Megan thought
   Jenny was a drag because her parents were strict and
   she was kind of needy and never had extra money
   to spend on things. And Megan and I had become
   friends quickly. Jenny wasn't wild about that. One
   day we didn't even know each other, and the next

I was joining their sleepovers. But the honeymoon
period didn't last long. Megan got fed up with my . . .
I wasn't always the most cheerful kid. My parents had
died, and I was adjusting to a new school and dealing
with this darkness I was feeling. I could be kind of an
asshole—still can.

[laughter]

That wasn't supposed to be funny, Gus.

Anyway, Megan saw me as a downer. Her life was sunshine and rainbows. I was a black cloud and Jenny was
too needy. She didn't want to be pulled under by us. She
wanted to fly.

[muffled sound]

What I mean is, the way the book describes Megan spending less time with us and more, maybe, with Ben—yeah,
I felt that too.

GULL: Do you need anything? Water? Okay. Megan
    stood you up at lunch. Then what?
WOZNEWSKI: We all ran into each other at our lockers
    that afternoon. We'd been talking for a long time
    about sneaking out to the School Forest. Just like
    in the book. That's what we were supposed to plan
    at lunch—it was supposed to be the weekend we'd
    finally do it. The Life Saver plan. But when Megan
    stood us up, that was kind of the end of that. None
    of us were in the mood. We decided to do what we
    always did instead.
        We went to the reservoir. That was our place.
    Usually, before we'd end up there, it would start out
    as a sleepover at Megan's and we'd sneak out to roam

around Shorewood. Just like in the book. The author got that exactly right.

GULL: What was exactly right about it?

[chair creaking]

WOZNEWSKI: Hmm? Oh. The feeling, mainly. Of being young and out in the night air by ourselves. Free. Something about the darkness, the anonymity of it, made me feel less exposed, I guess. I felt so examined most of the time. My aunt and my teachers were always watching me for signs of something. Depression, maybe. And high school is such a fishbowl, everyone staring at everyone else. Waiting for something to criticize. To be hidden, unexamined, was powerful. The only time I felt both protected and free. I think I've been chasing it ever since.

GULL: And you'd end up at the reservoir, you said. Where is that?

WOZNEWSKI: It's down by Spring Harbor, at the edge of Shorewood. On the lake. We always called it the reservoir, but it's a park. A little strip of grass that runs from a dead-end street out to the lakeshore. There's this old stone thing there that holds water. That's why we called the place the reservoir. But really it's a . . . what do you call that, like a man-made pond with stone walls, built to hold extra water? Like a giant, shallow well.

GULL: That's Merrill Springs Park. It's a spring-fed cistern that dates back to the thirties. Built by the Wisconsin ERA.

WOZNEWSKI: Uh, yeah. That place. Our late-night wanderings would always end up there. There's a path that cut from Lake Mendota Drive, which ran sort of parallel to Spring Harbor, down toward the park, between two houses; a no-man's-land where the two property lines met. The path let us out right at the dead end. We'd take that path down to the park and either sit on the rocks along the lake and stare out at the water or on the high stone wall of the reservoir. The water in it was very clear, but in the dark, with only the light of one streetlight at the edge of the park, it was like flat, black glass. Couldn't tell if it was, um, two inches deep, or two . . . million.

JOHNSON: Do you need to take a break?

WOZNEWSKI: No, I'm okay. Thanks.

GULL: You went to Merrill Springs Park the night Megan died.

WOZNEWSKI: Yes. We hadn't planned a sleepover that night. We'd kind of stopped doing those by then. Our last one had ended badly, and we hadn't all stayed over at Megan's in almost a month.

GULL: How did it end badly?

WOZNEWSKI: Oh. That. It was The Sweater Incident. We'd all gone to the mall earlier that week—not the week Megan died, but the week of the last sleepover. Jenny and Megan both liked this sweater at Limited Express. They thought it would be cute if they both got it and they could match. But it was like sixty dollars. Jenny didn't have that much money on her—or, probably, at all—so Megan lent it to her. It didn't seem like a big deal at the time. Jenny was excited, because they were going to be twins or whatever.

She worshiped Megan. We both did. That's what makes it so . . .

[throat clearing]

Later on, Megan's mom found out that she'd lent Jenny money. Mrs. Hollister didn't like that and got angry. Which is weird, because the Hollisters loved Jenny. And you'd think when you're that rich, you wouldn't . . . Anyway, Megan got in trouble and had to ask Jenny for the money back the next day. Jenny didn't have it yet, and Megan didn't like that. She wanted the whole thing over with. Now *she* was angry. She demanded the money. And Jenny said she'd bring it to the sleepover. We didn't know it would be the last one at the time.

I think it was Jenny's cousin Ericka who drove her to Megan's house. Yeah. Because it was Ericka who had to write Megan a check for the sixty dollars. Ericka didn't say a single word the whole time—she was never talkative, very stiff and superior. She helped Jenny unload her backpack and sleeping bag from the trunk of the car and handed Megan the check with a look that . . . wow. It was a death glare. A real ovary shriveler. Then she drove away.

The sleepover was tense as hell—we didn't sneak out that night, just went right to sleep—and Jenny and Megan were never the same after that. Megan forbade Jenny from wearing the sweater to school, or whenever they were together. At the time it seemed like one of those typical teenage girl spats, over pretty much nothing. And like I said, I was wrapped up in my own shit. But it definitely screwed up the friendship.

GULL: Because of the strained relationship, there was no sleepover the night Megan died, but you did meet up. At Merrill Springs Park.

WOZNEWSKI: Right. After dark. Jenny and I snuck out of our houses and rode our bikes over, and Megan walked from her house. We each had a backpack of contraband with us. The guy my aunt Shelly was seeing at the time liked to brew his own beer, so I stole a few bottles from the stash he'd left in our basement fridge and brought them along. They were a bitch to carry on my bike, kept clinking around. That beer was truly the most wretched thing I've ever tasted. But we were kids, and it was free alcohol. Megan brought a bottle of vodka. Not sure where she scored that. And Jenny brought a baggie of something she said was weed but smelled like a spice drawer. Oregano, probably.

GULL: No knife?

WOZNEWSKI: Like in the book? No. I mean, I didn't search Jenny's backpack, but I never saw a knife that night. I don't know if there's any truth to that part of the story. But it doesn't sound like Jenny.

GULL: And what did you do when you all arrived at the park?

WOZNEWSKI: Nothing. I mean, we never *did* anything on those nights. Just hung out. When I got there, Megan was already there. Jenny rolled up on her bike a few minutes later. We sat around, talking and drinking, sitting up on the wide stone lip of the reservoir and swinging our feet over the edge. What we always did, except this time it involved alcohol. That was going to be part of our big night out at the School Forest, too, like in the book. But when that fell through, we brought our contraband booze to the reservoir instead.

GULL: You weren't big drinkers.

WOZNEWSKI: Not then, no. I guess I can't speak for the other girls, about what they did when we weren't together. But when the three of us hung out, it was pretty innocent. We were freshmen, still couldn't drive, none of us had boyfriends yet—or at least none of us were seeing anyone publicly. We had sleepovers

and snuck out at night and hid from the Shorewood
cops. I think we ding-dong-ditched once—you know,
ringing someone's doorbell and running. That was as
criminal as we got. Until . . . yeah. Until that night.
JOHNSON: How about a piece of gum?
WOZNEWSKI: Thanks.

[crinkling wrapper]

The book did get one thing right about that night: Megan
was drinking vodka, and she got a lot drunker than us, a
lot faster. Jenny and I shared the skunky beers. I choked
down half a bottle. Maybe three-quarters. I don't remember how much Jenny had. It was a chilly, early spring night.
But Megan said she was getting warm, so she took off her
jacket. That's when Jenny saw the black sweater, the one
they'd fought over. We'd all been getting along up to that
point. Making jokes and enjoying being together again,
at our usual spot. It felt normal between us. But the minute Jenny saw Megan wearing the sweater, she clammed
up. Totally stopped talking, like a sea witch had stolen her
voice. Megan was oblivious, or pretended to be. She kept
babbling, keeping up the conversation for all of us. Jenny
stood up. She was on top of the stone wall, using it almost
like a balance beam. It wasn't too narrow, or that dangerous, but she . . .

Do you know what the reservoir looks like? It's a ring
of stone, much bigger than a normal well, and there's one
section of the stone that's taller than the rest. I always
thought it looked like a big chimney sticking up, maybe
twelve feet above ground level. At the bottom of the chimney thing, way down at water level, it has a hole. A little
archway, sort of, for the water to flow through. There's a
shallow creek that runs under that chimney, through the
archway, and out to the lake.

Anyway, Jenny was walking along the top of the reservoir wall. She couldn't make a complete circle because the chimney thing was in the way. She was walking away from where Megan and I were sitting, counterclockwise around the circle, and when she reached the tall chimney part, she had to turn around and walk back toward us. She wasn't acting drunk or crazy; her steps were steady and careful. There was enough room on the top of the wall for her to pass and walk behind us, as we were sitting there—the stone lip was pretty wide. But instead of doing that, she'd turn around again when she got to where we were. Back and forth, she kept going, between us and the chimney, like a tennis ball bounced between two rackets.

JOHNSON: How high was the part of the wall she was walking on?

GULL: Mr. Johnson, leave the questions to me, please.

JOHNSON: Sorry. I was trying to visualize.

WOZNEWSKI: It's pretty high. I used to walk back and forth along the wall sometimes too, but only for a few minutes, because I'd get this scary vertigo thing going on. Because it's deceiving. When you walk up to the reservoir from the park entrance, the stone wall is only about four feet high. But then the reservoir itself is set down into the ground, so the inside of the wall is high . . . maybe twenty feet or so, down to the water? I don't remember. If you fell off the wall on the ground side, you'd maybe scrape your knee. But if you fell on the water side . . .

GULL: Have you been back to the park since that night?

WOZNEWSKI: Never. I avoided it for the rest of high school. And I intended to go back and see if it still looked the same, but I never got there. There was always something better to do, another place to go

that was more pressing, or something that distracted
me. I didn't consciously avoid it, but I guess that's
what was happening. I don't ever want to go back
there now. Not after having to relive everything here,
for you. I thought I'd go my whole life without ever
telling anyone what happened there. But then, the
book.

GULL: So Jenny was upset, walking back and forth along
the wall.

WOZNEWSKI: She still wasn't talking to us. Megan and I
had been chatting about something, but then there
was a natural lull in the conversation, like sometimes happens. Megan watched Jenny for a while.
I drank my beer. Then she started saying Jenny's
name, all weird and drawn out. *Jeeeeeen-nyyyyyyyyyy.*
Almost like she was singing it. Jenny ignored her,
kept walking. Megan didn't like that. She got up and
walked toward Jenny along the wall. To get around
her, Jenny hopped down onto the ground, went past
Megan, got back up, and kept walking the wall. I was
getting annoyed—with both of them. Being a third
wheel is hard enough when the other two are getting
along. When they're fighting, it's painful.

Then I had to pee. The beer, you know. So I went
off to pee.

GULL: Where did you go?

WOZNEWSKI: To the edge of the park, behind the pine
trees that marked the border with the private property next door. The trees were tall and full, which
meant no one from the surrounding houses could see
us when we were at the reservoir. Must've been a bit
of a sound buffer too, because no one ever came to
tell us to shut up when we were down there. Even
though it was a public park, with a couple of houses

nearby, it felt private. Like it was ours. No one ever disturbed us there.

I didn't see how it started. I was still buttoning my jeans as I came out of the trees. When I looked up, Jenny had hopped off the stone wall again to pass behind Megan, who had sat back down on the wall, her back to me. As Jenny was stepping back up onto the wall, Megan reached out to grab Jenny's ankle. It didn't look like a strong grip, but it made Jenny stumble, and she fell. For a minute, I thought Jenny was going to fall down into the water. But as I said, the top lip of the reservoir wall was pretty wide. She fell hard on her knees on the stone and made a sharp sound. Not a scream—more like an angry screech. It must have hurt. She stayed on her knees like that for a while.

Megan was frozen, probably waiting to see what Jenny would do next. Jenny looked over her shoulder, back at Megan. The spot where I was standing was closer to the lake, behind where Megan was sitting, so she was between Jenny and me. The streetlight was off to their right, so Jenny's face was half in shadow. But from the part I could see, the look on her face was . . .

GULL: Was what?

WOZNEWSKI: There was pain. And something like the look her cousin Ericka used to give Megan, disgusted and angry and unforgiving. Then Jenny kicked her foot back, a donkey kick, and hit Megan square in the ribs with the bottom of her white Ked.

Maybe if Megan hadn't been drunk, or had been expecting a physical retaliation, she would have been able to brace herself. But the kick knocked her sideways, and her feet were already dangling over the edge of the wall. I guess her momentum and the weight of her legs dragged her forward. And down. She fell. There was no sound. Then a million years later, a splash.

GULL: And you were over by the trees, still? Near the lake?

WOZNEWSKI: Sorry, I . . . This is harder than I expected. Yes. I was still over there, I couldn't move. Jenny was frozen too, one leg still extended from the kick, like she was a sprinter at the starting block of a race. Then slowly she pulled both knees into her chest, stood up, and stepped down onto the ground. She looked around like she was searching for something. Her eyes found me, eventually. Her lips were moving, but I couldn't hear what she was saying. She was talking to herself, I think.

Then Megan started to moan. It echoed against the water and the stone walls, drifting up to us. Jenny flinched. She took a deep breath, then leaned over the wall to look down. I ran toward the reservoir. When I reached it, I put one hand on the tall stone chimney to steady myself. I couldn't make myself look down at Megan. Not yet. I focused on Jenny.

I was angry, asked her what the hell she'd done or something stupid like that. I knew what she'd done; I'd seen it. She didn't answer. Her eyes were wide and unblinking. Then, like something out of a horror movie, they rolled up into her skull until her irises disappeared and all I saw was white. I think she was about to pass out.

I was afraid of her in that moment, and of what had happened and was happening. I turned away, and that's when I finally looked down. Most of the water was in shadow, but a crescent-shaped sliver was lit by the pool of streetlight. Megan had fallen into the crescent. Lucky me, I could see everything. She hadn't fallen cleanly into the center of the reservoir; she might've been fine if she had. Because of the way she went down, sideways, she skimmed the inside wall on the way. There was a pipe sticking out, a bare spigot type thing, above the waterline. She hit it facefirst.

JOHNSON: Whoa, Petta. Are you okay?

[chair scraping]

Yeah, like that. Deep breaths.

WOZNEWSKI: I got it. I'm all right. I need to finish. The pipe . . .

[long pause]

[rustling, sniffling]

It, ah, ruined her face. Dented in the side of her head. She was floating, like, faceup in the water, staring at the sky, her head a weird shape and the dark water rippling around her black sweater and the sound of her moan echoing on and on, but she was dead by then, so I don't know how I could still hear it, but I could; I know that I did and I still do sometimes. Even though I try to block it out. Even now.

[heavy breathing]

One of her shoes had come off and was floating on top of the water. It was filling, starting to sink. A bright-white Ked. All three of us wore them. The vodka bottle was down there too, unbroken and half-empty, bobbing on top of the water. There was nothing we could do. She'd probably been dead before I reached the edge of the reservoir. That's what I tell myself. That there's nothing I could have done.

[pause]

Megan's death was an accident. I do believe that. Even though I've hated Jenny for it, and hated myself, for a long time. And I know that Megan was being nasty to her right before she died. By wearing the sweater that night, Megan was either trying to force things into being okay again, by getting it all out in the open, or trying to goad Jenny into a confrontation. Which is, I guess, what she got. But I don't believe Jenny meant for anything like that to happen when she kicked. The way Megan fell, it was . . . terrible, brutal bad luck.

After a while, Jenny started talking—it was an accident, it was an accident, it was an accident. She kept saying it over and over. Until the words didn't even sound like English anymore. *"Iddwuz annaxident"*—like that. I went to put a hand on her shoulder, to snap her out of it. I was about to slap her. I wanted to slap her. But she grabbed my wrist, and her hand was like a claw. Sharp and cold.

"We can never, ever tell people what happened tonight," she told me. *"Please."*

It was shitty of me, but I was relieved when she said it. I'd already started to dread what came next: going home to aunt Shelly, or to the police, and telling them what had happened. How could a fourteen-year-old have explained it all? I knew I'd have to tell the story of that night, over and over. To relive it, like I am now, seeing that image of Megan down in the water, over and over, her head like a crushed soda can, her gaping mouth filling with black water.

"No one knows we're here." That's what she said to convince me. *"We'll ride our bikes home, go to sleep, and tomorrow someone will find Megan. It was an accident; she was drunk and fell in and hit her head. Come on, help me gather these beer bottles."*

We left Megan's backpack but cleaned up everything that was ours. There was no sign we'd ever been there. Our footprints and bike tracks blended in with all the rest. Lots of families took little kids there, to play by the lake. It had these stone picnic tables that were popular with picnickers. And the ground was hard that night, still winter frozen.

We got on our bikes. Jenny rode alongside me all the way home, shooting me a strange look every few minutes. I thought it was nice at the time, like she was worried about my mental health or something. But after a while I realized it was more than that. She wanted to keep an eye on me, make sure I wasn't going to cave and go running to the cops. She wouldn't leave me until we agreed on what to say if anyone asked us: we'd both stayed home that night.

It was an easy lie for our families to back up, since no one knew we'd snuck out.

"Megan? No, we haven't seen her. We were supposed to hang out, but she blew us off. We didn't know she went to the reservoir that night."

That's what we told people.

"Remember, Petal: it was an accident." That was the last thing Jenny said to me before riding away. The last thing we said to each other in person, ever. And I kept her secret all these years. I said I would and I did. Until now.

14

MY CONFESSION HUNG in the air of Gull's office like steam in a hot shower. She stared at me for long enough that it got weird. She pursed her lips and swallowed, like she'd taken a bite of my story and was chewing it over until she found it credible.

"That certainly matches the police reports from back then. What was found at the scene, et cetera."

"Well, it should." I couldn't keep the irritation out of my voice. "It's the truth."

"Who do you think wrote the book?" she asked.

My stomach hollowed at the shift in questioning. And her words were as empty as my insides. She didn't want to be asking me that question, or to show me her losing cards. But she had to. Because she had no idea who ME Littleton was, any more than I did.

The detective wasn't totally useless, though. She had knowledge and access I could use. If I showed her a few of my cards in return.

"I've tried to figure that out. I got nowhere," I admitted. I was embarrassed by my sad little list of suspects, all with Facebook alibis. I wasn't about to mention any of them to her—she'd laugh in my face. "Can the publisher keep the writer's identity a secret? Is it like a reporter with a confidential source?"

The detective sighed and kicked a foot up onto her desk. She was wearing stylish black boots with wooden heels. No spurs.

"They can try. I've made inquiries. The publisher hasn't been particularly forthcoming. But things have escalated now." She meant Jenny. "My sergeant's on board. I can try to get the courts to force their hand, but it will take a while. In the meantime, I'll take another run at them, see what I can scare up. And I'm sure my officers have found the tape recorder and license by now. Might already be on their way to the lab for testing."

"Okay. Good."

Gus put his warm hand over mine, where it rested on my knee.

It sounds corny as hell, but getting the Megan stuff out in the open made me feel lighter. The telling of it had been like pulling my own rotting teeth. But sharing that toothache with Gull, and especially with Gus, was freeing.

"When you came to see me, you asked about a black Tesla," I said. "Why?"

Gull pulled her foot off the desk so fast her tipped-back chair hit the floor with a bang. Her mouth was a thin line.

"There's been one following me. I'll catch it in my rearview, and then it disappears. It's never gotten close enough for me to get a license number. I just know it's a Minnesota plate."

"Yeah," I admitted. "I've seen it too. At least I think I have, in front of Megan's old Shorewood house, when I first got here. But I didn't pay attention to the plate."

We stared at each other for a while over the desk.

"I'd appreciate it if you'd stay in town," Gull said finally. "I'm not ordering you, but I may need to talk to you again. We all want the same thing: to figure out what's going on here. I don't think I can do that without you."

She was trying to get me on her team. A good tactic, but not one I was susceptible to; I wasn't a joiner. I was grateful Gull existed, that we could share the burden of Jenny's death, but I didn't want to be her bestie.

"We'll stay," Gus answered for me. "You can call us whenever you need." He rattled off his cell number for the detective.

His natural, security-guard-given authority put the detective at ease. It calmed me too, enough that I didn't mind him hijacking the conversation. Letting others shoulder my burdens was new for me. A surprising, pleasant flavor on my tongue. Sweet, not bitter.

I could get used to not always being in charge. But should I?

Magic 8-Ball says: Reply hazy, try again later.

We left Detective Gull with her feet back up on the desk and a determined look on her face, as if she could think her way through to the other side of this case. I told Gus I didn't want to go back to the cottage, and I didn't want to go to his hotel. Staying in bed all day with him was tempting, but I'd spent too long squashing unwelcome feelings with sex and food and pot and music and movies. There was more I needed to say to him first.

I asked Gus to drive around. I showed him the places that had been important to me, giving him a tour of my building blocks, my atoms: the basic components that made me up from the inside out. We started on the west side with my high school, and the pizza place where I used to sling dough, now (surprise, surprise) razed and replaced by condos. At Bagels Forever, I tried to convince him they were as good as any bagel in New York. He refused to hear it but finished every bite of his pumpernickel.

We drove to the east side, and I showed him my elementary school, the park where I used to feed the ducks. Then I gave him directions to Maple Bluff. I was ready to see my old house.

Gus drove us there, and we parked on the street. It looked the same, though the layout of the front yard was different. Flowers where there had been greenery; open space where there had been old-growth trees.

The garage was still there, with the room on the second floor. I wondered what it was used for now. Was it still a guest bedroom? An office?

"This is where my parents killed themselves."

I thought he'd say something, but he just turned off the car and shifted toward me in his seat. He knew there was more and was waiting until I was ready to tell it.

I told him about finding them, about walking home from a sleepover and unlocking the front door of the house and calling out, then looking out the front windows and seeing a light on in the above-garage guest room. How I'd gone outside and up the stairs and opened the door and walked along the room's ocean-blue carpet until I saw their feet, shoes still on, stretched out on the still-made bed, side by side. I thought they were sleeping. I went to shake my mom awake, jiggling her shoulder until she rocked back and forth like a wooden doll, cold and still and lifeless.

A small curl of paper slipped out of her cupped hand. It was long and thin, like a fortune from a fortune cookie but torn from a larger sheet and ragged on one edge. In small script type was a single sentence.

The only way out is through.

I don't know if it was a message for me—some sort of deathbed wisdom she left behind—or a reminder for herself, in her last moments. Maybe both. I'll never know.

I'd picked up the paper, crushing it in my sweaty fist. That's when I realized something about the room was wrong, that I could feel the rumble of the Lincoln running in the garage underneath me and I had to get out before the air poisoned me too. I ran to the neighbors for help. There's a gap there, in my memory. The next thing I remember is waiting at the police station. They kept passing me from officer to detective to social worker. Finally, they called aunt Shelly to come pick me up. While I was waiting for her, alone in some windowless room, I unclenched my fist. The paper was still there. I never told anyone about it, and no one ever asked. It was damp and torn. The words were gone, a gray blur in their place. I didn't know what to do and I didn't want anyone to see, so I recrumpled the paper into a tiny ball and I ate it. Swallowed it. So it would always stay with me.

"I never forgot those words," I said to Gus, raising my arm and twisting it so the inside of my right bicep was exposed. Between a coiled snake and a snarling wolf head was a single line of black text. The only words I allowed on my body. A permanent reminder, in ink and blood.

The only way out is through.

For most of my life I'd misunderstood. I'd thought it meant the only way out of my tragedies was to do whatever it took to get through them. To survive them. But I was wrong. The real message, whether my mom had meant it for me or not, was this: *The only way through to the other side of a tragedy is to face it. To work through it.*

"And I can make it if I've got you," I said to Gus, embarrassed by the admission.

Gus was quiet, reassuring. He listened. I'd told him the things no one else knew. Things not even the book knew. For the first time, I was showing Gus the real Petta, the soft meat underneath my spikes. I almost couldn't do it, as doubts crept in about how it would change things. How it would change me, and us. It was scary as hell, and I almost stopped talking half a dozen times. But I kept going because he kept listening. He stayed. I told myself that meant I was doing the right thing. But I still wasn't sure.

"Where to next, boss?" Gus asked. I think he sensed I needed some distance from the house, and was trying to give it to me.

"I want to show you where I lived after."

When we were idling in front of aunt Shelly's old house on Rowley Avenue, I told Gus everything she'd done for me. The therapy she'd made me go to, the activities she'd signed me up for to keep me busy and out of trouble. The therapy didn't take, but I dove headfirst into the extracurriculars. I'd commit to two or three at a time, switching to something new when I'd learned the mechanics of badminton or pottery and my mind was set free to wander into dangerous territory. Or when the other kids became too friendly, asked too many questions. I overscheduled myself to the point of exhaustion, and aunt Shelly worried I was burning myself out. She was wrong. I was burning through, incinerating every bad thought and painful memory like fuel. Only then it started to be too hard to be around other people. I stopped the group activities and started taking solo walks. Anywhere, everywhere, for hours. And I'd never stopped.

When I had nothing left to tell, Gus's silence held the door open for doubts. Had I gone too far, said too much? Maybe I'd overcorrected.

As usual, Gus knew when something was up.

"What is it, P?"

"I need to know why," I said, after a long pause. "Why me?"

"Why you what?" His question wasn't terse or short. He placed his words in front of me, one at a time, like neatly wrapped gifts.

"Why are you still here? I treat you like crap, I'm a mess, I disappear, and now I've dumped all my baggage in your lap. People are dead. I'm being questioned by the police. There's an entire book about what a terrible person I am. And you still like me. At least I think you do." I waited for a nod, but he didn't give in to my fishing expedition. "I've never understood why you stick around."

Gus answered faster than I thought he would, like he had it in the chamber and didn't have to think.

"Because I like *you*, Petta. The person you are. You're tough. You're funny. You're never anyone but yourself. There's no one I'd rather eat dinner on my living room floor with, or watch movies with, or wander the city with. When we're together, I know you want to be there. Because if you didn't, you'd leave. And even when you leave, you always come back. I never have to guess with you. I know who I am to you. I like being that person. And I like you just for being you."

My chest hurt, but in a good way. Like it wasn't big enough to contain what was inside me anymore. Gus deserved a response. But I didn't have one yet. I wasn't the kind of person who could take a compliment like that and give one right back. Not yet. But maybe for the first time, I wanted to be.

My phone saved me. A text from Detective Gull.

Talked to the editor at Roebler House. Still not budging. Won't give up ID unless the court orders it. Working on that. But she did slip up. At end of convo she said: I'll tell HIM you'd like to talk.

I texted back: So the author is male.

Sounds that way. Any idea who?? Do you like Ben for this?

No, I don't, I texted, and shoved my phone in my pocket as Gus drove us the short distance to the cottage.

"Who was that?" he asked.

"Gull, with a quick follow-up."

I'm not sure why I didn't tell Gus what Gull had said. I didn't keep it from him on purpose. I was in my head, too distracted with running through every man I knew, every male on my suspect list.

Back in the cottage, neither of us knew what to do with ourselves after the day's revelations.

Gus tipped his head toward the bathroom. "Mind if I take a shower?"

I waved him toward it and collapsed onto the futon with a frustrated huff.

"We'll go get food after?" he called, bathroom door still open.

"Yeah, good," I said. "I'll eat whatever."

I stretched out on the futon and stared at the ceiling. The shower turned on, and Gus began to hum.

Who was the guy Jenny had talked to? Who would she trust with her darkest secret?

And had he killed Jenny because he was worried she'd talk to me and reveal his identity? Or had he finally discovered that she was the one who'd caused Megan's death?

There was still so much I didn't understand. Motivations, especially. Why Jenny had told her story after all these years, and why the author had turned it into a book, and why he was using it to torture me.

I got up off the futon and walked out the front door. Up the driveway and out to the street. I stayed away from Hollister Avenue, walking the opposite direction. I had The Itch again. I needed to move. My body was too antsy; I couldn't think.

It was blocks before I realized I should've told Gus I was leaving. Eh, he'd figure it out. He knew me. It wouldn't be the first time I'd disappeared on him, walking until my insides settled enough for me to be around another human.

Who is ME Littleton?

He could be someone I knew or someone I'd never met—never even set eyes on. Suddenly my suspect list seemed stupidly small. Megan had been secretive those last weeks. Maybe she'd had a whole stable of secret friends or boyfriends. Maybe she'd told them everything about me, about Jenny. Maybe she'd had a whole life separate from the one I knew. I'd been wrapped up in myself; I rarely cared what other people were doing unless they were right in front of me.

Megan had been my best friend at one of the most pivotal times in my life. But I'd hardly known her at all.

* * *

I don't know how long I walked. When I got back, Gus's rental car was gone from in front of the cottage and a damp towel hung over the shower curtain rod. He'd probably run out in search of Chinese food. It was his favorite; fried rice was Gus's version of comfort food. I went into the kitchen and cleared the mess on the table so we could eat there. I hadn't washed a single dish since I'd arrived at the cottage, instead pulling cups and plates out of the cupboard until it was empty and every available space was stacked with dirties. I started washing, ashamed that Gus had seen me living like a slob. I mean, he knew I was a slob, but my seedy side looked worse in the fresh surround-ings of the Airbnb than it ever had back home.

Gus hated eating Chinese out of the carton, even after I'd shown him how to deconstruct the white boxes so they'd reverse-origami into a plate. Gus liked a real plate, or better yet, a large, shallow bowl. He'd start with a bed of pork fried rice and add some of everything we'd ordered until there was no space left. There was no *my* food or *his* food, there was just our food. He was the perfect dinner companion, a generous spirit with adventurous tastes.

I looked down at my hands, resting in the soapy sink water. A pile of clean, dripping dishes sat drying on a towel nearby.

"Shit, Petta. You went and got yourself domesticated." It didn't feel like I'd thought it would to say those words out loud. It was good. The kitchen was clean, and so was I.

I dragged the velvet blanket off the futon and back to the bed. Later, I'd be snuggled under that blanket with Gus. The thought shot a spike of desire straight through my torso. I checked the fridge. We were low on beverages. I hoped Gus would bring something to drink along with whatever food he found.

The minutes ticked by, but Gus did not return. Dread replaced my desire, gathering inside me like a mound of sand rising at the bottom of an hourglass.

I checked my phone. There was no text from Gus, no call. That wasn't normal.

Where did you go? Are you grabbing food and drinks? I sent.

I waited, but there was no answer.

15

S USPICION IS LIKE carbon monoxide pouring from the tailpipe of an idling car. The poison will find a way inside you if you're stupid or careless enough to let it. Gus still had not returned, had not texted. And the cottage was filling with my suspicions.

Where was he? He was always checking up on me, keeping tabs on my whereabouts. It wasn't like him not to return a text. He was needy like that. And I needed him to be needy. He'd cared about me when any sane person would have abandoned my surly ass years ago. Was that the most generous love I'd ever known, or something else? I didn't deserve Gus, so my mind careened right into worst-case scenarios. And in doing so, some facts I'd ignored—niggling details that my new suspicions made me see loud and clear—reemerged.

One: Gus had been one of the first people to mention the book to me. He'd even bought a copy to show me, the same spine-damaged hardback from the drugstore that I'd held in my own two hands. That had seemed like an unfortunate coincidence then, but maybe it was more deliberate than that.

Two: Gus had tracked my whereabouts to Madison, then followed me here. He'd told me he'd gotten in the night before but that it had been too late to come see me. Too late since when? He knew I was a night owl. Then when he showed up, it was on the heels of the recorder being left on my doorstep. An eerie coincidence (there's that word again) in timing.

And three: There was so much I didn't know about Gus. We'd sometimes go weeks without seeing each other except at work, and I'd never asked him about his life. I'd been too selfish and self-involved. I only knew what Gus wanted me to know—a little bit about his mom and sisters, whom I'd never met. At my insistence, but still.

Who was Gus when he wasn't with me?

Could he have been ME Littleton all along?

The thought was there and then gone again, like a flicker of lightning in the distance. I couldn't imagine Gus writing a book. I'd never even seen him pick up a book until he bought that copy of *No One Suspected*. For me.

He was not connected to Megan, or to Madison, or to anything in my past. He was part of my new life, my unburdened self, in New York. I knew that, as well as I knew all of Sandra Bullock's lines in *Speed*. But if my life were a movie, those pesky coincidences, coupled with Gus's disappearance from the cottage, would have rocketed him to the top of the suspect list. The screenwriters would've had it all planned out, a way to link him back to my high school years, some convoluted connection that strained belief.

And that was the problem: I couldn't make myself believe Gus could be the guy.

He'd grown up on the East Coast; all his family was there. Could he have been Megan's secret summer camp romance, or a childhood pen pal? A cousin twice removed, maybe. I cursed myself for not listening more closely when Gus talked about himself. Megan's life before I met her was a mystery. Her past might contain all kinds of deep, dark things. What was she like when she was three? Or ten? Had Gus known her then? She and Ben had a secret relationship—why not something clandestine involving Gus too?

"No." I stood in the bathroom of the cottage, staring into the shower, the last place I knew for certain Gus had been. "Not Gus. She can't have him."

My life was not a movie. It was too slow and too sad. I was a terrible lead character, certainly not a hero; I was grumpy, withholding, introverted, and boring. Who would want to watch me eat garbage and scroll Netflix, or smoke pot and stalk the sidewalks for two hours?

Gus, on the other hand, shined. He was not a villain. He was innately good, the only pure human being I'd ever met. A bit clingy at times, but I was growing to accept that. Maybe even depend on it.

I checked my phone again. He still hadn't texted. The Gus I knew never would have left without a note or stayed away for this long without a text. Something was wrong.

I searched the folder on my phone where I tossed all the garbage apps I never used, looking for Find a Friend. I'd never used it to find Gus, or anyone. I wasn't even sure how it worked, except to turn it on and off. I opened it, and at the bottom of the window, I tapped the People icon. Gus was the only friend listed. I selected his smiling face, and a little wheel began to spin. I waited, heart thudding, for the on-screen map to zoom in on his location.

I dropped the phone when the map came to a stop, a small red dot pulsing inside a rectangle of green. My ears registered a crunch as the screen cracked against the weathered wood floor, the rest of my body screaming too loud to care.

Gus was not out getting Chinese food.

Gus was not out trying to find where I'd wandered.

Gus was at the one place I never wanted to return: the reservoir.

I paused only to make sure my phone was still working and ran for the car. It buzzed as I was backing out of the driveway, crushing a row of greenery under my tires as I went. I slammed on the brakes, and the phone slid off my lap and onto the floor.

Under normal circumstances, I'd be throwing f-bombs like crazy, but nothing about Gus being at the reservoir was normal. I was terrified into silence.

I fumbled for the phone. My palms were sweating, and it was hard to get my hands on it.

A message from Gus's phone.

Hide and seek time, Petal.

He never called me Petal. He knew better.

Three more buzzes.

Want to see your boyfriend again?

From Gus's phone, yes, but not from Gus.

Come to the reservoir.

Don't tell Gull or anyone else.

I didn't bother to respond. I drove like Meatloaf—a bat out of hell.

Underneath my fear, for both Gus and for me, was a thrumming anticipation. I was about to get my answers. One way or another, this would all be over soon.

The trip to the reservoir passed in a blur. I must have changed lanes, stopped at red lights, turned in at the *Village of Shorewood* sign. I have no memory of any of it. My attention was on Gus, so careful and kind and strong. Had they hurt him? Of course they had. He wouldn't have gone (or stayed) willingly. Whatever was happening to him was my fault. I was poison, and Gus had drunk more than his share.

He was a big man and knew how to handle himself. He would be okay until I got there. I would get us through this, no matter what it took.

These were the lies I told myself as I drove.

I parked a safe distance from the park, up on Lake Mendota Drive. I wanted to have the high ground, to approach on foot.

A Tesla sat ten feet past the nose of my car. Empty, with Minnesota plates. All Teslas looked the same to me, sleek and self-important. It was a good bet this was the one I'd seen, the one Gull had asked me about. But I didn't care anymore. The car was one worry too many, and knowing its owner wouldn't change what was waiting for me down at the reservoir. I was wrung-out and worried-out and ready to mow down anything or anyone that stood in my path. I only cared about Gus, and about ending this insanity.

The path down to the park was in the same place it'd always been. It cut downward along the tree line between two properties, leading from Lake Mendota Drive to the dead end of Spring Court where the park was located. When we were kids, the path was unmarked and hard to find, overgrown with weeds and blocked by unruly branches. Sometime in the last thirty years a sign had been put up, helpfully marking the top of the path. The ground was cleared and covered with wood chips. I brushed aside a large spider web and started walking.

The sun was a heavy stone, wallowing at the bottom of the sky. Evening inched closer as I neared the park. I paused, staying under the tree cover before emerging from the safety of the path. I wanted to see him, whoever he was, before he saw me.

I took out my phone, checking for new messages. Nothing. The last text had warned me not to tell Gull, but I've never been one for following rules. I couldn't see any way they'd know if I sent a text. In the movies, no one ever calls the cops at the crucial moment. I wasn't going to make that same mistake. Not when Gus was involved.

I'm at the reservoir. Something bad has happened. Come quick.

I slipped the phone into the front pocket of my jeans where I could reach it easily and willed Gull to check her phone, to hurry, to come put me out of my misery.

When I stepped out of the trees and into the street, the area was deserted. None of the windows in the surrounding houses were lit. It was a warm summer evening, everyone probably out living their lives—better lives than mine. I wished I were with them. I wanted to be anywhere else but the reservoir. But then I remembered Gus. My days of running away were over. I forced myself to keep going.

The stone reservoir was at the front of the park, right next to where the dead-end road met the grass. I stepped up onto its wide stone rim and scanned the area. The spring water below me was clear and calm, reflecting the puffs of cloud in the dusky lavender sky overhead. Beyond, past a small expanse of grass dotted with stone picnic tables, Lake Mendota spread wide. Waves lapped at the rocky shore. A narrow, shallow creek ran between the lake and the reservoir, passing under the taller, chimney-like section of the stone wall. The park was the same modest size as the private lots on either side. Tall trees marked the borders. It all looked the same as I remembered.

I closed my eyes and inhaled. The fishy funk of lake water. The wet stone of the reservoir.

I was fourteen years old again, waiting for my friends to arrive at our secret place.

I smelled my own panic sweat too, sour and skunky, and my unwashed clothes and hair. I opened my eyes.

That was when I saw the arm draped over the edge of the reservoir a few feet away from the chimney. I knew the weight of that arm, warm and sleep-limp across my body in the night. Gus's arm.

I leaped off the stone wall and ran toward him. A mix of guilt and dread and fury pounded through my veins. Was there a name for that feeling? The one that had dogged me my whole life, every time I made a mistake? Every time a person close to me died. First my parents. Then Megan. Then aunt Shelly. Now, maybe, Gus.

I found him on the ground, crumpled against the wall as if someone had flung him there. His face was in the grass. There was a smear of blood on his cheek, near his ear. He wore jeans but no shirt or shoes.

I could see how it had happened: a knock on the door as Gus was getting out of the shower. He pulled on his jeans to go answer it. They'd been after me but found him instead.

I'd had a lot of practice hating myself, but it had been amateur hour up until then. I'd gone pro.

I fell to my knees beside Gus, put my hand on his clammy chest.

"Gus!" I could feel the slow thud of his heart and let out a relieved sob. "Can you wake up? Please wake up."

I shook him. His head was heavy and limp. I cradled it in my lap and rubbed the dirt and blood from his cheek. He was alive, but out cold. The blood had come from his nose. A dark bruise bloomed at his left temple. The trees threw shadows over us like a net, disguising other injuries I feared he might have. I looked around, for help or for the person who had hurt Gus. I wasn't sure which I wanted to find more. I needed a confrontation, to take my anger out on someone. But Gus and I were alone.

"Screw it."

I reached for my phone—intending to call 911—but my fingers went cold and clumsy as I sensed movement at the edge of the park. The phone tumbled into the grass and came to rest against Gus's thigh. Someone was walking behind the tree line along the private property next door. A featureless figure, dressed in white. A ghost.

Then the ghost stepped out of the shadows.

Excerpt from
No One Suspected
The End

BULL AND I waited for Petal in the darkness, doubt settling upon my tensed shoulders. My determination was guttering, and I questioned every decision that had brought the elderly detective and me back to the Madison School Forest. The moon was high, the ivory color of an aged elephant tusk over the clearing, but the shadows behind the utility building where we hid were heavy. Next to me Bull was a stone, sitting on an old tree stump because he couldn't stand for long. I had to hold my breath to detect any life coming off the old man. He was single-minded, and certain of how he wanted this story to end. Two things I was not.

Bull had been helpful at first, using his police connections to find Petal in New York and feeding my well of bitterness as we launched a campaign of email and phone harassment. Enough that she ran from her life in the city, a haven that we had made hell. She came to us, like Bull had said she would. *You lay a trap right, and they can't help but walk right into it* was what he'd told me. I'd cheered our success, hungry for the next phase of the plan. By the time I realized our partnership was toxic and destined to end badly, it was too late.

He'd given me what I'd said I wanted but not what I needed, which was a guardrail to keep me from plunging off the cliff. Instead, he was fuel for my fire. If Bull had weighed in with logic instead of urgency, caution instead of emotion, things would be different now. But I couldn't see past my need for a dramatic final confrontation with Petal, to finally have the upper hand with her. I got that, in a way.

After Petal returned to Madison, Bull continued his campaign of torment. He called her hotel room and hung up. He found her rental car in the parking lot and set off the alarm. He sent his police buddies to search her belongings for illegal substances. But Petal was stronger than we thought. She didn't crack, and the police found nothing.

Then he told me it was my turn. I didn't know what that meant but pretended I did. I called her. She sounded exactly the same, and as we spoke, it wasn't her face that rose into mind from the past, but Miri's. The specter of my dead best friend urged me on, keeping my voice steady as I spoke to Petal on the phone.

"We need to have a conversation. Someone has been calling me, harassing me," I lied. "About Miri. I can't go on like this. I want it to be over. Would you meet me? In private."

"Why would I want to do that?"

She didn't let on that she had been getting harassed too. Maybe because she'd suspected it was me all along. I didn't know what to say to convince her, and she got annoyed and hung up. By the time I called back I'd steeled myself, trying to match her level of detachment.

"If the two of us don't talk about this, I'll have to talk to someone else. Like the police. Or a lawyer. I have evidence you don't know about. And I'm not afraid to use it."

A dry laugh drifted through the phone speaker.

"Midnight. Tonight. School Forest," I insisted. I liked the symmetry of that, the finality.

"Okay, Izzy. You win. I'll play your goddamn game. I'll see you at midnight. Don't be late."

Bull and I got there early and waited. I told myself it would all be all right, even though I knew that was a lie. I had no idea how it would be. But Bull could help me, no matter what came of our meeting with Petal. After, he could explain everything in terms the police would understand: why it had taken me so long to come forward and why it was important to get Petal there for a confession. He could shield me from any residual blame, from the stain of my decades-old secret.

But he wasn't interested in my welfare at all. I was a means to an end. He wanted justice and closure—but for himself, to right the wrong of giving up on Miri's case. The desire to make Petal pay was the thread holding us together, leading us out there, to that moment at the School Forest. Waiting.

I didn't know if I could face her.

Headlights washed across the clearing, and Bull struggled to his feet behind me. I couldn't see the car. A door opened and closed. I heard the crunch of feet on gravel. Petal emerged, thirty years older and thicker around the middle, crossing the grass toward the cabin where Miri had fallen. If I squinted, I could see the ghostly figure of my old friend standing there on the roof, a tiny bright speck in the night. The speck began to move. It teetered on the edge. It fell.

I looked away.

"Petal!" My voice was hoarse. I stepped out from the shadows and walked into the clearing. Bull and I had agreed that I'd approach her alone and he would only come out if I called for him. He was my backup. I wanted my moment with her. I needed it.

Petal stopped, halfway across the grass, and turned. She wasn't frightened or nervous. She was angry.

"You look like shit," she said when I was a few feet away. She crossed her arms over her chest.

I couldn't argue with her. My hair hadn't been washed in days, and I smelled like the cigars Bull liked to smoke in the car. Control slipped away as I remembered something I had forgotten: Petal was stronger than me. And always would be.

"Who's that with you?" she demanded, looking over my shoulder.

I whirled. It was Bull, hateful eyes trained on Petal. He wasn't going to give me my moment, and Petal wasn't cowering like I wanted. I swallowed my frustration, along with some bile.

"It's Detective Bull. Do you remember him? He helped me track you down. We laid a trap, and you fell right in." I laughed, but my voice was reedy, betraying my fear.

"Guess so." She didn't sound impressed. She sounded bored. "Can we get on with it? I'm not much for reunions. I'm sure you understand why."

I reached into my pocket and pushed record on an old mini-cassette recorder I'd found in a secondhand store. I should have turned it on the minute I saw Petal. But I'd been flustered and had forgotten. One more mistake.

Bull lurked like a shadow, waiting.

"I want you to admit that what you did to Miri was wrong," I said. "That she died because of you and that it was not my fault. For years, I've lived with the guilt. And I'm done."

A look passed over Petal's face, difficult to decipher in the moonlight. Disdain, perhaps. Or exasperation.

"Bullshit, Iz. None of us were innocent that night." She threw her arms wide, and I took a step back, nearly colliding with Bull. "We were all out here, all doing things no fourteen-year-old had any business doing. For Miri, it was stealing the car keys and drinking that vodka. For you, it was that goddamn knife."

"What about you? You were the one who picked up the knife! You hurt Miri! I only brought it to whittle with."

Petal laughed like I'd finally revealed the punch line to a thirty-year-old joke.

"Whittling? Jesus Christ. That knife never touched Miri, and you know it. And neither did I. She was my best friend. I could never have hurt her. You on the other hand . . . you were jealous of her. Crazy jealous."

Her version of the truth was an evasion, a perversion. Hearing it made me want to wring her neck, but that would be exactly what she wanted. It would prove that she was right about me. Petal held a power I hadn't felt since Miri was alive. As if she had absorbed Miri's life-force the moment it left Miri's body. I shuddered as the afterimage of my dead and broken friend danced in front of my eyes. I closed them, but Miri was still there.

I couldn't get the conversation back under control. In desperation, I looked back at Bull. He saw something in my face and nodded. An agreement was struck between us in that moment, though I didn't know it. He stepped out from behind me. I wanted to tell him to wait, so I could figure out what had been decided, but I didn't. He began to move. Though his gait was hitched, Bull's progress toward Petal was steady. He didn't have the strength or stamina to beat her in a struggle, and he was too old to inspire fear. He knew that and knew Petal would see it too. That's why he'd brought the gun.

It was cold gray steel, and Bull held it low at his hip. Petal didn't waste a moment and bolted for her car. She didn't get far. A second later, Bull shot. It all happened so fast I couldn't tell where the bullet hit, but Petal fell, losing control of her limbs as she hit the ground, tumbling along the grass before coming to rest with an arm thrown over her face. In the moonlight, the shadows were stark. Petal was still; I don't think she was even breathing. Life was not leaking out of her, as I'd imagined it would when someone got shot; it had fled, an antsy student kept too long at her desk.

"No! She wasn't—this isn't what we talked about!" My rage transferred to the man stooped in front of me. "Bull!" He had ruined everything. My chance to hear her say the right words—the words that would release me from my lifelong guilt—was gone. That's what the recorder had been for—not to give to the authorities. I hadn't even been certain I was going to turn Petal in. I wanted the words for myself. To replay, over and over, until I believed them.

"Hadda be done." Bull started making his slow, unsteady way toward the gravel parking lot, voice slurring with fatigue. We'd driven together in my car, stashing it in the trees near the road so Petal wouldn't see it when she arrived. I would have to get him back to the retirement home now, sneak him in so no one would wonder where he had gone and what we had done.

"No. It didn't. You didn't have to . . . kill her. I was going to get her to confess. I needed time. Why didn't you give me more time?" I was wailing, like an ambulance that would never come.

He stopped and turned, gun still at his hip.

"It was always going to come to this, sweetheart." Oh, how I hated being called sweetheart. "From the minute you showed up on my doorstep. And you know it. You should be thanking me."

"I never—"

"She wasn't gonna budge. I saw it in her eyes. In my business, you recognize these things. There was only one way to finish this for good. To get justice for your friend."

"Justice? This isn't—"

He shot me.

I don't remember, now, what point I was trying to make as I died. It's lost in the void; it belonged to my living self.

The bullet pierced the shell of my skull, entering through the meat of my cheek to the right of my nose. For so long I'd yearned to be free of my awful secret, to finally release the truth of Miri's death. I got what I wanted, in a way. I'd told Bull the truth, and I'd faced Petal one last time. But it wasn't enough. I wasn't enough, not ever. My time had run out.

*   *   *

None of that matters now.

Failure, success, revenge, justice.

In death, they're all on the far side of a wall I cannot climb.

I'd like to think that Bull will tell what happened, to Miri back in 1991 and, that night, to Petal and me. So Miri's family and mine can have some closure. But I know he won't. He will wipe the gun and put it in my hand and take my recorder and leave us there, me and Petal, the way we left Miri. Only fitting. He will drive my car back to Madison, leave it in the parking lot of my hotel. He will wipe away his fingerprints, and it will be like he was never there.

Miri died because of Petal; I know that now. It wasn't my fault. But Petal died because of me. If I could still feel anything, I would experience guilt for that. But my only sensation now is peace. All three of us are back together. Miri, Izzy, and Petal. Here in the lively hush of the forest, under the moonlight. Where death was our one last adventure.

CHAPTER

16

THE GHOST, DRESSED in white, faced me across the narrow expanse of the park. I was dressed in black. Gus, unmoving on the ground, was the pawn between us. The drone of a thousand insects filled my ears. I hadn't noticed them when I'd first arrived at the reservoir, but now it was like they'd crawled inside my head and started screaming. I repocketed my phone and got up from where I'd crouched next to Gus, knees and lower back protesting. I moved my body in front of his, not that I offered much protection. But I was braver with him at my back. He was my reminder that running wasn't an option. I'd stay and see this through. Both for me and for him.

The ghostly figure, now approaching, was smaller than I'd first thought. The closer it came, the more the ghost illusion began to break: feet striding purposefully across the grass, the cold glint of white teeth. Its left hand was wrapped around something. A purse or bag? No, smaller than that. Rectangular. A brick, maybe.

I took an involuntary step back, the heel of my boot hitting Gus's thigh. I imagined a brick smashing into the side of his head, of my head, crashing down over and over.

The wet, meaty sounds and splatters of blood. The grass beneath us turning from summer green to a gory, rusty red.

The figure stepped into a pool of light cast into the park from a streetlight on the dead-end road. Not a ghost, a person. And not the mysterious "he" I'd expected, but a woman. And the object in her hand was not a brick. It was a book.

Somehow, that was worse.

The book was black, making it hard to pick out a title from the shadows. A copy of *No One Suspected*, I thought. But as the woman tilted it toward the light, I could see sparkly, pink cursive looping across the cover. It glittered at me, a silent taunt. It was familiar, but I couldn't read what it said.

The woman's eyes found mine, cutting me like a scalpel. I knew those eyes, cornflower blue and piercing. My lips pursed, ready to call out.

Megan!

For the space of one unsteady breath, Megan stood there, looking the same as she had at fourteen. Petite and beautiful and clever and ruthless. Her expression was expectant, waiting for me to catch up, to catch on, to finally get the joke. But I held my tongue.

Another gust blew in off the lake, fishy and metallic. The woman's long hair swirled around her shoulders and across her face. She gathered it with her free hand, twisted and draped it over her right shoulder. Not Megan's coppery tone but a deeper red, with grayish roots beginning to peek out. Not Megan at all. Only a cheap copy.

The woman hugged the book to her chest, a move calculated to make sure I could read the writing on the front. I recognized it then: the book, the writing, and what it all meant. Puzzle pieces clicked into place.

Megan's diary. The sparkly glitter glue was ancient, dry and crumbling, transferring to the woman's creamy white sweater. Her tanned arm. Megan's blue eyes assessed me, waiting. But there were fresh crow's-feet at the corners, further betraying this woman's age.

"Bitty."

Her smile was praise, a reward for guessing correctly.

"You do remember me. I wasn't certain you would. Hello, Petal. Or I guess you prefer Petta."

I didn't care what she called me. But now that I was back at the reservoir, Petal seemed like the appropriate version of myself. I could step into her skin again, if I needed to.

"What did you do to Gus?" I asked.

She dipped her free hand into her back pocket and pulled out a Taser. The streetlight blinked off, leaving us in the dim in-between of dusk. Bitty pushed the button on the Taser, and it crackled to life—in case I had any doubts about who was in charge.

She put it back in her pocket and I sat down on the lip of the reservoir, tenting my legs over Gus. I leaned back on my arms, studying Megan's younger sister. Pretending I had all the time in the world. I wanted her to think I could sit there forever, if I had to, waiting for her to explain. I wanted her to believe she hadn't spooked me. But inside, my blood churned like a tornado. The stone underneath me was cold, and I shivered.

This place knew all my secrets. And Bitty was looking at me like she did too.

"The diary. Is that how you knew so much about the three of us? You used what was in there to write the book?"

Bitty bared her teeth. Not a smile, but one bloodsucker acknowledging another.

Megan had been obsessed with scribbling in that diary. At school, during sleepovers. She liked to record our midnight escapades on the streets of Shorewood, keeping a tally of how many times we evaded the local cops. She gave them silly nicknames: Mr. Clean for the bald one, Squatch for the hairy one.

Then, as she began to pull away, missing lunches and canceling plans, she stopped showing us the contents of her diary. She'd curl a hand in front of the page while she wrote. The diary had stopped being a record of our adventures and started keeping her secrets.

She must have written about Ben in those pages. I wanted to read what she wrote, to satisfy my curiosity about their relationship and to feed my late-stage jealousy over whatever they'd meant to each other. Megan would often smile to herself and giggle as she wrote. She wanted us to know she was withholding her deepest, darkest, dearest. And even more, she wanted us to wonder. Megan was an admiration vampire, and she fed on us.

I'd never kept a diary. Sure, I brought my battered notebook to sleepovers and pretended to write my desires on its pages. I kept up the charade for one simple reason: Megan wanted me to. I had secrets. Of course I did. But I kept the whispers of my heart to myself, as they were too painful to write down. Mommy and Daddy had been nearly perfect parents until they chose death over me—that wasn't something I wanted to put on paper. But I continued to fake it, because it made Megan happy. That's what she'd always wanted: for us to adore her, mimic her, please her. Follow the leader.

I understood Megan better after reading *No One Suspected*. She'd become more of a full-fledged person instead of a childhood icon lost to the fog of memory. I understood Jenny better too. We were more like enemies than friends in the days leading up to Megan's last. And after, we were forever tied, each propping up our own side of the same secret so it wouldn't spill. Until now.

"The diary's what started it, yes," Bitty admitted, picking a flake of glitter glue off her sweater. "I didn't know it existed, not for years. When our parents died a couple years ago, I was cleaning out their things. They'd never packed up Megan's room. They closed the door and pretended it wasn't there. We moved out of the house shortly after, and they left it all like it was. A mausoleum." She shuddered. "We were on them for years, Matt and I, to do something about the house. Eventually we convinced them to hire movers. None of us ever went back inside, but the help packed its contents in boxes and hauled it away to a storage locker. Still, my parents let the empty house sit, throwing away property tax money all those years, so they wouldn't have to face it. Once it was up to me, I drove up from Chicago to deal with the storage locker, cleaned it out, and found the diary."

I listened with one ear and tried to figure out a way to get that Taser away from her. Her eyes were saucers in the moonlight, her pupils like spilled pools of black coffee at their centers. And they were trained on me. She'd see any move I was planning before I took a single step. And I'd be useless to Gus if I ended up convulsing on the ground beside him.

Bitty held up the diary, opened it, and showed me its ruled pages, filled with colorful handwriting. Pink, green, and sky blue. Just like the page left on my car, the one that had nudged me to drive out to the forest.

"This was like a gift. Well worth sifting through all the other useless stuff from that horrible house. Megan was so much older, and over the years there was so much about her I forgot. Reading her diary was like crawling inside her head. There were things in there about you. Did you know that? And about Jenny."

I didn't take her bait.

She stepped closer. I wanted to back up, to keep the buffer between me and the mania shining from her eyes, but any further and I'd be over the stone wall. I stood so I could face her on my own two feet. I had a good five inches on her, but I didn't feel the advantage.

"Like right here," Bitty said, flipping forward a few pages and starting to read. I wanted to put my fingers in my ears and hum and squinch my eyes shut like a toddler. But I stood there and listened.

"*I can't stand to be around those two anymore. Like I told Benny yesterday, they're so boring. Jenny won't give me any space and Petal needs serious mental help. Like she's really screwed up, thanks to her parents. All I want to do now is spend time with Benny. He wants everyone to know that we're together but my parents probably won't be too wild about him and besides, keeping it a secret is kind of cool. I'll never forget that night I took him to the reservoir. After, he said he loved me. I didn't say it back though. I've never said it, not to my parents or to Jenny when she used to say it to me all the time. I don't know if I'll ever say it. I don't know if I can really love anybody.*"

I swallowed this new information, trying to get the bitter taste of it out of my mouth. Bitty was watching me.

"So what?" I said. "I knew about Ben already. You're wasting my time. Jenny is the one who cared, and she's gone. Because of you."

Bitty laughed like I'd made a joke. That was how she was treating all of it: like a goof.

"Did you know, every year on the anniversary of Megan's death, Jenny would send us a condolence card? And every year it would say the same thing: *I still miss her.*

After I found the diary, I wrote to her and asked if I could come for a visit. I thought maybe she'd like to talk about Megan and I could show her some things in the diary. That's how all this started." She waved a hand to encompass the two of us. "At first, all I wanted was to hear more about what my big sister had been like. Especially in her last days. I thought Jenny could fill in the blanks. And she did. But she had a lot to say about you too."

She retrieved the Taser from her pocket and pushed the button. White sparks leapt between the two prongs, searing my retinas and causing fingers of harsh artificial light to crawl across her face.

I closed my eyes.

"She told you that Megan died because of me." It wasn't a question. It was something I'd come to understand as clearly as my own shame. I forced myself to look at her again.

"Jenny said *you* killed her." Bitty's voice was a slap. "She told me everything that happened that night. Well, she told me the version she was ready to tell, at the time: she was the not-so-innocent bystander, the one who saw it all happen. Poor, pathetic little Jenny." Bitty was shaking her head.

I crossed my arms over my chest, trying to control my shivering. "And you taped her saying all that, on the minicassette recorder. Then you used the recording and the diary to concoct a fun-house-mirror version of the truth. First because of the lies Jenny told you. And then to punish me. You thought I was the bad guy, but you couldn't get to me, so you used the book to smoke me out." I paused. "How'd I do? Am I pretty close?"

Bitty tilted her head, studying me. She'd dropped the arm holding the Taser to her side. She didn't say a word. It was like she was waiting for something.

From me? Was I not following the script closely enough?

Then a voice came from behind me.

"Almost. But you left out one thing: me."

I whirled, tripping over Gus's legs. I caught myself against the low stone wall.

Matt stood on the other side of the reservoir. I backed up a few steps, keeping both twins in view, Bitty on my right and Matt on my left. It meant leaving Gus more exposed, but he wasn't the focus of their violence anymore. It was all me. I tried to give them what they wanted.

"Hi, Matt. Long time. What, exactly, was all you?"

"It was his idea to write the book," Bitty answered for him. "After I showed him the diary and played him Jenny's tape. But I'm the one who wanted to put your real name in it. I knew it would force you to pay attention." She stretched her face into another wooden, humorless grin. "Then I—"

"Elizabeth! Stop talking. You're only prolonging this. That's what she wants." Matt was angry, but something else lurked under the surface. Fear, I thought, of Bitty getting carried away and saying too much. Seeing it gave me a spark of hope.

"I suppose Matthew and Elizabeth are the M-E in ME Littleton. Very clever."

Bitty was a nickname, short for Elizabeth. Megan had given it to her. Because she was so itty-bitty when she was born, the smaller twin. The runt. Jenny had explained the nickname once, but I'd forgotten.

Bitty devoured my praise, tossing her head so that her sunset hair shone under the streetlight, which had clicked back on without me noticing. She was vain about her hair, I could tell. I wanted to rip it from her skull. But I kept my voice controlled.

"So Matt's the writer in the family. And Bitty, you exploited Jenny's pain so he'd have something to write about. You make quite the team."

My phone buzzed in my pocket, and I itched to check it. I slid my hand down toward it, but Matt saw. He growled in warning, and Bitty hit the button on the Taser again. I put my arms up, clear of my pockets. Bitty rewarded me by continuing to talk.

"It wasn't like that. Jenny loved our chats. She loved *me*. We talked for hours. She told me everything. At least I thought it was everything, at first. Matt and I couldn't just go to the police and tell them what we knew, not with secondhand information, after all this time. We didn't trust the authorities. They always seem to put the blame on the wrong people. Like they did with Megan. Blaming her for her own death. It was shameful. Matt said we should put the truth in a book for the world to read. And he was right. He's always had a way with words."

The Taser had drifted down again, held loosely in Bitty's hand. I would have gone for it if not for Matt lurking to my left. Keeping both in full view was like following a tennis match, head always swiveling. And two against one were not good odds.

"Bitty . . ." Matt's voice held a warning, but he didn't go so far as to threaten.

Bitty ignored her brother—I got the sense she had a lot of practice at that—and kept talking.

"Everything happened as Matt said it would. He wrote the story we wanted to tell. He's quite talented, don't you think? Once we found a publisher and it was released, we bought thousands of copies to make sure it would be a bestseller, visible in the public eye. It was only a matter of time before you or someone you knew read it. That's what we wanted: for your name to be forever linked to death, and for the whole world to know it."

"Well, mission accomplished, then, I guess. Gold star. But you didn't stop with the book." I couldn't keep the bitterness out of my voice.

"It wasn't enough. Not for me. The book was a success, but no one was talking about you, the real you. And then you gave us a gift. You came back, looking for us, trying to figure out who was behind ME Littleton. That's where I came in. I wrote the graffiti on the cabin and left it for you to find. Matt didn't think you'd go there, but I knew leaving you the diary page would make it impossible for you to stay away." She laughed, a sound like shattering glass. Matt and I both winced. "Everyone thinks I'm the quiet twin, the lesser. The runt. But I'm strong, and smart too. I made the cat posters. A fake lost pet to catch a real lost Pet. Can I call you Pet?"

"Bitty, enough with the idiotic wordplay. Let's get this over with," Matt urged.

The twins glared at each other. I reached into my pocket. The glass of my phone screen was cold against my fingertips.

"The poster was you?" I asked Bitty. I didn't care about her gloating confession. I'd heard enough. But I knew my best chance was to keep her talking until Gull arrived, to keep the twins bickering, facing off against each other so they wouldn't unite against me.

"Matt told me not to, but I did it anyway. Once we figured out where you were staying, I plastered them all over the neighborhood. I liked teasing you. And I knew getting you to call Jenny would confuse the both of you."

"But it didn't, did it, Bitty?" Matt was angry at her, fully loaded and not trying to hide it. I slipped my phone out of my pocket and palmed it against my leg. Neither of them noticed. Matt was still talking. "You almost ruined everything. Jenny could've told her who we were, long before we were ready. We agreed, in advance, how we were going to do this—get the book out there, and the rest would happen naturally. In time. But you couldn't resist pushing it, could you? You went too far, like you always do."

Bitty rolled her eyes at Matt and looked to me for support, cutting short my attempt to check my phone. I willed Gull to hurry and tried to give Bitty a smile, but as my lips stretched, the skin cracked, a trickle of blood painting my mouth red. I'd been licking my lips all night. A nervous tic. They were dry and tight. I licked them again, and the blood was coppery on my tongue.

"It's not healthy for you to get so worked up, Matty. The doctor told you, remember? And once I figured out what Jenny had done, I fixed everything, didn't I?"

Matt shook his head at her, as if he couldn't believe what she was saying.

"Our parents always told us: if there's a problem, take care of it. Simple. So I did," Bitty said.

"I think your parents and my parents would have gotten along," I told her. But my mind was clicking back to Jenny's time of death, and the posts Matt and Bitty had made on Facebook that day. The ones that had convinced me neither of them could have possibly killed her.

"How did you do it all? You threw a party that day. You baked a homemade goddamn Batman cake."

"Oh, that." Bitty waved a dismissive hand. "Juanita made it, in my home. She does all our cooking. I show up at the last minute and take the credit."

I don't think Bitty liked the look on my face, because she went on.

"I would have liked to make the cake, of course. I'm quite a good baker. I've taken classes. But I had to go up

there and make sure Jenny wasn't going to say or do something that would—"

"Bitty!" Matt's chest was rising and falling fast, too fast.

She lifted a single shoulder, deflecting his anger. "She
got a little upset. That's all. I was trying to keep her under
control the way Megan used to. I learned a lot from that
diary. Did you know she was going to test you and Jenny
with that trip to the School Forest? It was going to be about
loyalty, to see which of you would go through with it, but
also to see if you were still cool enough to be her friend."

Matt chimed in then: "Megan was smart. She realized
she only needed one of you. Two best friends is one too
many. She came up with a way to see who would win."

"Yeah. Jenny didn't much like it when I told her that,"
Bitty laughed. "At first, I fed her only the information
from the diary I wanted her to have. But on that last trip, I
had the diary with me. She grabbed it and read everything.
She was a mess. Crying. I still thought I might be able to
convince her to stay quiet, but then . . ."

Bitty's eyes glazed over. She was no longer with us in
the park. She was somewhere else. With Jenny. Killing
Jenny all over again. My empty stomach heaved.

"She broke down and told me the truth. She told me
what she'd done. Sniveling like a child the whole time."

"Bitty doesn't like people to show their weaknesses,"
Matt told me. "She thinks it's disgusting and degrading.
Don't you, sis?" There was an edge to his tone I couldn't
place. Like this was a discussion they'd had many times
before. And not in relation to Jenny.

"No. I don't like that at all." Gone was careless Bitty,
calm Bitty, hair-tossing Bitty. A vessel of vengeance stood
in front of me. She was looking at Matt, but my fingers
tingled with cold panic. Matt was looking at me, avoiding
his sister's gaze.

The way the twins needled each other reminded me of how Megan had treated Jenny. And that made perfect sense. They'd learned from the best.

"Why a book, though?" I asked Matt, to keep him talking. "It seems like a clumsy form of revenge. I mean, what if I never saw it?"

"It wasn't like that," Matt insisted. "It wasn't about revenge. Not at first. It was about airing the truth. Removing the taint of the suicide rumors. If we could do that and remain anonymous, that's what I wanted to do. We came up with the idea of using a pen name, because neither of us wanted to have to answer questions publicly about the book, or about Megan."

"We can say good-bye now, to that part of our lives. We never have to come back here again." Bitty spoke as if she was trying to reason with a child. She tucked the diary under an arm and began to tick items off on her fingers, keeping a grip on the taser. "First, we got rid of the house. Then we wrote the book, showing Megan was not to blame for her own death. And then we parted ways with Jenny."

"Oh, is that what we're calling murder now? *A parting of ways?*"

"And now it's your turn," Bitty said, ignoring me.

"*Now*, Bitty," Matt urged. "It's time." They both started walking, Matt around the left side of the reservoir's circular wall, and Bitty around the right. Closing in on me.

Bitty dropped the diary on the ground and raised the Taser. I hurried along the reservoir's wide lip, toward Gus, walking carefully until I could touch the tall portion of the wall, the one that looked like a stone chimney. I leaned on it for support. Under my shoulder, *1934* was etched into a small slab of concrete set in the mortar between the stones. The year the reservoir had been built.

As the twins neared, light glinted off something in Matt's hand. A knife.

"Megan wasn't always a nice person, but she was our big sister." Bitty lifted her chin, deflecting a challenge I wasn't planning to make. "Our parents were more interested in yachting in the Mediterranean and luxury suites in Las Vegas than looking after their children. When we needed help, Megan was always there. We did all this for her. And I'd do it again."

I tucked my body tight against the stone so neither of them could see what I was doing. I hoped it looked like I was cowering in fear. I flipped my phone around in my hand, attempting to shield the light of the screen with my body, and saw a text from Gull.

On my way.

All I had was hope: that Gull would arrive in time, that I wouldn't get stabbed or Tased before I could make sure Gus was safe.

"Are you sure you want to do this? We could all just walk away. I'm pretty good at keeping a secret." If I was going to go, it sure as hell wouldn't be quietly.

Bitty stopped moving and watched Matt, still approaching from the opposite side of the reservoir. Did he not want Bitty to have all the fun, or did she not want to be the only one with a murder on her shoulders?

Before Matt could close the last few yards between him and where I stood against the stone chimney, I started to climb.

Some of the stones stuck out more than others. I used these as hand- and footholds. I slipped a few times, rock scraping against my denim-clad legs and clawing at the soft skin on the insides of my arms. The mortar was crumbling away and I used that too, mashing my fingers between the stones until my already raggedy nails were torn and bleeding.

I looked down. Matt had reached the base of the chimney, but I had shifted around to climb up the opposite side. He would have to turn and run the other way around the perimeter of the reservoir, past where Bitty was watching us, or cross the narrow creek to be able to reach me.

I was almost at the top. I reached a hand up there and felt around. The chimney had narrowed as I climbed higher. The flat surface at the very top was small, maybe the size of two sheets of printer paper side by side. Barely enough space for my feet to stand, if I could heave myself up there.

I didn't look down at the water in the reservoir; I'd never be able to keep going if I did. I risked one glance behind me and regretted it. Matt had reached my side and was climbing with one hand, now inches away from my right foot, knife cocked and ready in the other hand.

Keeping an eye on the knife, I drew my right leg up and away from him, making one last push with my left, abandoning caution and attempting to fling my body across the top of the stones and drape it there like a sack of potatoes over a shoulder. But it wasn't enough. I wouldn't have been able to pull my body from the path of the knife in time if Matt hadn't hesitated. His face was scrunched into a mask of doubt, and the blade stuttered in the air as he brought it forward. At the last minute, in what seemed like slow motion, the blade struck the stone where my foot had rested one second before.

Bitty was the more ruthless of the pair, that was clear. And I could use that.

I shuffled through my mental Rolodex of badasses, trying to channel a little action-hero bravery. Because I had none of my own. The twins had me beat two to one, both with weapons and with Gus still on the ground. No

Gull in sight. How long had it been since I'd texted her? It felt like years.

"Jesus! You are bad at this. Why don't you go home and let the ladies figure things out, Matty-boy."

I only had what I'd ridden in with, and I was going to use it all: my shit-kicking boots, my brains, and my smart-ass mouth. "Shit, dude. Have you ever used a knife before? You probably only brought one because you thought it would be poetic justice, after writing a knife scene into the book."

Matt froze, his knife cocked to try again. Bitty was waiting on the ground, watching the two of us as if we were her favorite TV show. Which most likely was *Grey's Anatomy*. She probably called it *Grey's* for short and sipped her way through a bottle of Chardonnay while she watched each week.

Matt shook his head, but that stuttered too.

"Holy shit! I'm right. That's capital-P Pathetic. Seriously, you're not cut out for this."

I'd made it to my knees on top of the chimney-thing, almost confident in my balance and with all limbs at a safe distance from the knife, when he lashed out again. I'd gone too far, made him angry. I gripped the top of the chimney and flailed a foot at him. We collided—the knife stuck deep into the thick sole of my Doc Martens with a sickening *thunk*. The tip of the blade pricked against my heel.

"You prick!" I hugged the stone and kicked out again with my knifed boot like I was swimming the breaststroke, narrowly missing Matt's head. He ducked out of the way. Bitty appeared behind him like she was ready to tag in, Taser held high. But she was small, and I was out of reach. She rose onto her toes, stretching the Taser toward me.

With Matt still cowering, I banged the knife handle against one of the chimney stones until it wrenched free, tumbling down toward Bitty and Matt. It clipped the edge of a large, sand-colored stone and bounced, spinning off toward the center of the reservoir.

I'll never understand why Bitty lunged for the knife— maybe just reflex. She reached out with her free hand, leaning over the wall to try and catch it. She still had a death grip on the Taser, so no free hand to stop her fall when she lost her balance. Her momentum pushed her sideways, and gravity took over. I didn't miss the horror of this symmetry—it broke across me like goose bumps. For a moment, Bitty was airborne, like a football receiver lay-ing out to catch a pass. My mouth formed a silent O, and the breath emptied from my body. I leaned backward, as if I could counterbalance her. But I couldn't.

Her side struck the lip of the reservoir, and she crum-pled. The knife spun harmlessly past her outstretched hand. The weight of her upper body carried her over the edge and down, down into the water. A scream tore from her throat. It cut off as she struck the shallow pool.

Her fall had paralyzed me—brought back that night, with another Hollister, another fall. The same, but differ-ent. Images from the past had been coming in small waves ever since I'd returned to the reservoir. I'd been too wor-ried about Gus to give them space inside me. But Bitty's scream had them rushing back, hungry and clamoring to be noticed. They filled my mouth, tasting like mossy spring water, trying to drown me.

Damned if I was going to let them.

I pulled myself together, eyes scanning the park for Matt. I had a good view from my perch on top of the chimney. He stood a few feet from the edge of the reservoir where Bitty had fallen, breathing like he'd run a hundred-yard dash. His arms hung limp at his sides. He balled his fists and released them—once, twice—before stepping up to the wall. He peered over the edge, and I followed his gaze.

Bitty wasn't dead. But she wasn't unhurt either. She had one hand tight to her side, as if her ribs might disintegrate if she didn't hold them together. The other hand gripped the inner wall of the reservoir. She was pulling herself up, out of the hip-high water. One leg, her good one, was planted on the mossy floor. Once she'd gotten her balance, she pulled her phone out of her pocket and turned on the flashlight. The streetlight wasn't much help down there. Weeds grew up around her from the bottom, like stalagmites in a dank cave. A pool of crimson stained the water around her injured leg, and the stark white of bone winked at me through the ripples. A compound fracture. The shattered bottom half of her limb jutted out at a sickening angle. She was a mangled flamingo, her bad leg tucked as close to her body as the injury would allow.

"Oh, Bitty. Oh, no." Matt moaned her name, shifting his weight back and forth from foot to foot. He was a little boy again, out in the dark by himself and too scared to find his way home. "Bitty, Bitty. I can't."

She ignored him, searching the water for the knife or the Taser, finding neither.

I peeked at my phone while Matt was distracted. Nothing from Gull.

I looked down at Gus. He'd curled himself into a ball. I couldn't see his face. If he'd been conscious, I'd have gotten him on his feet and made a run for it. Bitty could rot down there in the water, for all I cared. But I wasn't leaving without Gus. To get to him, I had to get past Matt first.

I could handle one weaponless, whimpering twin. Still, I willed Gull to hurry.

"I'm all right, Matty," Bitty called up to him from below. "But you need to finish this. I can't—"

She cried out as her good foot slid across the moss-slick floor of the reservoir. I glanced up and saw that she couldn't stop her slow slide under the water. Matt ran back and forth around the stone circle, manic, trying to find a way into the pool. He ran behind me, splashing into the creek. He found the opening in the chimney underneath, but it was too small. Only an animal, low to the ground, would have fit. A cat, a raccoon. Matt was a big, nervous dog, whining and unable to reach his owner. In seconds he was back at the wall, peering down over the edge. Bitty had surfaced.

"Don't worry about me," she said, spitting water. "Get her, Matt. *Get her now.*"

He didn't have any weapons, but the gaze he trained on me was full of hate. The message was clear: anything bad that had ever happened to his family was my fault. And I needed to pay.

I forgot about Gull and crammed my phone in my pocket so I could keep my balance atop the stone platform and my center of gravity low. Climbing up there had made me feel safer, when he had a knife. Now I was trapped. I took a deep breath. The moment he made his move, starting to climb the chimney, I hit him with everything I had. I kept my voice low, gravelly. Almost a whisper.

"Matty, why are you letting her boss you around? You can make your own decisions. Why don't we call for help? They'll come get Bitty out of the well. Bring an ambulance, stocked with drugs. Wouldn't that be nice?"

He shook my words off like they were raindrops and kept coming.

Halfway up the chimney now. I might as well have been speaking a foreign language.

"I'll tell them it was all her. She's the one who killed Jenny. You wrote a book, that's all! It's not a crime."

He'd tuned me out. I guessed he was probably pretty good at tuning women out. I was only one in a long line of chatty women he'd chosen to ignore. He was an arm's length away, searching for a handhold, each movement methodical. He kept coming until I could smell his peppery cologne. He reached for me.

But I had an ace, waiting in the back of my mental deck ever since I'd read *No One Suspected*. And now was the time to play it.

"Hey Matty-boy, do you remember the skeleton trees?"

Of course he did. He'd written them into the damn book. But logic didn't matter when it came to childhood terrors, the kind that burrowed under the skin. That was one thing we had in common; something we both understood.

"Wh-what?"

Inches from my feet, his hand loosened on the stone; his foot slipped from its toehold. He slid, falling forward against the chimney, banging his chin as he caught himself. He wiped his mouth on the shoulder of his sky-blue polo shirt, leaving a red smear. The sight of his own blood made his eyes go wide.

Beneath us, Bitty swore quietly, then called up to her brother in a too-bright voice. "Matty, you're doing great. You've got her. Keep going."

She talked to him like Megan had when he was seven, coaxing him into doing something he didn't want to do. Like when he'd sneak into their backyard after bedtime and hide out in the Little House, refusing to leave because the night-world was too scary. Megan wasn't around to rescue him anymore, and Bitty—even before she'd been injured—was no Megan.

"Matty," I whispered. Only he could hear me. The rest of the world had fallen away, and it was just the two of us.

"They're watching. The skeleton trees have eyes. And they are watching you."

Matt sagged against the chimney. His face was a blanched moon in the darkness. His eyes were craters, dark and bottomless. I kept talking, repeating the same words, like a chant.

"They're watching you, Matt, and waiting. The skeleton trees. They've been waiting, all this time, for you. And now, they're coming. Coming for you. You should run."

"No! They're not here. They're gone. I had the skeletons torn down." He squeezed his eyes shut. Moisture rolled down his face; sweat or tears, I wasn't sure.

"Doesn't matter. Their eyes can still see you. They're watching, watching, always watching. And you know what, Matt? They did not like what you did to them. You hurt them, and they're angry. They've come back for revenge."

He went limp and slid the rest of the way down the wall. As soon as his feet hit the grass, I thought his knees would buckle, but they held. He shifted his body to the right, so the chimney both held him up and shielded him from Bitty's view. He started banging his head against the stone.

"Matt! What are you doing? Stop it!" Bitty had gone strident and scolding. When I heard the panic in her voice, I knew I had him. I kept going, though, kept talking. My tone was soothing where hers was shrill.

"I see them, Matt. Here they come. The trees. They have their eyes on you."

"Noooo." It transitioned from word to wail. "Not the Weery Wood."

"Weery what?"

"The Weeeery Wooood is waaaatching meeee."

His keening harmonized with another sound, too far away to pick out at first. It was a fleet of sirens, and they were getting closer. I'd never heard such a beautiful noise in my life.

One minute longer. If I could keep him in his terror trance for that long, we'd all come out of this alive. My throat was raw with the effort of adrenaline-charged whispering. I chanted in a hoarse, witchy tone.

"The skeleton trees have eyes. The skeleton trees are coming. The skeleton trees have eyes. The skeleton trees are watching."

Pushing another person into the arms of his demons put my stomach in knots. But it was either Gus and me or Matt and Bitty. And the contest wasn't even close.

I raised an arm and pointed, back into the trees at the edge of the park.

"Here they come. Look! There!"

As he spun to face his phantom attackers, I slid my body down the opposite side of the chimney wall, my shirt rucked up around my neck, belly scraping against the rough stone. I sucked in a loud breath through clenched teeth, but he didn't notice. His eyes were on the trees. He wasn't seeing the stately oaks and maples. He was seeing aspen, with their scarred white trunks. He was seeing the skeleton trees from his Weery Wood, and the Weery Wood was looking back at him.

He crumpled to his knees and I let go, dropping down to solid ground. I would have kissed the grass, but it hurt to bend. Bitty was screaming from down in the water, panting with pain and incoherent with rage. She went silent as a cavalry of cop cars filled the dead-end street with a seizure's worth of flashing lights.

Detective Samantha Gull led the pack. She pulled her sleek Dodge Charger onto the grass next to the reservoir. As soon as she got out of the car, I ran for Gus, splashing through the shallow creek to get to him. He was still curled into himself and groaned when I put a hand on his back.

Officers swarmed Matt, lifting him bodily off his feet and dragging him toward their patrol cars. Two ambulances pulled up, and behind them, a fire engine. The firefighters brought a ladder and climbed down to Bitty. I waved over a pair of paramedics to tend to Gus.

"He's been Tased and I don't know what else. Ask her. She did it." I pointed down into the water. With the help of a firefighter, she was limping toward the ladder.

They worked on Gus, checking for broken bones and setting up a gurney. I listened as they tossed medical jargon at each other and didn't hear anything too scary. Gus would be okay. I sat down a few feet away on the stone wall to give the paramedics space and allowed myself to relax a little.

That was a mistake. As soon as my adrenaline drained away, pain took its place. My throat was raw and my stomach and hands were scraped to hell and my muscles were cramping from being tensed for so long. A headache waited on deck.

Gus woke as they started rolling the gurney toward the waiting ambulances. I hurried to his side and pushed my way into his field of vision so my stupid face was the first thing he'd see. All my aches and pains started to recede. Relief was a rush of cool water down my throat; gratitude was a balm on my scrapes and bruises. Gus would be okay, so I would be okay.

"I'm here. You're okay. I'm here."

"You're here," he said, the words thick in his mouth.

"Yeah, dummy. That's what I said. I'm here and I'm not going anywhere."

"I'm going to"—he paused to swallow, which looked like it hurt—"hold you to that."

"Good. I need someone to keep me honest. Otherwise, I might do something stupid, like almost get us both killed."

"P, I feel like I'm going to pass out again any minute, but before I do, I need to say—"

Detective Gull appeared at my shoulder, patting Gus hard enough on the leg that he grunted. The paramedics worked around her, getting ready to load him into the ambulance. The self-satisfied look on her face was out of place, considering how little she'd contributed to the twins' final takedown. She swooped in at the last minute, ready to hog all the credit. But I didn't mind, at first. Not until she interrupted Gus and tried to steal the final one-liner.

"You know what they say—" she began, sighing and putting one boot up on the bumper of the ambulance and a hand on her hip.

I wasn't having it. This was my story, not hers. "Now's not the time, Gull. That crap might fly in the movies but not now."

Gull held her hands up in a don't-shoot gesture.

I climbed into the ambulance beside Gus, found his hand, and held on like my life depended on it. The paramedics closed the doors and we drove off. Into the—well, the sun had already set. But you get the idea.

17

MATT AND BITTY came out of that night fine, all things considered. He spent some time under psychiatric hold and she got her leg bone set and ribs wrapped. While all that was happening, I learned a lot more about how they'd pulled off their crimes.

Matt was the driver of the Tesla, of course—he worked for a big corporation based in Minnesota, and it was a company car. In Madison, a city lousy with Teslas, he'd blended right in and used the car to follow Gull and me around. The sneaky bastard.

Bitty was crafty too. Turned out that her pilot's license wasn't just a bougie hobby. She'd used her little Cessna to fly up and kill Jenny the morning of her own kid's birthday party. When Jenny finally admitted what she'd done to Megan and threatened to tell everyone who ME Littleton was, Bitty had killed her in a fit of rage. And been back home in time for cake, smiling at a houseful of kindergarteners hours after tasing and strangling Jenny. I take back my earlier comment—she wasn't crafty. She was stone-cold evil.

It irks me that they got out on bail and were allowed to go home to Chicago to await trial. I suppose that's the privilege money buys. But after the State of Wisconsin is done with them, Minnesota has requested a sit-down with Bitty. I'm looking forward to seeing that. In person. I owe it to Jenny. And to Megan. She's not around to look out for her siblings, so I'll make sure they get what they need. Or what's coming to them. Maybe both. Long before they get their due, I expect the twins will take their family money and their bestselling book profits and skip the country. I told that to the judge, but she didn't seem to care.

I don't like the twins very much, but I'm glad they're not dead—that our night at the reservoir didn't end with more death. I'm happy Ben was only peripherally involved in everything that happened. He really didn't know that Matt wrote the book. Gull questioned him for hours, and this time I believed what he said. He did call Matt the minute he left our coffee shop meeting, telling him I was in town and everything we'd talked about. Matt and Bitty already knew where I was, of course. Bitty had left the torn diary page on my car. Ben insisted he only fed Matt information because he was being protective of Megan's memory. I can't really fault him for that.

It was a bigger relief than I expected to know that Ben hadn't totally betrayed me. He wasn't the bad guy, or a murderer. He was a person who'd loved a girl once, and wanted to do right by her. And needed to get over the tragedy of her death, like me. Until my happy memories of Ben had been threatened, I didn't know how important they'd been. I'd needed to have one person from back then who I hadn't disappointed or who hadn't died on me, and he was it.

If Ben was my teenage test case, it was Gus who proved I wasn't totally broken. I could be a friend, a lover, a human. I wasn't a lost cause, no matter what *No One Suspected* accused me of or what I thought of myself.

Gus and I are going to be okay. Better than ever, actually. Even though we're still in Madison. Gus doesn't remember what the twins did to him after Bitty's first Taser zap, but he racked up an impressive list of injuries: severe concussion, internal bleeding, broken ribs and nose, dislocated shoulder. He's a big, tough doofus and he'll heal. Eventually. But for now, we've shacked up together in the Airbnb cottage. The owners were actually quite nice when we explained everything, which the police verified, and we assured them we'd be quiet and trouble-free tenants and would not get involved with any more murderers.

We're both on extended leave from our jobs. Gull helped out with that, talking to our bosses and getting us some excused absence time. Gull isn't so bad, I guess. But don't tell her I said that.

I'm not cut out to be a nursemaid. But there are lots of things I'd do for Gus that I wouldn't do for anyone else. He's got me wrapped around his not-so-little finger. I'll still snap at him or storm out the door to walk off my frustration. I don't want him to think I've gone soft, even though I feel like a giant marshmallow most of the time. Gooey and defenseless, filled with the sweetness of relief and love and freedom.

Is this what it's like to be normal?

I wouldn't know, and the not-knowing is like walking around with my shoes untied all the time. If I no longer have a good excuse to act like a miserable bastard, who even am I? Assholery was, like, my whole thing. Imagine if John Wick gave up beating the shit out of people to open a puppy rescue in Iowa farm country and lived happily ever after, falling in love with a perky barista. Would you want to watch that?

Yeah, me too.

I can't shake the idea that Jenny's death was partially my fault. More Bitty's fault than anyone else's, but it probably wouldn't have happened without my involvement. Gus doesn't like it when I go down this road, but I can't help it. There are too many parallels—too many (say it with me) coincidences. Jenny wasn't to blame for Megan's death, but it wouldn't have happened without her being at the reservoir that night. And while I wasn't to blame for Jenny's death, it wouldn't have happened if I hadn't come back to Madison on the trail of that book.

I was that domino in the middle, the one that you think, for a minute, might not tip and keep the cascade going. But then it does, and all the rest of them fall.

It was my choice to come back to Madison. I thought there was some big mystery to solve (and there was). I saw the cat poster and texted Jenny's number. Matt and Bitty were the bad guys, but maybe they wouldn't have escalated to murder without my involvement. I try not to think, *What if I'd called instead of texting her?* I might have recognized her voice, and we could've had a real talk after all those years. But then again, she probably wouldn't have answered.

I could go back into the dark, if I wanted. I could reconjure the scared teenager who felt abandoned and betrayed by her parents. The fierce young woman who threw herself into the abyss of New York City because it was the only place noisy and vibrant and chaotic enough to quiet her demons.

Or I could build a new, more solid identity on top of the old rubble. I want that solid life, I really do. And I have a way out. I have Gus now. Well, I've had Gus for a while, but the difference is that now he has me too. We're a team. And he won't let me backslide. He's lifted me out of my wallow, keeping me floating and happy and stupidly in love.

He's too nice to say so to my face, especially after that whole gallant speech about liking me just because I'm me, but he likes the new-and-improved Petta much better. Don't tell Gus—in fact, I might use my life-saving Doc Martens to kick the crap out of anyone who lets this slip— but I like this new version of me better too. She's much easier to live with.

As far as what's going to happen next, I have no idea. I quit Facebook. And learned a valuable lesson about social media: most of it is garbage, and people can construct a whole life that has nothing to do with reality. Also, it's a worthless alibi.

I've slayed most of my demons, but that doesn't mean I can see the future. Or that I'm equipped to wrap all this up with some profound life advice. Like I told Gull, perfect endings like that only happen in the movies. My story doesn't have a moral. But I guess there's one thing I've learned. Something I'd tell Young Petta if I could go back in time and meet her, in all her flannel-and-black-nail-polished glory.

Here it is: You never know when you're going to come across The Thing. The person or place or moment that will change your life. It could be during a Pap smear, even. Or when you return to a place you swore you'd never lay eyes on again. And there will be no swelling soundtrack or glorious burst of fireworks when it comes. The Thing could be as humble as a plate of well-cooked food, as complex as the person you love, or as magical as a movie.

Hell—what do I know? It might even be a book.

ACKNOWLEDGMENTS

Thɪs ʙᴏᴏᴋ ɪs the years-long result of writing, read-ing, learning, revising, rejection, success, failure, and more writing. While all of those highs and lows happened to me alone (sometimes all in my own head), that doesn't mean I didn't need a lot of help and support along the way.

My gratitude goes out to:

The team at Crooked Lane Books, for saying yes to this novel and being such a great support along my debut publishing journey. Extra-special thanks to my Badass Editor (her official title) Sara J. Henry, who plucked my query out of the pile and saw potential in my manuscript. Her suggestions and support have made this an infinitely better book, and not only because she called me out when a line was too corny. Thanks also to Ben LeRoy, who called to say the words every aspiring novelist wants to hear. Rebecca Nelson answered every question I had almost quicker than I could ask them. Copyeditor Rachel Keith kept me in line when my tenses slipped. Madeline Rathle and Dulce Botello in marketing helped this first-time author tell the world about her book.

My beta readers, who helped shape several messy drafts into a coherent manuscript. I've had great readers over the years, on projects of all lengths (shout-out to my stalwart Myna Chang!), but on this particular book, these fine folks came to my rescue with smart feedback and/or much-needed conversation: Carmen Baumann, Marcy Dilworth, Krista Galm, Laila Miller, Mike Osborne, and John Reddan.

My writing groups, who span the globe. To the SU and WAB gangs, my continued appreciation for creating online communities where we all feel safe sharing our work.

My longtime friends, some of whom I've known since middle school. Carmen Baumann, Paige Bodmann, Liz Preston, and Lissa Sundberg: you guys are the best. I spent some time as a youngster getting up to some (pretty innocent) midnight mischief in both Maple Bluff and Shorewood Hills. Those nights helped inspire this book, so to the comrades who were out there under the stars with me, thanks for the memories. And to my fellow West High Class of '94 alums: Go, Regents! None of you appear in these pages, I promise.

Thank you to Madison, Wisconsin. Is it weird to thank a city? Too bad, I'm doing it. I've been hard on my hometown in this book, and part of the fun of writing *I Know What You Did* was creating a main character who grew up in the same time and place as I did but had an opposing view on almost everything, including where we came from. To write this book, I tried to see Madison through her eyes, not my own. Because of her difficult childhood, she sees its faults more clearly than its merits, and I do the opposite. Madison isn't perfect, but it's special. It has shaped me, and it has been good to me. I hope it continues to get even better, so that every Madisonian can feel at home here the way I do.

Thank you (yes, you) for reading this book. Books need readers—without you, we'd be typing into the void. And authors need people to talk about their books. I humbly ask that if you love a book (not mine specifically, but any book that grabbed you and wouldn't let go), please request it at your local library, give it as a birthday gift, talk about it or review it online, preorder the follow-up novel, share the cover on social media. Whatever way you are comfortable supporting books and authors (many of which require spending no money), we are grateful. We'll keep writing books if you keep reading them. Deal?

I saved this one for last: Many thanks to my family. I won't list all your moments of love and support and kindness here (there isn't room). Thank you to my mom and dad and the rest of the Johnsons; to my sister Shelby and the Steels; Don and Derew and Michele and the rest of the Osbornes. To my husband, Mike, and our kids, Devon and Rhys—I love you, and thanks for letting Mom write. And an extra thank-you to Rhys, who has no idea he inspired a part of this book. When he was a toddler, after I picked him up from day care one afternoon, he piped up from his car seat in back: "The skeleton trees have holes, and the holes are eyes." We'd just driven past a group of leafless, spindly (frankly creepy) aspen trees. That phrase stuck in my brain and I wrote it down. Years later, a version found its way onto these pages.